PRAISE FOR SHADOW OF A SMILE

"From the moment you enter Meredith Springfield's world, you will feel as if you are alongside a dear friend on her amazing journey to self-discovery. Valerie Joan Connors' writing is so vivid, so intimate, that Meredith's travails and triumphs become your own. I miss her already, now that she's gone on with her life and I must go back to my own. A story of love and lies and life, *Shadow of a Smile* is a must read."

—Linda Hughes, author of BECOMING JESSIE BELLE and
WHAT WE TALK ABOUT WHEN WE'RE OVER 60

"*Shadow of a Smile* examines the large price paid for secrets and coverups, not just by the perpetrators but also by generations before and after them. Ms. Connors has written a novel for anyone who likes family and relationship stories that are emotional, complex, and altogether satisfying."

—George Weinstein, author of HARDSCRABBLE ROAD and
THE FIVE DESTINIES OF CARLOS MORENO

With extraordinary deft, Valerie Joan Connors explores how we take responsibility for our actions and their consequences. In Meredith Springfield, Connors has created a woman who discovers truths about her own relationships and the consequences of her actions and how close her life has comes to mirror her mother's. We follow Meredith on her journey along roads her mother traveled with all their twists and turns and nests of lies and secrets. *Shadow of a Smile* has layer on layer of emotion, anger and pity, joy and sadness—interwoven, juxtaposed, and "back to back."

—Rona Simmons, author of THE QUIET ROOM

"Valerie Connors has a distinctive voice. Each scene is filled with secrets and longing. Each character is brave and steady and real."

—Nicki Salcedo, Author of ALL BEAUTIFUL THINGS

SHADOW
of a
SMILE

SHADOW
of a
SMILE

VALERIE JOAN CONNORS

Marty —
You're the best. I
appreciate you more
than I can say —

Valerie Joan Connors
6-22-14 Launch

DEEDS PUBLISHING | ATLANTA

Published by Deeds Publishing
Marietta, GA
www.deedspublishing.com

Printed in The United States of America

Library of Congress Cataloging-in-Publications Data is available upon request.

ISBN 978-1-941165-19-5

Books are available in quantity for promotional or premium use. For information, write Deeds Publishing, PO Box 682212, Marietta, GA 30068 or info@deedspublishing.com.

First Edition, 2014

10 9 8 7 6 5 4 3 2 1

ACNOWLEDGMENTS

FIRST AND FOREMOST, I WISH TO thank the writers in my life. You encourage me to soldier on, even when it seems there are far too many obstacles standing between my keyboard and me. Thanks to you, I keep putting words on the page, and putting words on the page is what makes me happy and nourishes my soul. My fellow writers understand the journey, the struggle, and the reward. Your friendship and counsel are invaluable.

If I could buy a house on a cliff overlooking the ocean, or a log cabin in the mountains, or a lake house with a big, screened porch, I would invite all the writers I know to come and spend weeks of uninterrupted writing time, in rooms with a glorious view. I would do it because I understand the need and the desire for such a place, where a writer can bring amazing stories to life, if only given the opportunity, away from all the distractions of the real world and their day jobs.

I will always be grateful for the Atlanta Writers Club, a wonderful organization and an amazing group of people who came into my life at a critical time, when I was only beginning to consider myself a writer, even though I'd already finished writing my first novel. Marty Aftewicz recruited me to the club and Clay Ramsey brought me onto the board of directors. George Weinstein suggested I would make a good president, and because he did that, many doors have been opened for me, and many opportunities to further my writing career have come my way. I will always be grateful for having these people in my life. Their friendship, support, and encouragement are a great gift.

Thanks to Bob Babcock, Jan Babcock, and Mark Babcock of Deeds Publishing, for believing that my words were worthy of publication. It's a pleasure to work with you, and I hope our collaboration will be long and fruitful.

I'm grateful for the time I spent in California in the late eighties, mostly in San Diego, with visits to Los Angeles, Santa Barbara and points north. Those memories inspired some of the details in this book. They also touch a very special place in my heart, and speak to one of the underlying themes in this book, that the happiest and saddest times of our lives are so often experienced back to back. To Dawna Love, who remembers it all, and offered a helping hand when I needed it most, thank you for still being my friend all these years later.

And to my original family, thank you for giving me the gift of music and the part of my brain that yearns for a creative outlet. And thank you for giving me the courage to share my work with the world. When I hear *The Shadow of Your Smile,* I imagine my father at the baby grand, my brother at the electric piano, and sometimes I hear my mother's voice. I love you all very much.

Finally, I want to thank my husband, Patrick, for never once complaining about all the hours I spend in front of my computer, and for minding the details of our life while I follow this dream.

To the ladies in the garden, who share my path and understand my dream.

"Now when I remember spring,
all the joy that love can bring,
I will be remembering
the shadow of your smile."

The Shadow of Your Smile
Music by Johnny Mandel
Lyrics by Paul Frances Webster

CHAPTER 1
Meredith

I WAS BORN IN LOS ANGELES the day Marilyn Monroe died, August 5, 1962. Shortly thereafter, my father was killed in a car accident on Highway 101 between L.A. and Santa Barbara, on his way to play the saxophone with his band at one of the hotels along the beach. A drunk driver going sixty miles an hour veered into his lane and hit him head on. Many things about my father remained a mystery to me until I reached my thirties, but his secrets paled in comparison to my mother's. People say that you never really know someone, and on some esoteric level, I had always believed that to be true. But when you start to peel back the layers of a person's life once they're gone, when they no longer have the opportunity to color the truth, you begin to understand how accurate a statement that really is.

A short time after my father's death, my mother and I moved back to Milwaukee, Wisconsin where she'd grown up. We lived with my grandparents, so my grandma could take care of me during the day while Mom went to work as a hairdresser at Pearl's House of Curls.

We stayed with my grandparents until I was four years old and my mom had finally saved enough money to buy us a little house of our own on Elderberry Lane. Grandpa helped us set up a hair salon in the basement so mom could work from home once I started school. That way she could always be there waiting for me when I got out of school at three o'clock and walked the few blocks back to our house. The salon had its own separate entrance on the side of the house, part way down the driveway between the street and the small one-car garage. Above the door was a green and white striped awning, just big enough to cover the entrance that led customers down a flight of stairs to the basement. My mother had special ordered a small neon sign that read, "Anastasia's," to put in the window beside the door.

Unlike me, all of my friends had two parents when I was growing up. Because of that, I felt a vaguely disturbing sense of being diminished in some way, not quite on equal footing with my peers. People seemed to be a little uncomfortable when my mother was around, particularly women, although it wasn't until I was much older that I began to understand why. Eyebrows were raised and knowing looks were exchanged when my mother showed up alone at my school events, and my friends' mothers seemed to cling to their husbands when she was around, as if to establish property rights. My mother was quite beautiful as a young woman, and she aged very gracefully. Her vocation may have had something to do with that. She paid close attention to fashion, and as far back as I can remember, always looked more put together than the other moms. No one ever saw my mother with curlers in her hair, or without makeup.

While we were living with my grandparents, we went to the Episcopal Church in our quiet Milwaukee neighborhood every Sunday. After moving into our own house, we gradually stopped going to services except on Easter Sunday and Christmas Eve. As a result, my religious education was somewhat stunted. Over the years I went to church with friends sometimes, and was exposed to the different philosophies of various denominations, but this only added to my religious ambiguity. There were so many different points of view, and each group was certain that theirs was the *real* truth. How was I to know who was right? As a child, after a particularly frightening experience at Catholic mass with a friend's parents, where I understood precious little about what was being said, I had found myself grappling with the concept of a person's soul. After a couple of days, I initiated conversations about it with my mother and each of my grandparents, and determined that in my way of thinking, when a person died, something that looked a great deal like Casper the Friendly Ghost would float out of them. Casper would either head straight to heaven, straight to hell, or be stuck in some middle ground for a period of time until a final ruling could be made. As an eight year-old, this was both confusing and more than a little bit disturbing. Another one of my friends told me that her parents believed there were only a finite number of souls to go around, and that when people die, their souls are recycled into newborns who arrive on earth the same day. To me, that seemed like a fairly reasonable explanation—which explains my connection with Marilyn. Not only was I born the same day she died, but in close geographic proximity as well. The latter, I figured, significantly increased my chances.

Like me, Marilyn grew up without a father. So, besides potentially sharing a soul, another thing I had in common with Marilyn was that neither of us had a proper set of parents to raise us. And then there was the blonde hair. I didn't learn until much later in life that she wasn't a natural blonde, but that didn't change the way I felt about her, nor did it diminish the connection I felt we had.

I left home after college and moved to Chicago to take a job teaching English in a high school. It wasn't that I didn't love my little family, my mom and my grandparents. I was just tired of being the poor little girl who grew up on Elderberry Lane without a father. I wanted to simply be known as Meredith Springfield, a high school English teacher, who might have cosmic ties to Marilyn Monroe.

Another thing Marilyn and I had in common was our tendency toward unhealthy relationships with men. Like Marilyn, I had one sad relationship after another, including two broken engagements. But finally, I decided that I was better off on my own and that's how it stayed for a long time.

In April of 1991, I got involved with Derek Carpenter, the man who did my taxes. We'd been seeing each other for nearly a month by the time he admitted to me that he was married. He was separated from his wife, and had been for several months, but still married just the same. Unfortunately, by that time I had already developed some fairly deep feelings for him, and I couldn't bring myself to get all indignant about it and simply walk away. At least that's what I told myself when I couldn't sleep at night, knowing there was another woman out there who might or might not wish to have her husband back at some point. Derek was with me in my condo in downtown Chicago on a Thursday night in January of 1992 when my grandmother called to tell me that my fifty-two year old mother had just died of a massive coronary.

"I'll pack a bag and get on the road right away."

"It's snowing like crazy up here, Meredith. Maybe you should wait until morning. There's no rush now, I mean she's already—"

My grandmother had put her hand over the receiver, but I could hear her sobbing in the background. No one should have to see her child die, even if that child is fifty-two years old.

"Don't worry, Grandma," I said. "I'll drive carefully. I'll be there as soon as I can."

I hung up the phone and stood there for a moment, stunned, trying to make some sense of what I had just heard. My mother was in reasonably good health, as least as far as I knew. She had smoked for years, but lots of people did that, and twice a year she took a two-week vacation to California that she referred to as being "for her health," whatever that meant. I always just assumed she needed a break once in a while like the rest of us. My mom worked long hours in her hair salon to supplement the insurance money she had been receiving since my father's accident when I was a baby. It seemed perfectly natural to me that she took those trips to relax and recharge her battery. And like most children, my little world revolved mostly around me, so it never occurred to me to ask any questions about my mother's travel plans. I enjoyed staying with my grandparents while she was away. Then my mother would come back two weeks later. It was part of our lifestyle, a normal routine.

Derek put his arm around my shoulders and pulled me in close to him, ready to hold me up if necessary.

"I'll come with you," Derek said.

"Don't be ridiculous," I said. "How am I supposed to explain you?"

"What do you mean, explain me?"

"You know," I said. "You're someone else's husband. There's no way I'm bringing you to my family—what's left of it anyway."

That sounded so harsh, and I immediately regretted having said it. But I was having trouble getting my head around what was happening. I wanted to be alone, but at the same time that was the last thing I wanted.

"Meredith," he said, "Vanessa and I are legally separated. I agreed to hold off on the divorce until she gets her head together a little. She's still very unstable after what happened with Lily. But we live separate lives. Besides, it's not as if she doesn't know about you. You're practically pals. Can't you leave that little detail out of the introduction? Come on, honey, let me be there for you."

I desperately wanted to say yes. For once in my life, I thought, it would be nice to feel like I didn't have to be the strongest person in the room. What I really wanted to do was lie down on the floor and cry like a baby, and let Derek gather me in his arms and rock me until I stopped. I wanted him to tell me that everything was going to be fine.

"Come on," he said. "I'll run to my apartment and get a change of clothes while you pack a bag and be back for you in an hour. We'll take my car and I'll have us there before midnight. I'll make a reservation. What part of town do your grandparents live in?"

"No hotel," I said. "We'll have to stay with Grandma and Grandpa. They'll want me at the house, at least for tonight. I'll tell them that you're a friend who offered to drive me because I was too upset to go on my own."

"Of course that's what you'll say, Meredith," he said. "It's the truth."

But it didn't feel like the truth, exactly. He was a friend, yes, but he was my boyfriend, not just a buddy, and I had never been too upset to manage the events of my life before. I had been on my own a lot and was proud of my independence, but at that moment I realized I *should* have been too upset to go on my own. My mother had just died. I supposed I was in shock, and it would all hit me once I arrived in Milwaukee. Meanwhile though, it was as if it were happening to someone else. In any case, I decided that having Derek with me would be better than being alone. And like he said, I didn't have to introduce him as my boyfriend who was still technically married to another woman. As far as my grandparents were concerned, that wasn't really relevant. It was just my guilt, that despicable little thread of not-rightness that was woven through every minute of every day.

I called my grandmother back.

"Hi, Grandma," I said. "I'm just packing a bag and I'll get on the road, but I wanted to let you know I'm bringing a friend with me. His name is Derek. We've been dating for a little while. He didn't want me driving alone tonight in the snow. I hope you don't mind."

"Of course not, honey," she said. "We have plenty of room for your young man," she hesitated, "but, well, I know you're a thirty year-old grown woman, and what you do in your own place is entirely up to you. I mean, I'm not judging you, it's just that—"

"It's all right Grandma. I don't expect us to share a bedroom. Please don't give it another thought."

"Okay, that's fine then. I'm glad you have someone to travel up here with. Drive safely, dear. Your grandfather and I will be waiting."

"How is Grandpa holding up?" I asked.

"Not well," she replied. "He's been sitting in his big reclining chair in the den with the lights out ever since we got back to the house, staring out the window. He'll be better once you get here. We both will. Just be careful, please."

After Derek went home to pack a bag, I took a suitcase out of the hall closet and started putting things into it. I soon realized that there had been no rhyme or reason to the things I was putting into the bag. I didn't know how long I'd be gone, or what we'd be doing exactly. My mind refused to focus. But I finally managed to tell myself I'd need my black dress, some warm clothes, pajamas and cosmetics, so I dumped everything out onto my bed and started over. I had just finished zipping up the suitcase when I heard the knock on the door.

"Come on in, Derek," I called. "I'm almost ready."

When the knocking continued, I hurried to the living room, tossed my bag on the chair, and pulled open the door.

"It's not locked, Derek—"

But it wasn't Derek standing in my doorway. It was Vanessa. And just looking at her I could tell she was completely wasted. Her eyes were glassy from the alcohol, her cheeks flushed, and that far away stare told me she'd taken something else as well. Most recently, it had been the anti-depressants she liked to mix with her drinks. It wasn't the first time she'd been to my door, but the first time she'd come when Derek wasn't there.

"Oh, hi Meredith," she said. "Is Derek here?"

"No, Vanessa," I said. "Not right now, but he'll be here any minute. But listen—"

"Are you two going on a trip or something?" Vanessa slurred, obviously having noticed my suitcase. "Where are you off to?"

She was talking very loudly, but not angry, at least not yet. The last time she'd been at my condo she had made a terrible scene in the hallway, and one of my neighbors threatened to call the police if we couldn't make her quiet down.

"I can't remember the last time Derek and I went on a trip together," Vanessa said. "It must have been before Lily—"

And there it was. The moment she said her daughter's name, I knew we were in for trouble. Her face grew dark, and her whole body language changed. I could see the rage and desperation washing over her. I knew that Derek would arrive soon, but I had to do something to diffuse what would surely turn into a disaster if I'd let it continue.

"Vanessa," I said, putting my hands on her shoulders and forcing her to look at me. "Listen! There's no time for this right now. Yes, we're about to leave town, but it's not a vacation. I just found out my mother is dead, and Derek is going to take me to my grandparents' house as soon as he gets back here. I'm begging you, Vanessa, just this once, please don't make everything about you tonight. Please."

Something in my voice had reached her, even through her drug and alcohol induced stupor. It was almost as if I had slapped her, the change was so sudden. She stood up straight, and put her arms around me.

"I'm sorry, Meredith," she said. "Really sorry. I'll go."

Then she released me as suddenly as she had embraced me, and as she turned to leave, to my great relief, I saw Derek coming out of the elevator.

"What's going on, Vanessa?" he asked. "Why are you here?"

"It's okay, Derek," I said. "Just help Vanessa get a cab, okay? I'm ready to go as soon as you are."

Vanessa didn't hate me. I knew that. I'd even picked her up a few times when she was too drunk to get herself home and Derek was out of town. She called my number on a regular basis, looking for him for one reason or another, something with the house, or the bills. And she was always very cordial, as was I. However, she had no intention of relinquishing the hold she had over him any time soon. He was free to carry on with his life, up to a point, but no further. She had been in rehab twice for her alcoholism and substance abuse, and she occasionally ended up in the psych ward when she'd lose control of herself, perhaps threatening suicide in front of someone who was bound by law to report it.

"What was it this time?" I asked.

"No idea," Derek said. "By the time I got her into the cab, I'm not sure she even knew who I was."

"Will she be all right?"

"I don't know," he said. "But I gave the driver an extra twenty and asked him to make sure she gets inside the front door."

"Are you sure you should leave?"

"Yes," he said. "She's a grown woman. I'm not going to babysit her. It's emotional blackmail. She's been doing it for years and it's not fair. But it's like with a bully, if you don't let them think they're getting to you, it isn't fun anymore and they'll go and pick on someone else. If Vanessa had her way I'd follow her around twenty-four hours a day to make sure she didn't do anything stupid. It's exhausting, and I'm not going to live like that anymore."

He picked up my suitcase, and switched off the lamp on the coffee table beside the door.

"Is the stove turned off? Your iron unplugged?"

I laughed. We both knew that we didn't have to worry about either of those things. I hardly ever cooked anything, and if it didn't come out of the dryer ready to wear, it went to the cleaners.

"We're good," I said. "Better get going."

My heart ached for Vanessa, but she was toxic. I couldn't help her, and Derek had spent years trying. She was a raging alcoholic before what happened to Lily, and afterward, Vanessa gave up even trying to get straight. I often hoped that she would meet someone new who could make her want to start over again and do something with her life besides getting wasted. But sadly, the type of person she would be likely to attract in her condition probably wouldn't be a positive influence.

As Derek drove us north on I-94 toward Milwaukee, the windshield wipers clearing the snow off of the glass, I found myself doing something I did as a child. I leaned my head against the window and tilted my head back so I could see the snow coming down from high above the trees. It was magical when I was young. I used to think about climbing to the tops of those trees where I imagined the snow originated, to see what the world looked like from way up there. That night it only made me think of my mother, and growing up with just the two of us in our little house. It wasn't easy financially, but we got by. My grandparents helped us with the unexpected costs of maintaining our house, like when we needed a new roof or had to call the plumber. They also paid for my tuition at the University of Wisconsin. In high school I did a lot of babysitting to earn money for clothes, and in college I waitressed at a diner on campus. I made enough to pay for my books and some of the groceries, and that helped Mom to save for her trips to California. As I got older, I realized that it had probably been very important to her to visit the place where my father had lived and was now buried. But it was obviously very painful for her too, because she never said much about her vacations when she came back home, so I didn't ask a lot of questions. If she'd wanted me to know what she did out there on the West Coast, she would have told me. And except for doubling the cost of the trip, there was no reason she couldn't have taken me with her if that's what she'd wanted to do. I would have enjoyed seeing Disneyland. What child wouldn't? The one time I asked about that, she assured me that if she ever decided to include Disneyland in her vacation plans she would definitely take me with her. But she never did, and I didn't ask about it again.

My mother probably worried about money a lot more than she let on, but we managed to get most everything we needed and even a few of the things we wanted. It was never our financial status that made me feel inferior to the other kids. Lots of families struggled financially. It was the glaring lack of a daddy. Mom was pretty, everybody said so, and I never understood why she didn't remarry. She didn't even date. That was another one of those threads running through my childhood that seemed a little off, but I accepted it without giving it too much thought. We accept so many things as children, without questioning. Then as adults we learn how very complicated life can get, how complicated we can make it by letting our hearts make our decisions for us.

"Where did you go?" Derek asked.

"Just thinking about my mom," I said. "I can't believe this is happening. I know that once we get to Milwaukee it's going to be plenty real, but I just can't get my head around it. I've been after her for years about her smoking, but other than that she seemed fine."

"I'm sorry, Meredith," he said. "I wish I could do something to make this easier."

"Thanks," I said. "And thanks for coming with me. It will be nice to have someone to lean on. My grandparents are devastated. They may end up leaning on you a little, too. I hope you're okay with that."

"Anything I can do," he said.

For the most part, Derek was a very good man. He was hardworking, honest, and kind. The only downside was the fact that he still legally belonged to someone else. His marriage was very sad. Things had begun to fall apart when their daughter drowned in Lake Michigan a year or so before. The little girl had only been five years old when it happened. Vanessa felt responsible for what happened, and arguably she was. When I first learned about it, I couldn't believe she hadn't gone to prison for child endangerment or worse. But I didn't want to probe into the details because it hurt Derek so much to talk about his daughter's death, and his wife's involvement in it. Lily's drowning was the most devastating consequence of Vanessa's drinking, although with several DUI's to her credit, it was a miracle she hadn't killed anyone else. You'd think she would have learned something from what happened to Lily, but instead she used more alcohol to try to numb out some of her pain and guilt. When that didn't work, she added narcotics into the mix. After the first round of rehab, she seemed to be making some progress, but it didn't stick, and after only two months of being clean and sober, she fell back into her old habits. She tried rehab again, which also resulted in a brief period of sobriety followed by a disappointing relapse. After that, Derek gave her an ultimatum. He said she needed to clean up her act, or he was going to leave her, because he wasn't going to watch her kill herself. When Vanessa continued to drink, he moved out of their house. For him, the marriage was over. When he brought up the subject of divorce however, she threatened to commit suicide. So there we were, in a kind of purgatory, where all of us were able to go through the motions of living each day, but none of us could make plans for the future. The three of us seemed inextricably joined together. Vanessa knew Derek was involved with me, but accepted it, knowing she still held the upper hand. She had him paralyzed.

"Sorry, Derek," I said. "I'm afraid I'm not very good company."

"No worries. I don't expect you to be. In fact, for the next few days you have complete amnesty. No apologies necessary."

"Here's the exit," I said. "Why are you so good to me?"

"Because I love you, silly."

When we arrived at my grandparents' home, it looked as though every light in the house was on. I saw my grandmother's face in the kitchen window and bet she had been standing there watching for us for a very long time. A moment later she and my grandfather were waiting inside the open front door. I ran to them, leaving Derek to get our luggage, and threw my arms around them both. As he approached us, my grandparents tried to pull themselves together to meet my boyfriend. Their strength of character simply amazed me.

"I'm so sorry for your loss," Derek said, hugging my grandmother.

Derek said the same thing again, as he took my grandfather's hand in both of his.

"I'm Derek Carpenter," he said, as we crossed the mud porch into the living room. "Meredith's friend."

"Of course, dear," Grandma said. "We haven't heard much about you, but we're looking forward to getting acquainted."

"We're Ben and Martha Burke," Grandpa said.

My grandparents looked better than they had sounded on the phone, and seemed to have pulled themselves together some, for my benefit no doubt.

"You must be hungry after your long drive. Come into the kitchen and I'll fix you something."

"Thanks, Grandma, but we're fine. We stopped for a bite an hour ago. Let me fix you a cup of tea and you can fill me in on the details. This is all just so unreal and out of the blue."

We sat at the kitchen table, Grandma with her tea and the rest of us with bourbon in highball glasses, mine with ice and water, the men with theirs neat, while Derek and I learned the painful details of the past twenty-four hours.

"Her cholesterol was very high, had been for years," Grandma said. "The doctor has been after her to quit smoking forever, but she just wouldn't listen. He warned her that something like this could happen. Naturally, she didn't want you to know how bad it was, because she didn't want you to worry."

"But why didn't she listen to the doctor?" I asked. "She was a young woman. Mom should have had so many years ahead of her."

"You know your mother. I suppose I should say knew her," she paused to regain her self control. "No one could ever tell her what to do. She was headstrong, always, and did exactly as she pleased, no matter what the consequences were for you or anyone else—"

"Martha, that's enough," my grandfather said.

"What consequences?" I asked. "What do you mean, Grandma?"

"Your grandmother is just upset, honey, that's all. She doesn't know what she's saying."

My grandfather tossed his remaining bourbon down his throat and poured a couple more fingers' worth into the glass.

"Anastasia has been taken to the Lowery Funeral Home where she'll be cremated. It's what she wanted."

"How do you know that, Grandpa?" I asked. "She never said anything like that to me."

"She had a will," he said. "Gave us a copy. There were specific instructions about her final wishes. She wanted to be cremated immediately, and there are to be no services."

"What?" I asked. "No services? Who does that? We have to do something."

"No," he said. "She was very clear about it. The strange thing is, there was a letter. It was sealed, and addressed to the legal firm whose name was printed on the folder her will was in. The instructions said that it was to be mailed immediately upon her death."

"Where is it?" I asked. "I want to see it."

I started to get up from the table, but my grandfather raised his hand as if to stop me from going any further. I paused for a moment, frozen in place halfway to a standing position, and sat back down in my chair.

"Your grandmother mailed it this evening. Walked it down to the post office while we were waiting for you to get here. Anyway," my grandfather said, "it's done now. All that's left to do is clean out her house and put it on the market. That is, unless you want to keep it. It's yours, of course, along with everything inside. That, she was very clear about, too."

"But we have to let people know. If there are no services, how will people know? A person can't spend more than half a century on earth and then simply cease to exist, just like that, with no explanation and no funeral."

Then it occurred to me that when someone dies, that's exactly what happens. One second they're here and the next they're gone. It's final, in the blink of an eye. All that's left is a body. The person you have loved your whole life is gone, forever. What remains is just an accumulation of flesh and bone that needs to be disposed of in one way or another. In my mother's case, turned into ashes. For all I knew it had already been done. I realized my hands were balled into fists and I was holding my breath. The corners of my vision had begun to blur. I tried to breathe normally, and dug my fingernails into the palm of my hand, hoping the pain would be a distraction from my thoughts so that I could focus on the conversation I was having.

"What about her clients?" I asked. "How will they know she's gone?"

"There'll be a notice in the papers," Grandma said. "The funeral home will take care of that once we give them the details for her obituary. Is that something you could do, honey? Maybe your friend, Derek, could help you."

"Sure, Grandma," I said. "We'll do that first thing in the morning. Then I'll call the school and have them arrange a substitute teacher for my classes next week while I get Mom's house in order."

"That's fine, dear," she said. "Now, it's late. You kids must be exhausted. Let's get you settled in and see if we can all manage a little sleep."

That didn't seem likely, but my grandmother probably needed some privacy and tucking everyone into bed was the only way she was going to get it.

Grandpa went straight to bed while Grandma helped us get settled in the two unused bedrooms upstairs. When everyone was behind their closed doors, I changed into my pajamas and sat on the bed where I had spent so many nights as a child. One of my biggest fears as a little girl was that something would happen to my mother and then I would have no parents at all. And now it had actually happened. I was an orphan.

It had only been two weeks since I had spoken to my mother on the phone. We usually talked every Sunday, but the last weekend we had just played phone tag all day and were never able to actually connect. She sounded fine, but she wasn't. And she knew it, too. Yet she hadn't said anything to me. Mom didn't want me to worry, they said, but instead all she did was set me up for a cosmic two by four across the side of my head that came completely out of nowhere. Was that better that letting me worry? I didn't really think so. And maybe I could have done something, but I supposed it was too late for that now. My mother was gone, and she wasn't coming back.

I took a notebook out of my bag and tried to begin writing my mother's obituary. I was exhausted, but certain I wouldn't be able to sleep. As an English teacher and an aspiring novelist during summer breaks, I had been in the challenging position of having to summarize three hundred pages of prose into a two- or three-page synopsis. That's difficult, but not nearly so difficult as trying to summarize fifty-two years of life into several paragraphs. She was a mother, a daughter, and a hairdresser, and she vacationed in California twice a year. Sometimes she attended stylists' conventions, at least that's what she'd said, but mostly she said her trips out west were for her health. Having grown up in Wisconsin, it seemed perfectly logical that getting out of sub-zero temperatures a couple of times a year would be good for her. I was usually too wrapped up in my own life to care very much about the details. But that night, sitting on the bed at my grandparents' house where I had spent the first four years of my life, I started to wonder about what the draw really was. And I couldn't stop wondering what the consequences were that my grandmother had referred to at the kitchen table. I always thought my mother's life was an open book. She moved to California when she graduated from high school, because she wanted to start her own life in a place that was warm and sunny. Who could blame her for that? She fell in love, married, had a baby, and lost her husband in a tragic car accident. Naturally she came back to Milwaukee where her parents could help her. She never seemed like much of a rebel to me, or headstrong for that matter, as Grandma had called her. My mother worked hard and took good care of me. On the surface it all seemed pretty straightforward. But I was about to find out that my mother's life had been anything but ordinary.

I heard a light tap on the door, and Derek poked his head in.

"I couldn't sleep either," he said. "Are you okay?"

"I'm fine. I've just been sitting here thinking. I tried to start on the obituary, but my writing skills have deserted me."

"I'll make a few calls in the morning," Derek said. "I can stay through the weekend to help with the heavy lifting over at your mother's house, but then I'll have to get back. I've got a crazy week coming up. Will you be able to deal with all this on your own?"

"Sure. Don't worry. And you don't really have to stay the whole weekend. I can just drive my mother's car back to Chicago after I clean out her house and get it listed with a real estate agent. I'll probably be back by the end of next week."

"I know I don't have to stay, Meredith. I want to stay."

"Thanks," I said. "I think I'm going to be very sad."

He put his arms around me, and for the first time since I received my grandmother's phone call, I cried. I stood there, in his arms, and cried for a very long time.

CHAPTER 2

"GOOD MORNING DEAR. WERE YOU ABLE to get any sleep?" my grandmother asked, as she pulled a coffee cup off the shelf and filled it for me.

"I think I finally fell asleep a little after three. Where's Derek?"

"He's outside shoveling snow off the driveway with your grandfather. He's a nice young man, Meredith. Why haven't we heard about him before?"

My heart skipped a beat, and I felt myself beginning to flush. I was totally unprepared for the question, but also determined not to lie to my grandmother, at least not directly.

"It's just that I've had such bad luck with men in the past. I'd tell you and Mom all about how wonderful someone was, maybe even bring him up to meet you, and then a few weeks later I have to tell you that he actually wasn't quite so wonderful after all. Derek is the first truly decent man I've met in a really long time. I didn't want history repeating itself. So I decided to keep it to myself for a while, that's all."

That wasn't really all, and it certainly wasn't the main reason I hadn't talked about him, but it was true. I supposed that was something. Under different circumstances, my grandmother would have probed further. My mother definitely would have, under any circumstances. Grandma knew there was more, but she took me at my word and let it drop.

"I understand, dear. But I'm pretty sure you found a good one this time. Come here. Look."

I went over to Grandma who was standing in front of the kitchen sink, looking out the window. Derek and my grandfather were out in the driveway, bundled up so that only their faces were showing. Grandpa stood outside in the cold, while Derek shoveled the fresh snow away so my grandparents could get their car out of the garage. Then my grandfather lowered his head and pressed his hands to his eyes. After a moment we saw Derek lay down his shovel and put an arm around my grandfather's shoulders. Derek stood there next to him like that until Grandpa pulled himself together, then he picked up the shovel and continued clearing away the snow.

"Yes," I said. "He's a good man."

I saw my grandmother wipe away her own tears that she had tried so hard to contain.

"Your grandfather's heart is broken," she started. After a moment she continued, "And so is mine."

"I know, Grandma. Mine, too. It's all so sudden and horrible. It just seems impossible that this is really happening."

"We should go over to the house after breakfast and get started. The sooner we start, the sooner we'll be finished. And if we wait for this to really sink in, I think the job is going to be a lot harder."

Grandma fixed us comfort food for breakfast: oatmeal with cream and brown sugar on top, eggs, bacon, home-fried potatoes, and blueberry muffins. She must have been up since before dawn. These were all the things I loved as a little girl, and things she hadn't allowed my grandfather to eat for years. They usually had a poached egg on dry whole-wheat toast and a bowl of Grape-nuts with skim milk. But that morning, we needed something, anything, to soothe us even a little. I think we all tried our best, but most of that beautiful breakfast ended up in the dog's bowl.

On the short drive between the two houses I had spent so many happy days in over the years, I remembered the first time my mother let me walk the ten blocks between them on my own, and how many times I'd made the trip on my bicycle in the years that followed. Suddenly it was all changed. The house at the end of this journey would belong to another family soon, and my mother would never be there again.

As we turned onto Elderberry Lane in my grandfather's car and approached my mother's house, my hands began to shake, and my stomach felt as though a thousand butterflies had made their home inside of me. Her car was parked at the end of the long driveway that runs past the side entrance to her salon, with its small, green and white striped awning, to the single car garage there had never been room to put a car in. It would have looked as though she were inside waiting for us, if not for the fact that the front porch light was still burning in broad daylight. I felt a strong urge to run all the way back to Chicago, get into my own bed, pull the covers over my head, and try to wake up from this nightmare. I knew that the moment I walked into her house there would be no denying it. My mother was gone forever, and I was alone. At least I would be, soon enough. My mother was an only child, and my grandparents were old. They were in good health now, but they were both in their early seventies. When they were gone, there would be no one. No relatives, and no children. I knew it would happen one day, but with my mother's death, that day just got at least twenty-five years closer than I thought it was.

"Are you ready, Meredith?" Derek asked. "We don't have to do this today if you're not ready."

"No, I'm okay. Like Grandma said, this isn't going to get any easier. Besides, I'll have to get back to work soon. The new semester is just starting, and I don't want the kids to fall behind. Best to get started while we're all still in shock, I suppose."

"She's right," Grandpa said. "Even if we don't get much accomplished today, we can at least make sure everything is locked up tight and the stove's turned off."

In my mother's house, unlike mine, there actually *was* a possibility the stove had been left on. Mom cooked at home all the time, even when it was only for herself. Though she could have easily managed the price of a restaurant meal once in a while, she preferred her own cooking. I had preferred her cooking, too.

The street was quiet, and there were four inches of fresh snow on the sidewalk that led to the front porch. It was freezing outside and the sky was a low gray ceiling that felt heavy and close, but at least the snow had stopped falling.

We all climbed out of the Buick, trying not to slip on the icy driveway. Grandpa took the spare house key out of its hiding place in the planter at the top of the stairs on the front porch, first sweeping away accumulated snow with a gloved hand. My heart was pounding as he opened the door to what was once my mother's house and stepped inside.

The television was still on. She must have been watching the evening news when the pain in her chest started and she called 911. That made me think about how many times I had heard people say, "When I heard the news, I nearly had a heart attack." But my mother actually had. I wondered what the newscaster had been talking about when it happened.

"Meredith?" my grandfather said.

I realized I had been just standing there, one step inside the front door, with Grandma and Derek standing out in the cold.

"Sorry," I said, as I moved inside.

From the corner of my eye I saw something dart across the room toward us and it startled me enough to make me jump and cry out. It was my mother's cat. She started butting me with her head and rubbing herself against my legs, all the while howling like a wild animal.

"Oh my," Grandma said. "We forgot all about the cat. She must be starving."

The beautiful white cat with one green eye and one blue, kept moving between us, yowling. She was looking around the room as if to say, "I'm really glad to see all of you because I'm awfully hungry and I've been alone here all night, but where is my mother?" I wondered the same thing. But that brought about an image I did not want in my head.

"Thank God the paramedics didn't let her outside last night," she said. "Poor thing would have frozen to death. Come on, Blossom, let's get you some food."

We all followed my grandmother into the kitchen. None of us had any idea where to begin. It was all simply too horrible.

"Well," she said, "we needn't have worried about the cat going hungry."

My mother had been about ready to eat dinner. She had made a casserole; macaroni and cheese with crab, and lightly browned cracker crumbs on top. The casserole looked as if it had just come out of the oven, except around the edges where Miss Apple Blossom had helped herself. That had been my all-time favorite meal as a teenager. It's a wonder I didn't weigh two hundred pounds, but now that I thought about it, that might have explained my mother's cholesterol problem. We didn't eat food like that all the time, but in the harsh Wisconsin winters, my mother said we needed food that would stick to our ribs. Unfortunately for her, it stuck to the inside of her arteries as well.

"Meredith?" Derek said. "Are you alright? You look really pale. Come and sit down for a minute. I'll get you some water."

"I'm fine," I said. "Here's what I think we should do. Grandma, if you want to start in the kitchen, I'll start in the bedrooms. Grandpa, maybe you could start sorting out the garage. See what you can use and what we should donate. A lot of it is probably yours anyway. Derek, if you wouldn't mind, it would be a huge help if you could get out the phone book and find a real estate agent to list the house with. See if someone can come over on Monday to start the paperwork. Also, see if you can find a charity that picks up donated household goods."

For a minute I expected to hear someone tell me I was awfully bossy, and ask who died and left me in charge. But then, we all knew the answer, didn't we. I think everyone was glad to have some direction, because they all got busy with their assigned tasks. Grandma threw away the casserole and gave Blossom some cat food. Then she washed the dishes, cleaned out the refrigerator and pantry, and put the perishable food in boxes on the front porch where it would stay cold. Then she started pulling dishes out of the cupboards and lining things up on the dining table.

She and I would decide which things each of us wanted to take home, and what remained would be donated to charity.

We'd do the same in all the rooms of my mother's house. We would save the things we wanted, and in a few days a big truck would come to haul the rest away. Most of my mother's possessions, things that had meaning or a purpose for her, were no longer necessary. Her death had invalidated them. We'd keep the photo albums and the good china, sure. And I'd keep her jewelry and other mementos that had sentimental value. But the coffee maker she used every morning, her furniture and cooking utensils, sheets and towels, these things would end up in someone else's home; someone who couldn't afford to buy them new. In my rational mind, I realized that was good, and something my mother would have wanted. She had been a very generous and caring person.

I was dismantling my mother's existence, piece by piece, and it was very strange and unsettling, like taking down the Christmas decorations after the holidays were over. Only these things would never be put back together. I missed my mother so much that I didn't see how life could go on without her. At the same time, I was certain that it would. We just had to get through the next few days, and finish dealing with the business aspects of her death. Then we could begin to heal, in our own familiar environments, far away from her empty house. It seemed simple enough. I had thought that we only needed to endure a few horrible days and the work would be done, but cleaning out my mother's home had only been the tip of the iceberg.

I went into the master bedroom and sat down on her bed. There was a paperback novel on the bedside table; one of those Hollywood noir detective novels set in the forties. Her nightgown and robe were laid neatly across the foot of her antique four-poster bed, her slippers carefully lined up on the hardwood floor below. There was a laundry basket in the corner of the room, filled with neatly folded clean clothes that were ready to be put into the dresser drawers. If I went into her bathroom, I knew exactly what I'd find; the hair and makeup products she had used for years, and the small, hand-painted ceramic vase she found at a garage sale that she kept her tweezers and nail clippers in. I'd see the framed needlepoint I made her for Christmas one year during college when I couldn't afford to buy her anything nicer. I had spent countless hours working on it, painstakingly cross-stitching the deeply philosophical words, "bloom where you're planted," that had been my mantra in those days. I had already spent twenty years in Milwaukee by the time I was half-way through college, and found myself wanting to be anywhere but there. But I had no money, no job, and no plans, so I tried to convince myself that I should try to be as happy as I could be in the life I'd been assigned. I hung onto that idea long enough to finish college, and then I blew out of town like my hair was on fire.

"Making any progress?" Derek asked.

I realized I'd been sitting on the bed for half an hour and hadn't lifted a finger yet.

"Just trying to figure out where to start," I said.

"I called the real estate agent your grandfather recommended. Someone will be out here on Monday at 1:00. I explained the situation, and they said we should clear out all the closets and cabinets, and take out half the furniture. Some furniture makes it easier for prospective buyers to picture their own stuff in the house, but too much of it makes the place look smaller. I also found an organization that will come and pick up the things you don't want to keep. They'll be here with a big truck on Tuesday. All you'll have to do is pack the smaller things up, and point out what goes and what stays. Their guys will do all the heavy lifting."

"Thanks, Derek. Thanks for being here, and for being so great about all this."

"No problem at all," he said, "but I think we should give it another hour or so and then get out of here for a while and go try eating again. I'm worried about your grandparents. As hideous as this is for you, at some level you realized you would probably be facing it someday. But she was their daughter, and the last thing anyone wants to imagine is losing their—"

His voice caught in his throat, and although he tried valiantly to regain control before I realized he was thinking about Lily, it was too late. Her memory was still so close, the pain of her loss so terribly fresh and raw.

"Derek, I'm so sorry. Damn it. Yes, let's do a little more, then get out of here for a while."

Derek went out to the garage to help Grandpa. Then I remembered the salon. We had a fully functional hair salon in the basement with a truckload of equipment and supplies. It was all far too much to think about. But they say the best way to eat an elephant is one bite at a time, so I brought an entire box of heavy-duty trash bags into the bedroom and started unloading dresser drawers.

As I filled the bags with neatly folded stacks of my mother's clothing, I started a pile of things that I wanted to keep for myself. There was no explaining my choices; my mother was a petite size six and I'm four inches taller and generally wear a size eight. It wasn't as if I could wear her clothes. It's just that there were some things I'd seen her in so many times that I couldn't bring myself to put them inside a trash bag, only to have some other woman somewhere end up wearing them. It wasn't completely rational, but it allowed me to continue the task at hand, and at the time, that was the important thing. I tried with all my might to avoid thinking about the reality of what I was doing, and simply soldiered on. I knew that if I thought about it too much, I would end up in a blubbering pile on my mother's bedroom floor clutching her bathrobe, and there was no time for that sort of thing.

As it turned out, my grandparents, once they got started, were making pretty good progress as well. So instead of going out somewhere, Derek brought back sandwiches for everyone and we were all able to eat a little bit. After lunch, we all got back to work and tried to stay focused. I asked Derek to start pulling together my mother's financial records that she kept downstairs, the salon books as well as her personal ones. Since he was in the tax business, I figured he was much better equipped for the task of closing out her accounts and filing any necessary paperwork than the rest of us. I've never been a numbers person. I'm a right-brained, letters person all the way. But Derek, bless his heart, was able to find some of the first clues that led me to the truth about my mother's life, and my own.

By four o'clock we were all about done in. We were exhausted in every way. I looked around my mother's bedroom at the sea of trash-bags lined up in rows on the floor and the open closet that I hadn't even touched yet. There was still an unbearable amount of work left to do, but I reminded myself it was only Friday, and I had checked out of work for the whole next week. I didn't have to finish all of this today. So while Derek and my grandparents started loading boxes into the back of both their car and my mother's, I put my shoes back on and searched through the mess for my purse. I found it buried under a stack of sweaters on the cedar chest at the foot of the bed. I tried to raise the lid, but the chest was locked. Somewhere in my mother's things I would find the skeleton key that opened it, but chances were I had a lot of work to do before that would happen.

We arrived at my grandparents' house in our two-car caravan, with the trunks so full that both cars were noticeably lower at the back end. Once the cars were unloaded into the formerly immaculate two-car garage, and the boxes of various sizes and shapes were stacked in uneven rows against the back wall, we gathered at the kitchen table for a drink. I made the tea for Grandma and me, and Grandpa poured bourbon for Derek and himself. We sat together, relieved to be finished with our day's difficult tasks, while my grandparents tried to get to know Derek a little better. This made me uncomfortable, to put it mildly, but they were talking about something other than the death of my mother, so I tried to relax and join in the conversation. But then I noticed the blinking red light on the answering machine.

"Looks like you have a message," I said. "Want me to get it?"

"Sure, honey," Grandma said, so I pushed the play button. A man's voice began in a slow and gentle tone and I immediately wished I had kept my big, fat mouth shut.

"Good afternoon, Mr. and Mrs. Burke. This is Dale Lowery down at Lowery Funeral Home. I am terribly sorry to disturb you during this very difficult time, but I just wanted to let you know that your loved one's cremains will be ready for you to pick up tomorrow afternoon, any time after three o'clock. Once again, I want you to know how deeply sorry we are for your loss, and how much we truly appreciate that you have chosen Lowery Funeral Home for your bereavement needs."

My grandma excused herself and left the room. Grandpa stared into his glass of bourbon for a moment and then poured in some more. Derek looked at me with eyes that asked, "What do we do now?" In answer, I got up from the table, ran to the hall bathroom and threw up. I kept throwing up until there was nothing left in my stomach. Even then, I kept on heaving. When I finally started to get my stomach under control, I noticed the cramping that had started in my intestines. Before long I was sitting on the toilet having massive explosions of diarrhea, and heaving over the small wastebasket I held on my lap, on the off chance that anything still remained in my stomach. I felt like I might die, and then for a while I hoped I would. My grandma had started tapping on the bathroom door every few minutes to see if I was okay. When I was finally able to get off of the commode, splash some cold water on my face and sit down on the edge of the tub, I let her come in. She was a brave woman to enter that room, and I loved her very much for doing it. Grandma ran cold water over a washcloth, wrung it out, and held it to my forehead as she sat down next to me on the edge of the tub.

"You're a very stoic person, Meredith," she began. "You always have been, even when you were a little girl. Remember when that old cocker spaniel of yours ran away for a couple of days? Most children would have been hysterical, but not my granddaughter. You just got busy making posters to put up around the neighborhood. You rode up and down the street on your bicycle for two days, putting up the posters everywhere and calling for that dog. There were no tears at all, until he got home. When you knew he was safe, you gave him a good talking to. You weren't sobbing, just crying quietly, while you told him how much he scared you, and that he should never do that to you again. But later that night I sat with you on the edge of this same bathtub with a cold cloth on your head after you finished throwing up and all the rest of it, just like tonight. Sometimes you have to just go ahead and let things out, Meredith. It's going to come out one way or another."

"I don't know why I'm like this. I guess I always felt that Mom had enough to worry about without listening to me whine about my little problems. I've always tried to be self-sufficient."

"Yes, I can see that," she said. "But it's okay to let people know when you're hurting. Your grandfather and I were awake most of the night, crying in each other's arms. We probably didn't sleep more than a couple of hours between us. I won't be surprised if we do it again tonight, especially after spending the day going through her things. What's happened is awful, and it hurts like nothing I've ever been through in my seventy-two years. But one way or another, I'm going through it. Maybe I could hide my head in the sand and put it off a little while, but sooner or later I'm going to have to accept that your mother is gone, and feel all the pain that comes from knowing it. We'll get through this together, honey. Don't feel like you have to carry it all alone."

"Believe me, if this is what happens to a person when they bottle up feelings, I'm going to make a concerted effort to avoid doing it ever again," I said. "What's Derek up to?"

"He and Grandpa went to the store to get you some Popsicles."

With this announcement, I burst into tears. My mother always got me Popsicles when my stomach was upset. It was a way to gradually convince my stomach and mouth to accept nourishment and I could eat them lying down if I had to. The cool sweetness always made me feel better. I used to say that my favorite flavor was red. That made my mom laugh.

Derek helped Grandma with dinner while I lay on my bed, hoping that soon I would have the energy to join what remained of my family. It was horribly quiet in the house that night. Even the dog was quiet. Their old golden retriever, Duncan, occasionally poked his head in my bedroom door to see if I was ready to play yet. Each time I'd call him over and he'd sit next to the bed so we were at eye level. I would pet his soft fur for a while, telling him what a good dog he was, until he'd suddenly decide he had somewhere else to be, and someone else to attend to. He had loved my mother desperately, and it was as if he were going from room to room looking for her. But all he found were a bunch of humans who were doing the same thing, expecting to see her appear in a doorway at any moment.

"Want some company?" Derek asked.

"Yes, please. Sorry I've deserted you," I said.

"Don't be silly. How are you feeling? Ready for another red Popsicle?"

"Maybe later. What's everybody doing? It's so quiet in the house."

"They're in the den. Ben is reading, and Martha is knitting something. I was sitting at the kitchen table going through some of Anastasia's financial records. She kept clean books. Did she do them herself, or did someone help her?"

"She always did her own bookkeeping, but she had a CPA who she turned everything over to at the end of the year. The same woman did her tax returns as far back as I can remember."

"That's good," he said. "We might want to talk to her at some point. Your mother's bank statements have all been neatly reconciled and I see how everything ties back to her sales receipts from the salon. There's also a recurring monthly deposit of a thousand dollars. Was she receiving a settlement of some kind?"

"Yes, there was a life insurance annuity she'd been receiving ever since my dad died, right after I was born."

"Really?" He looked at me, puzzled.

"Yes. Why?"

"Well, you're almost thirty years old. It's unusual for an insurance policy to pay out that big an annuity for thirty years. There's usually some kind of cap on it. Usually a policy will have a face value that could be paid out in a lump sum or spread out over a period of time, but even if you forget about the time value of money, a thousand dollars a month for thirty years would be three hundred and sixty thousand dollars. It must have been an expensive policy. But I thought your father was a musician, just starting out."

"He was. Now that you mention it, that doesn't really seem right, does it."

"I'm sure there's an explanation, but we may want to talk to your mother's accountant. She'll probably be able to clear things up."

"I can ask my grandparents, too. They might know something. Have you eaten?"

"Martha ordered two pizzas from that place she said you like. It was really good," he said. "There's a bunch of it left. Want to try a slice?"

"Oh, God no," I said, and the look on my face must have been a clear reflection of how his question had made me feel inside, because he actually took a little step away from me.

"Sorry, honey," he said. "Let me know if you want something later, okay?"

"Okay," I said. "Meanwhile, turn on that little TV in the corner and keep me company for a while."

As we watched *The Golden Girls*, Derek sat on the floor next to my twin bed with Duncan curled up at his side. The TV show was a nice distraction, and with Derek and our beautiful old dog there to protect me, I felt safe for a little while, and comforted. My stomach muscles had relaxed. Although I wasn't hungry and perhaps never would be again, I no longer felt like the slightest movement of my head would bring on another bout of nausea. For a long time I had been flat on my back, afraid to move, but I finally turned onto my side so that I could rest a hand on Derek's shoulder. The next thing I knew, my bedroom was dark and

I was alone. The clock radio on the nightstand said it was three in the morning. I'd fallen asleep way too early, and I was wide-awake with nothing to do until dawn, and no one to talk to. So I took my copy of Stephen King's *Needful Things* out of my bag, and read until I smelled the coffee brewing in the kitchen.

CHAPTER 3

THEY DID KNOW SOMETHING ABOUT THE annuity payment, I was almost certain, but it was obvious that my grandparents didn't want to talk about it. Grandma said it really didn't matter now, but that it was probably exactly what my mother had said it was, a life insurance annuity payment from my father's death. It wasn't so much what she said, as the way she said it, and the fact that she very quickly changed the subject. But given what had happened and the kind of emotional struggle we were all going through, I decided to just let it go. I would talk to the accountant in a few days and she'd clear everything up for me.

After breakfast Saturday morning, the four of us headed back over to Elderberry Lane to continue the daunting task of packing up my mother's abbreviated life. My goal for the day was to gather everything that my grandparents wanted to keep, and bring it back to their house while Derek was still there to help with the heavy lifting. We'd even be able to fit some of the smaller furniture inside his Ford Explorer. After spending most of the day emptying linen closets and sorting through the storage cabinets in my mother's tiny but heavily loaded garage, I drove her car back to my grandparents' house with Grandma riding shotgun, while Derek took Grandpa to the funeral home to pick up my mother's ashes.

"What are we going to do about Blossom?" I asked. "We can't just leave her over there all alone."

"Well, your grandfather is allergic, or so he says," my grandmother said. "Sometimes I think men just say that because they don't like cats and want an excuse to keep them out of the house.

Anyway, we can leave her at your mother's house for now. But I suppose we'll have to take her to the pound, unless you want to take her back to Chicago with you?"

"No, not the pound!" I said, louder than I meant to.

"Okay, Meredith, not the pound," she said. "We'll figure out something."

"I'll take her back with me if we can't find another arrangement. Mom would be furious if we took her cat to the pound."

"Yes," she said. "You're right, of course she would. I don't even know what I'm saying these days, Meredith. You'll have to excuse me, I'm just—"

"It's okay, Grandma. I know."

When we arrived at my grandparents' house, Grandma and I milled around in the kitchen making a half-assed attempt at getting dinner started, both knowing that any minute two men would return to the house carrying a box that contained the charred remains of my mother and place them on the kitchen table. I imagined all of us standing there, staring at them, somehow unable to find our way to the moment beyond that one.

An hour later they arrived carrying a large, pastel-colored gift bag, with the words "Lowery Funeral Home: The Best Choice For Your End-of-Life Needs," printed on it in raised gold lettering. Inside, to my extreme relief, was a tastefully decorated ceramic urn. It was ivory with multicolored flowers growing like vines up the sides. My grandmother must have chosen it.

For a minute I felt a very creepy sensation that made the hair on the back of my neck stand up. I thought I might faint, or start throwing up again. It was a sense that something unspeakable had just happened. My mother was inside that urn. I started seeing all sorts of horrible images in my mind, and hard as I tried, I couldn't chase them out. I realized I was doing the exact thing I feared we'd all do, get trapped in that horrible moment, unable to move past it. I took a deep breath to clear my head.

"What are we supposed to do with them?" I asked, when I was finally able to speak.

My grandparents looked at each other, exchanging some secret knowing with one another, then looked back at me.

"We're supposed to take them to California," Grandma said.

"What?" I asked. This was truly unexpected information.

"That's right," Grandpa said. "And it's not us actually, it's you. You're supposed to take the ashes to California and spread them in the Hollywood hills, near that big sign."

"The Hollywood sign? Mulholland Drive?" I asked.

"Yes, I suppose," he said.

"I'm not even sure you're allowed to go up there," I said.

"I don't know about all that," he said. "But that's what the will says."

"Well how on earth am I supposed to do that? I can't just drop everything and go to California."

"It doesn't have to be right away," Derek said. "You can wait until summer vacation, after school is out."

"And you know this how?" I asked.

"Your grandfather told me."

"It's stated in the will," Grandpa said. "Your mother wanted you to take the ashes to California yourself, and she knew it might take some time before you were able to do it. She just wanted it to be done as soon as possible, but within a year's time."

"This is all too weird," I said. "I think there's something about Mom that you're not telling me. What is it, Grandma? When I asked you about the insurance money this morning, you couldn't change the subject fast enough. Please, tell me what you know."

My grandparents exchanged another one of those looks, and then Grandma left the room for a few minutes. When she came back, she was holding a skeleton key.

"For the cedar chest in mom's room?" I asked.

"Yes," my grandmother said. "Your mother had her secrets. She promised to tell you everything someday, but she just kept putting it off. I told her it was a mistake; that you were a grown woman and had the right to know about your past. And she also promised I would never have to be the one to tell you any of it. I used to get so angry with her, that she finally agreed to write everything down. At least she told me that she would. Whether she did that or not, I don't know. The last time she went to the doctor, he threatened to put her on some kind of medication she didn't want to take, and I think it scared her. Anyway, she gave me this extra key to the cedar chest and said I should give it to you if anything happened to her, in case you couldn't find hers. All this intrigue is just so ridiculous!"

My grandma was white as a sheet, and her hands were shaking, as were mine. I had started to feel as though my reality was beginning to unravel. There was a loose thread in the tapestry of my life. I was terrified to discover what would happen if I started picking at it, but had the feeling I wasn't going to have a choice in the matter.

"We're good people, Meredith. Your grandfather and I didn't approve of many of your mother's choices, but we loved her. Your mother was a very stubborn woman. I tried for years to talk some sense into her, but what could we do? She was our daughter."

My grandmother had started sobbing, and my grandfather put his arms around her for comfort. Sensing their embarrassment, Derek had left the room.

"You'll get to the bottom of this soon enough, Meredith," Grandpa said. "Please don't make your grandmother talk about it. You can see how upset she is."

"Of course," I said. "Come on, Grandma, I'll help you with dinner."

After a few awkward moments, we got busy cooking and setting the table for dinner. Derek rejoined us and tried making small talk. It was a fork-in-the-lip meal if ever there was one, and right after we'd finished eating, Derek went to the guest room to start organizing his things to leave in the morning.

"I can stay if you want me to," Derek said. "I'll just have to make a few phone calls, but I can stay a couple more days at least. I hate to leave you in the middle of all this, especially with this latest turn of events. What do you suppose that's all about?"

"I have no idea. My mother had a simple life. She ran the salon, went to her book club, and occasionally took a vacation to

California. She hadn't had a date in years; not that I'm aware of. I can't imagine what the big mystery is, but I'm sure it's no big deal. I'll sort it all out and have the whole story for you when I get home next weekend. It's the beginning of tax season and you know you need to get back. I'll be fine, Derek. Don't worry."

"Maybe it has something to do with your father, or his family," he said.

"From what my mother told me, he was an only child and his parents were dead. He didn't have any living relatives."

"That seems a little odd, doesn't it? No relatives at all, at his young age?"

"I never really thought about it," I said. "I always just took my mother at her word. Why wouldn't I? But now that you mention it, maybe it is a little strange."

"And this whole California thing," Derek said, "what's up with that?"

"That's where she met and married my father. I always assumed she went there to get away from the cold winter weather, and that maybe the place held happy memories for her, that's all. She used to stay in different hotels where my father had performed in L.A. or up the coast in Santa Barbara. I can understand why she might want to visit those places, to feel close to him for a while, although she never really talked about that. She'd just go away for a couple of weeks and come back with a tan, looking rested. That was a good enough explanation as far as I was concerned."

"Promise to keep me posted?" he asked.

"I promise. You'll be able to reach me at my mother's house. I guess it's technically my house now. Anyway, I think I'll stay over there for a few days, and give Blossom some company. I feel like spending a few nights in my old room, thinking about what's happened. I'm going to be very sad for a while, there's no getting around it, so I might as well get started."

"Meredith, you're the most pragmatic individual I've ever met. That's one of the many things I love about being with you. The absence of drama, even now."

"I've never been one for drama, that's true. I think it's a waste of energy."

"You're right about that. But don't be afraid to lean on me if you need to. She was your mother, and we all only get one of those."

That was true, and especially relevant since I never had a father to back her up. I was parentless now. The thing I had feared all my life had really happened. It was like being someone who only has one kidney; when that one goes you're totally screwed. While I was certain I'd live through it, my life would never be the same again. I'd have to learn whom I would be without my mother to bounce things off of. She'd always been the one I called when I had some good news, or bad. And I had always known she'd be there for me.

There had been plenty of room for girl talk in my house, in fact, that was about the only kind of talk there was. We had very few secrets from one another. At least that's what I thought. My mother was my very best friend and confidante. Some things you just can't talk about with your boyfriend, or even your closest girlfriends. It was going to be different now. Who would I trust with my most personal thoughts and fears now that she was gone? Where on earth would I find anyone else who would love me so unconditionally and listen to me talk without judging me? I realized I would have to keep my own counsel on some things, from there on out. I decided that it was part of growing up, but a harsh reality for sure.

Derek left right after breakfast Sunday morning and I headed over to my mother's house in her car, with my small suitcase. I hated leaving my grandparents alone, but had the feeling they were a little relieved to see me go, thus sparing them from further questioning about my mother's choices.

For the third day in a row, I entered the house having completely forgotten about the cat, and when she arrived like a streak from my peripheral vision, she scared the hell out of me. I put on a pot of coffee and turned on some lights in the house. Then I switched on the television and built a fire in the fireplace. When the coffee was ready, I poured myself a cup and headed to my mother's bedroom, turning on more lights as I went. It was still chilly in the house, so after I slipped off my shoes, I replaced them with my mother's fuzzy bedroom slippers. It sent a chill down my spine, and made the hair at the back of my neck stand up again. The realization that my mother's feet would never be inside those slippers again made my stomach clench. I feared a repeat of Friday night's performance at my grandparents' house. To make matters worse, it occurred to me where my mother's feet actually were at that point, in an urn on my grandparent's mantle, and I slapped my hand over my mouth and ran for the bathroom.

I didn't lose my breakfast though, and I was grateful for that. In a few minutes my stomach settled down and my heart rate returned to normal. I cleared off the clothes that were still stacked on top of the cedar chest, sat down on the floor in front of it and put the skeleton key my grandmother had given me into the lock. My mother's cat slipped into the room when I wasn't looking, but didn't startle me for once. She just curled up on the floor next to me and made herself comfortable. I was suddenly overwhelmed by a deep appreciation for her company. This job was not going to be easy.

I smelled the unmistakable scent of cedar the moment I opened the lid of the chest. It was filled all the way to the top. I removed the extra comforter she kept handy for cold winter nights, the southwestern style blanket that I got for Christmas one year and used to keep on the foot of my bed, and several angora sweaters that were stored in zip-lock bags. There was an afghan my grandmother had crocheted, a bundle of silk scarves, and a hand-embroidered tablecloth that we used to use at Christmas time. I found myself wondering what her thought process was as she decided why these things, to the exclusion of others, would be selected to go into the chest. Most curious, however, was the fact that she kept these ordinary things under lock and key.

When I came to a small cardboard box with a floral pattern on the top, that looked as if it might have once held a large photo album, I was sure I had finally reached my goal. But I only found a christening gown, a silver rattle with my name engraved on it, a baby book, and what was probably my first pair of shoes. I picked up the baby book and leafed through it. In the back of the book were some loose papers. Among them were two notecards with congratulations from people whose names I didn't recognize, and an envelope with the words "birth certificate" printed on it. I realized that I had never actually seen my official birth certificate. I had never been married, nor did I have a passport, since I had never had the opportunity to leave the country. My mother had taken care of any other business during my life that would have required proof of my age and citizenship, like when she enrolled me in school. She would have had it with her when we went to get my driver's license too, but I supposed I was too excited to notice.

My heart beat quickened as I opened the envelope and removed its contents. It was a photocopy that looked as if it were made from microfilm. The background was mostly black and the printing was white. There was my name, Meredith Jean Springfield, and my birth date, August 5th, 1962. My mother's name, Anastasia Burke Springfield, was typed neatly in the appropriate place, but the box that should have contained my father's name was completely blank. It should have read, Howard Springfield. But not only was my birth certificate minus a father, I saw that my place of birth was listed as Milwaukee, Wisconsin. Not anywhere in California. This wasn't possible. My mother and I had left California right after my father was killed, but I was born in Los Angeles. It had to be a mistake, but the document looked official so it must have been listed in the public records that way.

I picked up the phone to call my grandmother and dialed six of the digits before dropping the phone back onto its cradle. My grandmother didn't want to talk about whatever it was my mother had kept a secret from me all my life. She wanted me to find out on my own, and that's what I was going to do, even if it meant putting an airplane ticket on my already over-burdened credit card and heading to sunny California right away.

I put the baby book back into the box, keeping the birth certificate out, and started to replace the cover when I noticed something else. In the bottom of the box was an envelope with some old photographs sliding out of it. Some were black and white and some were color, and I could tell that some of them were taken with a Polaroid camera. The Polaroid snapshots didn't have dates on them, but the others, the ones that had been developed commercially, had dates stamped on the edges. Those photos had been taken in 1960 and 1961. There were a variety of people captured in the photographs, and they were taken in different places, often at the beach, but the same two people were in the center of every single one of them. I recognized one of the people as my mother, although she looked very different than the mother I had grown up with. She wore sparkling dresses and jewelry, or sexy swimwear, things I never saw her in. But what struck me the most was the look on her face. She was happy. In all my thirty years, I had never seen her look like that. The other person in the photographs, the one with his arm around my mother, also looked happy. Although I did not recognize him, having never seen his face in these photographs or any others, I had no doubt in my mind that the man with the big smile, often pictured with a shiny silver saxophone in his hands, was my father.

One day, when I was still a little girl, it occurred to me that I had never seen any pictures of my father. When I asked about it, my mother had said that right before we left California, when she was packing up our things, she discovered there had been a leak in the attic where all her photos were stored, and they had all been ruined. So I had taken her at her word, and never asked about it again.

In one of the black and white photographs, my parents stood arm in arm on the sidewalk in front of a hotel. The beach was visible in the background, with what looked like the end of a beautiful sunset over the water. Beside them on the sidewalk stood a large sign advertising a band called The Starlighters, with a special guest appearance by a woman with my mom's maiden name. Anastasia Burke. My father, I was sure that's who he was, wore a dark suit and what was likely a white shirt, with a very wide tie. His hair was combed back, and he was beaming at my mother who was wearing a full-length sequined dress that was skin tight, and outlined the curves of her slim body. She wore a white gardenia tucked behind her left ear, in her long, wavy, blond hair.

They looked like they were ready for the stage, or had just finished a performance, and they were laughing, my mother's head thrown back. The people in the background were dressed much more casually. A similar photograph, this one in color, showed my parents standing with the beach behind them. The beautiful sequined gown she wore was red, and her scarlet lipstick matched it perfectly.

In another photograph my mother stood on the beach, ankle-deep in the surf, wearing a white, one-piece bathing suit. My mother had been stunning. I always thought she was pretty, but in what I considered a somewhat modest and motherly way. The young woman in the photograph had a body that could stop traffic. Gorgeous legs, firm, full breasts, and that smile of hers. She was glowing.

I wondered why my mother had never shared these photographs with me, why in fact she had outright lied about them having been destroyed, and I also wondered what she had been doing on the stage. Special guest what? Had my mother been a singer? That had to be it. In my entire life she had never mentioned playing any musical instrument, and I had definitely never seen her with one. This was all so strange. I was looking for answers in my mother's cedar chest, but so far I had come up with nothing but more questions. There was a story here. Of that, I had no doubt.

I had begun to believe that my mother had lived a very different kind of life than the one I knew about, but figured that maybe she held these mementos in private because they were simply too cherished to share with anyone, even me. I couldn't hold that against her. She had loved the man in the pictures, and he had been tragically ripped from her arms by the accident that had taken his life. I wondered how often she took these photographs out and looked at them, and whether they made her smile or cry, or maybe both.

I felt dizzy, and lightheaded. According to my birth certificate, I was born in Wisconsin, not California, and the space reserved for my father's name had been left blank. My mother had lied to me and I didn't know why, but I was damn sure going to find out.

I had so many questions and didn't know where to start. My grandparents certainly had some of the answers. But had they been covering for my mother all those years? Had they been lying to me, too? I was outraged, confused, scared, and a little sick to my stomach. For thirty years my life was what my mother told me it was. I trusted and believed her. Why wouldn't I? We believe what our parents tell us, because if our parents don't tell us the truth, what hope do we have of living a sane life? I had begun to doubt everything I believed to be true about my mother. I had to find some answers, but I needed to clear my head so I could figure out where to begin.

I pulled on my boots and puffy ski parka and went out the front door of my mother's house. As I trudged down the side-walk, the snow crunched under my feet. The air was biting cold and I could see my breath. It was quiet except for the rhythmic sound of my footsteps, and the whiteness of the sky made it difficult to identify the horizon line where the snowy ground and the clouds met.

Walking usually helped to clear my head, and the icy Milwaukee air was like a cold glass of water to the face. I found myself on a familiar path, down to the end of Elderberry Lane and around the corner to the grade school I attended in the late sixties and early seventies. The building looked much smaller than I remembered, and it was beginning to show signs of decay. As I passed the houses nearby, I saw that they were showing their age as well.

The schoolyard was empty. I tried to picture what it would be like the next morning when all the children returned after the weekend, bundled up in their winter coats, hats and mufflers. As I walked through the fresh snow onto the playground and sat down on a swing, I found myself thinking about a scene in the movie *A Christmas Story* where the little kid puts his tongue on a frozen metal pole on a dare and gets it stuck there. I wondered how many times my own mother warned me not to put my tongue on the metal playground equipment when it was freezing outside? What a ridiculous idea that was. Why would anyone want to put her tongue on filthy metal playground equipment, whether it was freezing outside or not?

I thought about my mother, waiting for me in the kitchen of our house on Elderberry Lane when I'd come home from school. Sometimes she'd be wearing an apron, and taking a pan of peanut butter cookies out of the oven, just for me. She never ate them herself. But I used to love watching her making the little crisscross marks with a fork on top of each one. She loved baking for me, because she knew how much I loved the things she made, and we often made together. Then I thought about how many hours she must have worked, every day of the week, and many times in the evening, so that we could afford to live in that little house where she could have fresh, warm cookies waiting for me when I came home from school. She had loved me very much, that was clear. But she had not been honest with me, and I couldn't imagine what she was hiding that was so bad she felt that she had to keep it from me all these years.

I began to notice how cold it was outside and decided to head back to the house. The answers I was seeking might be there somewhere, and I would spend a little more time looking for clues in order to spare my grandparents from any unnecessary embarrassment, but ultimately they were going to have to tell me what they knew about my mother. I would try not to get angry with them for keeping secrets, she was their daughter after all, but I couldn't help feeling betrayed by all of them.

As I turned back down Elderberry Lane, I saw an unfamiliar car pulling into my mother's driveway. I saw a man in a black overcoat get out of a white Mercedes 450 SL with a large manila envelope in his hands. As he approached the front door, I hurried toward the house, hoping to catch him before he got back in the car and drove away, thinking no one was home. I wanted to know who this man was, and what was in that envelope.

I reached the driveway in time to find him coming back down the front porch steps, the envelope still in his hands.

"Can I help you?"

"Are you Meredith Springfield?"

"Yes."

"I'm Stephen Kensington, your mother's attorney. Can we go inside? I have some things to deliver to you."

"Of course," I said. "Come in, please. It's freezing out here."

As I stepped inside and held the door open for Mr. Kensington, once again my mother's cat shot through my peripheral vision and startled me.

"Are you all right?" he asked.

"Yes, sorry. That damn cat scares me every time I walk into the house. I keep forgetting about her. Guess I'm a little jumpy. Please, sit down. Would you like some coffee?"

"That sounds good, thank you," he said. "I'm sorry to intrude like this and very sorry for your loss."

"Thank you," I said. "It's all been a little overwhelming. So you're my mother's attorney?"

I poured two cups of coffee and brought them into the dining room where Mr. Kensington was draping his coat over the back of a chair, the manila envelope still in his hand.

"Yes, your mother had been my client for thirty years," he said. "I handled the legal matters for her business, prepared her will, and have managed your trust fund ever since you were born."

"Trust fund? What trust fund?"

"I should probably start at the beginning," he said. "Your grandparents have probably already told you that your mother left all of her assets to you, as her only heir. And perhaps they also told you that she wished for you to take her ashes to California."

"Yes. They said her will stated that a letter was to be mailed, to you I assume, in the event of her death, and that they had already done that by the time I arrived in Milwaukee."

"That's right," he said. "I received the letter yesterday. Fortunately, I was in the office. I usually work at home on Saturdays. Anyway, my instructions were that in the event of her death, I should deliver this envelope and its contents to you immediately. I came by last night, but no one was here, so I thought I'd try again today. If I hadn't found you this time, I would have tried your grandparents' house, and was just about to head over there when you arrived."

"So, Mr. Kensington, what's in that envelope you've brought me and what's this about a trust fund? I'm not aware of any trust fund. No one in my family has enough money for any kind of trust fund."

"On the contrary, Miss Springfield—"

"Please, call me Meredith."

"On the contrary, Meredith, someone in your family apparently has a great deal of money."

"I don't understand what's happening here. I'm very confused about the things I've already discovered today, and now you're talking about something that doesn't make any sense."

"I'm sorry, Meredith. I know this must be very confusing, which is why your mother wanted the letter to come to me immediately, so I could get to you and begin to explain things as soon as possible."

"Well then please, Mr. Kensington, enlighten me. I'm beginning to feel like I've slipped into an alternate universe. It's a little unnerving."

"Understandable. Let me see if I can help. First of all, this envelope contains three notebooks, journals I suppose you would call them, given to me by your mother for safe keeping."

He opened the metal clasp on the envelope and pulled out the small stack of spiral notebooks, bound together with a leather tie. They were small, maybe half the size of the ones I'd used in college. When he handed me the notebooks, I noticed a white envelope tucked under the binding on top of the stack.

"I'm to instruct you to read the contents of the envelope first, before you begin reading the notebooks."

"What's this about, Mr. Kensington? Why all the intrigue? What was my mother up to?"

"I really don't know that much. All she told me was that there were events in her past that you needed to understand, but that she did not want you to discover them until after she was gone. I'm really sorry to be so mysterious, but this is what she asked me to do. She said that the notebooks would explain everything, including the trust fund. Which brings me to the next item. I'm supposed to give you this."

He handed me a window envelope with my name, and my mother's address. Through the cellophane window I could see the words "pay to the order of," and realized that the envelope contained a check with my name on it.

"May I open it?" I asked.

"Of course, please."

I carefully opened the envelope and unfolded the contents. The words "Meredith Springfield Trust Account" were printed on the stub. When I saw what was on the check itself, my breath caught in my chest, and I dropped both check and envelope onto the table.

"This is a joke, and not a very funny one I'd say. Who put you up to this, Mr. Kensington? Who would do something so cruel when I've just lost my—"

"I understand your shock, Meredith, but I assure you it's no joke."

"But where would my mother get this kind of money? She ran a hair salon in her basement, for God's sake. If this is for real, then where in hell did it come from?"

"It's all explained in the notebooks. You'll have to read them to find out."

"Do you mean to tell me you have no idea about any of this?"

"Your mother specifically instructed me not to read the contents of the notebooks, and I gave her my word. All I do know is that a large deposit was made into this account the day you were born and additional deposits have been made periodically over the years. The deposits were made via wire transfer from a bank in California."

"From whom?" I asked.

"I don't know. It wasn't my job to ask. It was my job to invest the money in low risk, liquid assets and deliver the balance of the account to you in the event of your mother's death. I wish I could tell you more. I could have my office look into it further if you'd like, but you should probably read whatever is in these notebooks first. If they don't answer all your questions, let me know and I'll help in any way I can. But for now, if there's nothing further, I'll be on my way. And again, I apologize for the intrusion. I know this must all be rather overwhelming."

"To put it mildly," I said. "What exactly do you recommend I do with a check for more than half a million dollars?"

"I'm afraid that's entirely up to you, Meredith. I'd recommend putting at least some of it in an interest bearing account until you decide what you plan to do. But the money is yours, so you can do with it whatever you see fit."

It was a rhetorical question. Lawyers take everything so literally.

Somewhat dazed, I shook his hand and walked Mr. Kensington to the door. As he pulled out of the driveway, I stood at the front door watching him go, the check still in my hand. Blossom meowed and rubbed at my ankles, and I couldn't remember whether I'd fed her yet or not. I thought I had, but she seemed awfully insistent, so I headed for the kitchen.

"Okay, kitty, let's get you some breakfast. I need another cup of coffee. Actually, what I need is a drink, but I guess it's a little early for that, isn't it."

I realized how nice it was to have a pet in the house, especially for someone living alone. That way you don't have to feel like such a moron when you catch yourself talking out loud to an empty room.

While the cat scarfed up her can of food, I leaned against the counter watching until she licked the bowl clean. I was stalling, there was no doubt about that, eager to begin reading the spiral-bound notebooks, but terrified at what I might find in them.

An attorney whom I'd never heard of before had just handed me a check for more money than I ever dreamed of having, and gave me no clue where it had come from, only that it was from a bank in California. Just an hour before, I had discovered that my mother had been lying to me for thirty years, and I saw my father's face for the very first time in my life. I asked the empty room how much stranger my day could get, and later I wished, once again, that I had kept my mouth shut. As it turned out, my day would get much, much stranger.

At the dining room table with a fresh cup of coffee, I carefully unwrapped the leather strap that held the notebooks together.

The envelope that had been secured to the top of the stack had my first name printed on it in my mother's careful handwriting. My own hands were trembling as I opened the envelope and took out the letter that was folded up inside. There were two pages, also handwritten, the text slanting upward as it approached the right margin. My eyes welled up before I read a single word. This was my mother's voice, coming to me from beyond death, and it comforted and alarmed me in turns. But I had delayed as long as I could. It was time to take a deep breath and dive in to my mother's personal thoughts; time to find out exactly what in the hell was going on.

August 5, 1980
My Dear Meredith,

As I write this, you are out with your three closest girl-friends celebrating your 18th birthday. You girls looked so grown up when I dropped you at the mall near the multiplex for pizza and a movie, that I almost called you back so I could get one more look at you. But you're a young woman now, and I can't call you back anymore. I have to let go of you, and trust that our relationship will remain strong enough to bring you home to me from time to time once you're off on your own and no longer under my roof.

You've been the most important person in my life for eighteen years, my precious daughter, and I hope that after you've read the contents of these pages you will understand why I couldn't tell you before. I wanted to tell you everything, and several times I came very close to it, but in the end I decided that my secrets shouldn't have to be your secrets. At the same time, you deserve to know the truth about your life, your mother, and your father. Your grandparents know some of it, but not all. If you're reading this, it means that my life has ended and possibly your grandparents are gone, too. In any case, I'm glad that I wrote everything down, because while I was not courageous enough to tell you this story myself, I feel you have the right to hear it, and hope to God you can find it within yourself to forgive me. The decisions I've made were based on what I believed was best for you and for everyone else involved.

Your grandmother insisted that if I wasn't going to tell you the truth myself, I should at least write it down for you so she wouldn't have to be the one to fill you in. My parents didn't approve of many of my choices, and if they'd known the whole truth about my life, well who knows what they would have done. Anyway, I told her that I would put it in writing for you in case something happened to me, but I had already written much of it down.

I started keeping a journal in 1960 when I moved to California. I was twenty years old, only a little older than you are as I write this. I was fearless, as I embarked upon the adventure of a lifetime, and documented most everything, good and bad, that happened to me in those early years. I'm sorry, Meredith, if anything contained in these pages hurts you. Please believe me when I say that's the last thing on earth I ever wanted to do. I robbed you of a father, and for that I will never forgive myself, but at first I felt I had no choice. As time went on, I had told you and everyone else so many lies it was impossible to go back. So anyway, here it is. The truth. All of it.

Please read the notebooks in chronological order. As I write this, there are two of them, but by the time they reach you there may be more. I tend to write when I'm very happy or very upset, and not very much, if anything, when things are going smoothly. Anyway, regardless of the number, after you've finished reading, I prefer that you destroy them, but I'll leave that up to you. You're very likely a grown woman by now, perhaps with children of your own, and I trust that you are able to make better decisions in your life than I did in mine.

All my love,
Mom

I put the letter down on the table and noticed the cat had curled up in the chair next to mine. With her tail wrapped around her, she formed a perfect circle. She was dozing, occasionally opening her eyes to make sure I was still there. Maybe she was as curious as I was to find out what secrets those notebooks held, or maybe she knew much more about my mother's secrets than I would find in their pages. If she could talk, I wondered whether she would tell me.

When the phone rang, I nearly jumped out of my skin. My mother's cat was not moved.

"Hello?" I panicked for a second when I realized there was a very good possibility the call was not for me, and worse, that it could be someone calling for my mother, not knowing she was dead, and I would have to break the news to them.

"How are you?"

Derek's familiar voice came as a relief.

"Having a very strange day," I said.

Rather an understatement, I thought.

"What's strange about it?"

"It's hard to know where to start, Derek, and I think it's going to get a lot stranger. To begin with, I was looking through an old cedar chest in my mother's room and I found some pictures of her from the early sixties, and she was with a man I'm pretty sure was my father."

"Pictures you hadn't seen before?" he asked.

"Never. She said that she didn't have any pictures of him, but I'm almost sure that's who the man in the pictures is, because he's holding a saxophone."

"Right. I remember you saying that he was a sax player. So I guess it's strange she had the pictures and didn't show them to you. Is that it?"

"No, it gets much stranger. I went for a walk this morning and when I got back to the house there was a lawyer in the driveway."

"How could you tell?"

"I couldn't tell by looking at him, Derek," I said with a smile. "I didn't find out until I actually met him. But he was my mother's attorney. Remember the letter my grandmother said she mailed on Thursday? Well, it arrived in his office yesterday and he just happened to be there to get it. The letter was to notify him of my mother's death, and his instructions were to make a delivery to me, which he did this morning. He brought me an envelope full of my mother's journals, and those are supposed to explain everything. But here's the really strange part."

"Tell me."

"He handed me a check for $533,000."

There was silence on the other end of the phone line. I knew he was still there, because I could hear him breathing.

"I'm sorry, Meredith," he chuckled. "It sounded like you said $533,000."

"That's right. That's what I said."

"Where in the world would that kind of money come from?"

"Good question," I said. "It's from my trust fund. I, Meredith Jean Springfield, apparently have a trust fund. I accused him of playing a very mean trick on me, but he assured me it was for real. Maybe you could look into it for me and help me figure out what's going on."

"Something really strange is happening, Meredith, you're right. I thought there was something crazy about that annuity of your mother's, and now this. It's like you won the lottery."

"On the surface at least, but I'm going to have to get to the bottom of all this. The attorney said I should find some answers in the notebooks, so I'm going to pour a fresh cup of coffee and get started. I'll tell you all about it when we talk later tonight."

When I hung up the phone I felt a brief pang of loneliness. It was good hearing Derek's voice, familiar and warm. He was a tie to my real life in Chicago, where I was an adult with a job, a mortgage, and grown-up responsibilities. Here in Milwaukee I still felt like a child, even at thirty. In my mother's house, I was always the child. In this town, I had always been Meredith Springfield, the little girl who grew up on Elderberry Lane without a father. Who would I be now?

The cover of each of the notebooks was a different color, with the year printed in the upper right corner. The one on the top of the stack was blue, the color of the ocean. The year was 1960. Pasted inside the front cover was a black and white photograph of my mother, standing next to her Ford Fairlane, the car my grandparents helped her buy when she graduated from high school. You couldn't tell from the picture, but I knew it was powder blue. She drove that car all the way to California and back, and who knew where else in between. The car in the picture was parked in the street outside my grandparents' house. My mother was wearing a wool coat, buttoned up to her throat. It looked as though the hat, gloves and muffler she wore were soft and fuzzy. There were two suitcases on the ground next to her at the end of the freshly shoveled sidewalk. She was waving at the person taking the picture, probably my grandfather. She looked confident and happy, and I wondered what was going through her mind, faced with saying farewell to her parents and heading west all by herself. That innocent girl who grew up in Milwaukee, Wisconsin with both of her parents was about to go off on her own and discover what it's like to be free. The date on the photograph was January 16, 1960. I started reading, and didn't stop until I'd finished the first notebook.

CHAPTER 4
Anastasia

JANUARY 16, 1960

IT WAS FOURTEEN DEGREES OUTSIDE WHEN I left Milwaukee this morning. I put on a very happy face for Mom and Dad when I drove away, because I didn't want them to be sad. I know that Mom probably cried for the rest of the day, although I tried not to think about that. I'm a little scared about making this trip alone. Five days on the road is a long time. I could get a flat tire, or get in an accident or something. But mostly I'm glad to be heading away from the cold weather. When I get to California it's going to be warm and sunny, and I absolutely cannot *wait* to see the ocean!

I drove about four hundred miles today, in order to spend the night at Aunt Edie's house in Jefferson City, Missouri. I only made one sightseeing stop, to see the world's largest catsup bottle in Collinsville, Illinois. It's actually a 100,000-gallon water tower that's used to supply the sprinkler system in case there's a fire at the plant. I didn't stop for long though, I just picked up a brochure, snapped a photo with my new Polaroid camera and got right back on the road. Since I haven't seen Aunt Edie for a couple of years, I thought it would be nice to visit. Besides, it's one less motel to pay for along the way. I'm going to have to be very careful about how I spend my money, at least until I find a job.

For the past eighteen months since graduation, I haven't spent a dime on anything that wasn't essential. My paychecks from the salon and all my tips have gone straight into my bank account for this trip. The way I figure it, if I find a fairly cheap place to stay, I'll have enough money to last for a month. Hopefully by then I'll have found a job. My friend, Sarah, told me that her cousin, Jill, got a job as a hair stylist at a television studio, and she makes really good money. I'm going to try that, too. Between all the TV and movie studios in Los Angeles, I should be able to find something, especially since I finished my cosmetology certification. I might have to take some more classes to get a license for California, but hopefully that won't keep me from getting a job right away.

I started on Route 66 in Chicago and I'll follow it all the way to sunny Los Angeles. It's hard to believe this is really happening, at last. I've been looking forward to this trip ever since my senior year in high school. Finally, I'm on my way.

Aunt Edie is calling me to dinner, so I have to stop here for today. More tomorrow night when I reach my motel in Oklahoma City.

JANUARY 17, 1960

OKLAHOMA CITY, OK

The price was right on this motel, but it's a real dump. I think I'm going to wedge the desk chair up under the doorknob when I go to bed. The lighting in the bathroom is terrible, just one bare bulb. I hope I don't really look like this! It was nice staying at Aunt Edie's house. She's a very interesting person, and still quite attractive, even though she must be close to fifty by now. Mom said that when they were in high school my aunt was really popular, but for some reason, she never married. It made me a little sad thinking about her living all alone like that, but it doesn't seem to bother her. She has a really good job as a journalist for the local paper, and lots of friends too. I guess I can see some advantages to being single at her age, especially if you can afford it. But I want to get married some day and have three or four children.

Anyway, at dinner Edie told me that my parents had already called twice before I arrived, even though I promised I would call and check in with them as soon as I walked in the door. It must be hard for them, knowing I'm out here in the world all by myself. I guess I don't blame them for being worried. But I'm being very careful, and don't plan on doing anything stupid, so I'm sure that I'll be just fine. Although, if I'm honest, it's actually a little creepy here and I'll be glad to get back on the road in the morning. My room is clean, technically speaking. I mean the toilet and sink appear to have been scrubbed recently, and I'm sure the sheets are fresh. But the rest of the room looks like a million people have traipsed through it in dirty shoes. It's more the feeling of dirt than actual dirt, I guess. I don't know. Anyway, I walked over and got a sandwich from the deli next door and brought it back to my motel room for dinner.

My car is parked right outside the door and I didn't want to lose my parking place. Also, everything I own is in the trunk, so I wanted to hurry back and keep an eye on it. There are a couple of longhaired guys in the room next door who look a little shady. They were in the parking lot drinking beer when I walked over to the deli. One of them said something to me as I walked by and the other one laughed, but I just ignored them. I can hear music coming from their room. Well, I should say I hear the bass line of what must be music. All I hear is thump, thump, thump. I'm thinking I'll get on the road really early in the morning. I feel safer when I'm moving.

JANUARY 18, 1960

SANTA FE, NM

New Mexico is so beautiful! Last night I was in the capital of Oklahoma, and tonight I'm in Santa Fe, the capitol of New Mexico, and it's so much different from anything I've seen before. The hills and the desert are so open and rugged. It's a little bit cool outside, but nothing like it is back home. When I called to let my parents know I was here, Dad said they got more snow last night in Milwaukee! No thanks. I'm headed to sunny California.

This motel is a lot nicer than the one I stayed in last night. Those guys next door kept me up half the night with their loud music. I even called the office to complain, and heard their phone ring a few minutes later. They finally turned the music down, but then I was afraid they'd come over and yell at me, or worse. Anyway, I finally got to sleep, but the moment I woke up, I showered, dressed, and got the heck out of there! As I was pulling out of my parking space, I gave my horn a good loud honk so those guys next door could see what it's like to try and sleep when other people are making noise.

A few minutes ago, I met a nice family in the room next door to mine. They're much better neighbors than the ones I had last night! They're on their way back to Georgia. The kids have this adorable southern drawl. When I first heard them, it made me laugh. But it didn't take long to get used to it. They invited me to join them for dinner, since I'm travelling alone. I think that's so sweet of them. Maybe it's true what they say about people from the South. Anyway, we're going to walk over to the Bob's Big Boy in a few minutes for burgers and fries. I'm starving! So that sounds really good. Hard to believe it, but day after tomorrow I'll arrive in Los Angeles. I'm so excited!

JANUARY 19, 1960

FLAGSTAFF, AZ

There's snow here in Flagstaff! I guess it's winter everywhere in this part of the world, so I shouldn't be surprised, but I thought I'd left all that behind in Wisconsin. The man at the front desk said that it gets below freezing here at night almost half the time. Then it gets warmer during the day so the snow starts to melt, but it freezes right up again. I thought it would be hot here in Arizona, since it's the desert. But no, there's snow. It's beautiful here, though.

All of the country I've driven though so far has been beautiful in its own way. The landscape in the place where I start the day is completely different from where I am at the end of it. It's amazing. I don't know why anyone would spend all that money to travel to other countries when there's so much to see right here in America. But there's something extra special about this place. I can't really put my finger on it, but it makes me feel happy just being here. Maybe it's because I know that tomorrow I'll go to sleep in California. Since it's my last night on the road, and tomorrow is a very special day, I'm going to get my clothes ready, put some curlers in my hair, and get a good night's sleep. Get ready, L.A., here I come!

JANUARY 20, 1960

LOS ANGELES, CA

Today I saw the Pacific Ocean for the first time. My eyes tear up every time I think about it. In my whole life, I have never seen anything so magnificent. It was seventy-five degrees this afternoon when I got to Los Angeles. I followed the map to the hotel where my friend Sarah's cousin, Jill, stayed for a while when she first moved here. There are millions of places to stay in Los Angeles, but since I don't know anyone else that I can ask for a recommendation, I figured it was as good a place as any. Besides, it's not far from the beach. Well, it's kind of far, actually it's too far to walk, but by car it only takes a few minutes.

As soon as I brought my bags inside and called Mom and Dad to let them know I had arrived safely, I got right back in the car and drove to the beach. I parked the car, took off my shoes, rolled up the cuffs of my blue jeans, and walked straight out to the water. It was unbelievable. I just stood there, crying, with my feet in the salt water for the first time. Having grown up on the Great Lakes, huge bodies of water are nothing new to me, but this is a whole different thing. The ocean is an incredible shade of blue in the bright sunshine, with a white border where the waves crash onto the seemingly endless, jagged shoreline.

There were quite a few people on the beach, even though it wasn't exactly hot out, especially with the wonderful breeze. I can't even imagine how crowded this beach will be in the summertime. But even on this winter day, there were lots of striped umbrellas next to matching beach chairs, and lifeguards perched up in their stations, keeping a lookout over the handful of people who were swimming. The water was pretty cold, actually much colder than I expected, but it is January after all.

Back at home, there are icebergs on Lake Michigan. Here it's sunny and warm, and the sky is perfectly blue. I stood at the edge of the water and turned in a complete circle so I could take everything in. I wanted to create a panoramic picture in my mind so I will never, ever forget this day. Although I don't imagine I ever will. This place seems to go on forever, all of it wrapped up in an endless blanket of sunshine, like the biggest gift I could ever possibly ask for. The Pacific Ocean is truly the most amazing thing I've ever seen. Even if I live to be a hundred years old, I bet I'll never see anything more beautiful. I'm never, ever leaving this place.

JANUARY 21, 1960

My first morning waking up in California, and guess what I did? No surprise, I got up, pulled on my clothes and went straight to the beach. I didn't stay long, because I have a lot to do today, but I think that any day that begins with a walk on the beach simply has to be an excellent day. I called Sarah's cousin, Jill, this morning when I got back to my room, and caught her on her way out the door to go to work. She gets off at 4:00, and she's going to pick me up and show me around a little. It will be so nice to have a friend here.

L.A. is so big, and I've never been too far outside of Milwaukee before now, so it's strange being in such a huge place where I don't know a single person. Once I get a job, I'll meet some people there and eventually I'll know lots of people, just like I did at home. But meanwhile, Jill seemed awfully nice on the phone, so

I'm really looking forward to getting to know her. This weekend she's going to take me on a tour of the movie studio where she works. I'm very excited!

JUNE 14, 1960

So much has happened since my last entry. I got a job at a hair salon about five minutes before I ran out of money. Jill got me an interview with the lady she worked for before she got the job at Twentieth Century-Fox doing hair and makeup for the movie stars. It wasn't the fanciest salon in the world, but it kept me from starving to death.

The ladies in California are a lot different than they are in Wisconsin. You wouldn't believe how many of them have blonde hair, although a lot of them didn't start out that way, and most of the women who walked into the salon asked for a beehive. I did more backcombing and hair spraying than you can imagine during the couple of months that I worked there. But when the boss's husband made a pass at me in the supply room and she walked in and saw it, she accused me of coming on to him and fired me right on the spot, without even giving me a chance to explain. It wasn't my fault he was a horny old coot, but she fired me anyway.

I had moved into a tiny studio apartment near the salon right after I got the job, so I could save money on gas. There were roaches in the kitchenette the size of small bats, and sirens blaring outside all night long. My parents would have had a fit if they'd seen the place. Anyway, when I got fired from the salon, Jill asked me to move in with her for a while. I think she might have talked to Sarah and told her what happened, and Sarah asked her to help me out. In any case, I'm living with Jill now, in a better part of town. The apartment is really small, but it's a lot nicer than the last one.

After about two weeks of being unemployed, I was starting to think about getting in my little blue car and going back to Milwaukee, much as I hated the idea, when I ran into one of my customers from the salon. She works in the bar at a hotel right along the beach in Santa Monica, and she told me that they were looking for a waitress. I got the job, and believe it or not, the same day Jill came home from work and said there was a chance for me to get on at Twentieth Century-Fox as a shampoo girl! It would be crazy to give up a chance to work at a movie studio, but the job didn't pay very much at all, certainly not enough to live on. So now I have two jobs! That's why I haven't written in such a long time. I work days at the studio and nights at the bar, so I don't have time to do much of anything else. But I'm having fun and managing to put some money away every week, even now that I'm paying Jill some rent. She's been such a good friend to me. I'll always be grateful for her help.

She introduced me to some of her friends, and since I've been working in both places, I've made lots of other friends, too. Not that I have much time for socializing, with two jobs, but so far I haven't really missed Wisconsin. Sure, I miss my parents, but I talk to them every week and we write letters as well. I just love it here!

AUGUST 13, 1960

Guess what? I'm a singer! Can you believe it? I can't. I mean, I always sing in the shower, and while I'm doing housework, or whenever I'm in a really good mood, but I never would have thought of myself as a singer.

Let me back up. One night a few weeks ago, I was working at the bar, and we were getting ready to close. The guys in the band were sitting at the bar having a drink before packing up their things to head for home. Jake, the drummer, had just broken up with his girlfriend, and he wasn't in a hurry to get back to his empty apartment. Anyway, the bartender asked them if they'd mind playing a couple more tunes while we finished cleaning up. They all said sure, and took their drinks back up to the bandstand.

Like I said, I always sing when I'm doing housework, and the band was playing *The Shadow of Your Smile*, which I adore, and

I started singing along. When the song was over, the saxophone player, who's gorgeous by the way, asked me to come over to the bandstand.

"Where'd you learn to sing like that?" he asked.

"Like what?" I replied.

"Like an angel with a devil inside her."

Then I got embarrassed. I probably turned fifty shades of red. He asked me to come up on stage and sing it again, with the microphone this time, just for fun. I thought, what the hell, and went up and did it. And you know what? I was pretty good! So every night for the rest of the week while they were at the hotel, I got to sing a couple of songs with the band after we closed up for the night. It's so much fun! Who knows, maybe someday I'll get to sing with the band *before* we close the bar, while people are still there to hear me.

The band is playing at another hotel for the next few weeks, up in Santa Barbara. But Howard, that's the sax player's name, said that they'd be back in September. I can't wait!

SEPTEMBER 17, 1960

I'm happy and sad, all at the same time. Isn't that odd? Howard and the band were back at the hotel tonight. I was so happy to see them, especially him. He looked so handsome, relaxed, and happy. He was practically glowing. And, it's no wonder. While he was up in Santa Barbara he'd gone and gotten married. Married! I didn't even realize he had a girlfriend. Apparently she's some high society girl from Brentwood and her family is loaded. Her father is a big deal in the entertainment business or something and her mother inherited millions.

Frankly, I sort of thought Howard was flirting with me, and I secretly hoped that something might happen between us, even though he's a few years older than me. But it looks like it won't be happening, so that's why I'm sad. The happy part is that he's asked me to rehearse with the band and he said that maybe I could fill in for his singer while she's on her honeymoon. I told him I could only do the L.A. gigs because of my job at the studio, but he said that would be fine since they didn't have anything scheduled out of town until his regular singer got back. So I have to practice like crazy for the next two weeks!

The bar manager is being really nice about letting me take the time away from waiting tables on weekend nights when I'll be singing, so everything seems to be falling into place. It's funny. I remember my girlfriends and me at sleepovers in high school, singing along with our favorite records and holding a hairbrush like it was a microphone. But I never dreamed I would have the chance to be on the stage for real! I always knew that coming to California was the right thing to do. My life is magical.

OCTOBER 1, 1960

Tonight was unbelievable! Just imagine me, Anastasia Burke, on stage, in a glittering black dress that I borrowed from my friend, April, who works in the costume department at the studio. She asked her boss and everything, and he said it would be okay as long as I was extra careful with it. I'm not sure who else wore this dress, but I like to think it was someone famous and ever so glamorous, because I feel like a movie star in it. I really hope he won't get in trouble, though. I'd feel awful if he got fired for letting me borrow clothes, although the dress I wore tonight had been in an old storage room for years, so I doubt anyone would care.

I sang beautifully, if I don't mind saying so, and the audience applauded for me! I'd say it was like a dream come true, except it wasn't ever a dream I really had, not seriously anyway, until it dropped into my lap. But it was by far the most exciting and overwhelming night of my life and I'll never, ever forget it. I sang *Good Morning Heartache*, not like Billie Holliday or anything, but everyone still seemed to like it, and of course we did my favorite songs, *The Shadow of Your Smile* and *I've Grown Accustomed to Your Face*. It's such an amazing feeling, standing on the stage with the band, and having everyone in the audience looking right at me. It was scary at first, because I thought; what if they don't like my voice? Or what if they get up and walk out? Or worse, I was afraid they might all just start talking to each other and ignore me completely, and I'd still have to stand there behind the microphone until the song was over. But as I looked around the room, people were watching me and smiling. Some of them were tapping their feet, or bobbing their head to the beat of the music. They were enjoying themselves, and so was I. It was truly a magical night.

Meanwhile, it's 3:00 in the morning and I'm sitting in my bedroom in this glorious dress because I can't bear to take it off. But I have to get some sleep now because my shift at the studio starts at 11:00 in the morning, and I'll get to wear a different dress tomorrow night, thanks to April's boss, and the fact that I promised his wife free hairdos, at their home, for the next six months. Oh well, it's worth it to feel this glamorous, and married or not, I'm pretty sure Howard thought I looked good, too, because he couldn't seem to keep his eyes off me. Too bad for him—he had his chance and decided to go off and get married instead. So he's just plain out of luck.

NOVEMBER 26, 1960

It's been a crazy couple of months, for sure. When Howard's regular singer came back from her wedding and honeymoon, she announced that she was pregnant and wouldn't be returning to the band. She said all those smoke-filled bars they played in wouldn't be healthy for the baby she was carrying, which makes a lot of sense when you think about it. So, believe it or not, I'm her permanent replacement. Since I'm singing with the band on weekends and we sometimes have to travel, I quit my waitressing job at the hotel, but I still work at the studio during the week.

A few days ago, the most amazing thing happened! In fact, I wouldn't even believe it myself if I didn't have the photograph to prove it. I went over to the wardrobe department at Twentieth Century-Fox to have lunch with April. While I waited for her to finish up so we could go eat, I started looking through a pile of old dresses they were going to get rid of. Since I'm singing with the band on a regular basis now, I need to have some dresses of my own, and she thought we might be able to salvage something out of the studio's throw away pile and make alterations to fit me.

Anyway, I'm standing there in front of the mirror, holding this old rag of a dress in front of myself, trying to imagine what it might look like if it was cut down to my size. The dress was black with silver sequins. At one time, and on a woman who was much larger than me, it was probably quite stunning. So anyway, I'm standing there with this tattered old dress in my hands, and you'll simply never guess who walks in. It's only the most gorgeous woman in the entire universe. Marilyn Monroe actually walked up to me and said, in her sexy, breathy voice, "Honey, you're much too beautiful for that ugly old thing. What's your name?"

So I told her. We started talking, and I said that I sing with a band and that we were just digging through some old dresses to see if we could find something for me to wear on stage. Of course, I know she's a singer, too, and then I realize I'm nothing at all compared to her. I couldn't even believe we were actually having a conversation! I told her that I work as a shampoo girl at the studio during the week, and she said, "I'll ask for you next time. Meanwhile, I have a couple of dresses that would look gorgeous on you. They'll need to be cut down a little, but I'm sure your friend here can help with that. I'll have them sent over." Then her assistant walked up and said, "There you are, Miss Monroe," and rushed her off to look at some costumes. I'm pretty sure I thanked her, but as she walked away, she turned and smiled at me, and gave me a little wink. I'll never forget that smile. The next day, she came back to the wardrobe department to drop off the dresses personally, instead of having them sent over. When April called to tell me that Marilyn Monroe was there, waiting for me, I ran across the lot as fast as I could, so she wouldn't have to wait long. She brought me two of the most exquisite dresses I've ever seen. One of them was white with tiny crystal beads all over the bodice, and the other was red with sequins all over it.

She wanted to see me in one of them, so I put on the red one and my friend pinned it on me so that it looked smooth and sleek on my body, at least from the front. Then Marilyn told me I looked beautiful and let April take our picture together.

I'll never understand why such a famous, talented and utterly amazing woman would take the time to even look in my direction, but Marilyn did. I'll carry the memory of that moment with me for the rest of my life! Every time I put on one of those dresses, I'll feel her energy and be reminded that I'm the luckiest girl in the entire world.

DECEMBER 31, 1960

Howard was drunk tonight. It's New Year's Eve, so everyone was drunk. Well, everyone but me, it seemed like. I doubt that anyone else even noticed, but several times he staggered while we were performing and I was afraid he might fall right off the damn stage! He had another fight with his wife, Victoria. That's been happening a lot lately. In fact, he's rented a small bungalow by the beach where he stays sometimes so he can be away from her. She's so controlling, especially with her money. Howard's wife never lets him forget that she's the one who owns the mansion they live in, and that if it weren't for her father's connections in the music industry, he wouldn't have a chance of making it in the business. Thanks to his father-in-law, Howard might have an opportunity to sign a recording contract one of these days, but only if he "behaves himself." That sounds strange to me though, because as far as I can tell, Howard always behaves himself. Well, until tonight anyway.

Tonight was different. He was so drunk that I was afraid to let him drive back to his bungalow, so I gave him a ride home. When we got there, I helped him inside and tried to put him to bed so he wouldn't drink anymore. That was a big mistake, I guess, because we both ended up in his bed. I thought he had passed out the minute he fell onto his bed, so I took off his shoes, and unbuttoned his shirt, thinking I could roll him over onto each side and pull his arms out of the sleeves. I planned to cover him up with a blanket and leave. But that's not exactly what happened.

Before I knew it, he reached up and pulled me down onto the bed with him and rolled over on top of me. I had fantasized about being kissed like that, but had no idea the effect it would have over me. Pretty soon we were both ripping our clothes off. It was like something had taken control over me, and I couldn't do anything to stop it. Nor did I want to. My first time ever in bed with a man, and he was both drunk and married. Not exactly the way I envisioned it, that's for sure, but I love him. I've loved him for a long time. I just didn't want to admit it to myself. It was wonderful being with him, in spite of everything. I had wanted him so badly that I didn't stop for one second to consider what I was doing. I knew it was wrong, and I did it anyway. What kind of woman am I?

After he fell asleep, I got dressed and came home. Tomorrow is going to be awkward. Hell, maybe the rest of my life will be awkward, and maybe I'll be punished in some horrible way. I probably deserve that. But I wouldn't take it back, even if I could. It was incredible, and God help me, I can't wait to do it again.

JUNE 17, 1961

After that night in December, Howard and I were together for two glorious months in his bungalow by the beach. We couldn't be seen together in public, but that was okay because we wanted to be alone, just the two of us. He said he was never going back to his wife and that he'd find a way to get along without her financial support. I thought he'd divorce her and we could live happily ever after. But then in February, she called to tell him she was three months pregnant and he ran to her, just like that, and left me behind. The baby is due in August.

They say that spring is for lovers, a time of renewal and joy and other assorted bullshit. But this spring felt like the end of my life. I felt sick inside, and couldn't eat or sleep for days on end. I wanted to die, and on a few occasions I considered it. One night in particular, I was driving home along the coast highway, and I thought about how easy it would be to drive straight off the cliff and end up in a flaming heap on the beach. All I'd have to do is hold the steering wheel straight for a few extra seconds instead of making the curve. I thought about my parents and what something like that would do to them, but they'd just think it was an accident. And accidents happen all the time.

But then I thought about Howard. What if he really did leave Victoria for good one day? It could happen. So I decided to stay alive for a while longer to see how it all panned out. What the hell, why not?

I'm still singing with the band, though. Some days I think I hate Howard more than anyone on earth. Other days, I'm pretty sure I'm still in love with him. But it doesn't matter, because he's not going to leave his wife any time soon, now that they're having a baby. Of course, that doesn't stop him from complaining to me about her. She's fat, crabby, and very demanding, according to Howard, and it gives me some satisfaction knowing that she's making his life miserable. He deserves it.

I've started seeing a nice man I met at the studio. He's one of the writers for a TV series. We have fun together, but it's nothing serious and so far I've managed to do a good job of escaping his advances. I'll probably have to break it off soon, and stop leading him on, but for now it's a good diversion. Besides, it drives Howard crazy, which makes me feel a whole lot better about things.

NOVEMBER 11, 1961

Howard and Victoria had a baby girl. She was born on July 20th, two weeks ahead of schedule. I guess old Vicky just couldn't wait to break my heart and decided to start early. I don't really think she knows anything about the time that Howard and I spent together, or I doubt she'd let me continue singing with the band. She'd probably hire a hit man instead. Heaven knows she can afford it.

Anyway, Howard was thrilled to greet his new baby girl. They named her Melody, which I guess is sort of cute for someone whose father is a musician. Anyway, he and Victoria seemed to be almost happy together for exactly two months before they started bickering again. She had started coming to the clubs sometimes to watch us perform, but she always stayed in the back of the room and left when we stopped playing. That was perfectly fine with me. I did not relish the idea of shaking her hand.

Since October, Howard has started spending weekends at the bungalow again. He tells her it's because now that he's a father, he has to be more careful. It's dangerous driving home to Brentwood late at night after playing a job and having some drinks. The truth is that he wants to be with me, and may God help me, I want to be with him. He says that he doesn't love her anymore, but that if he leaves her she'll never let him see his daughter again. And I understand that, I do, but I'm pretty sure that he's still *acting* like he loves her so she won't be suspicious.

I try not to think about that, but after all, he is still her husband, at least until his career takes off. Then maybe he can do something about that, but for now I'm stuck being the other woman. When I'm with him it's wonderful and I don't think about the rest of it. But when he's at home in his Brentwood mansion, and I'm alone in my little bedroom in the apartment I share with Jill, I'm sick about the situation I've put myself in. I swear I'm going to break it off and never see him again. But when he's in front of me, I'm helpless to do anything but love him.

FEBRUARY 4, 1962

The sun was an angry red ball of fire on the horizon tonight that melted into flaming pink clouds on either side. It looked as if it would sink into the water and make steam rise up out of the Pacific Ocean with a hissing sound, rather than disappearing around the curve of the earth. Its reflection on the water was almost too beautiful to bear. Back home in Milwaukee the temperature may not even have been in double digits, but here, although the air was cool on the beach, a light sweater over my bare shoulders was enough to keep me warm.

Last night I wore my red sequined dress, the one I save to wear on stage when I know we're going to have a big crowd. I noticed it was beginning to get a little tight around the belly, and soon others would notice as well. So this evening, I had planned to tell Howard about the baby. I'd picked up dinner for Howard and me from the deli near Jill's apartment, where I'd gone to get some clean clothes and sort through my mail. On the drive back to the bungalow, all I could think about was how my news was going to change everything, and how happy Howard and I were going to be. But when I got there, a strange car was parked in the driveway and Howard's wasn't there. I thought I remembered him saying that his car needed to go into the shop for repairs, so I assumed the strange car in the driveway belonged to one of his musician friends and was on loan to him until his car was fixed. It looked familiar, but I couldn't place it. Also strange was that all the curtains were drawn, in spite of the fact that the sun had only just set. Still, I was eager to see Howard and couldn't wait to tell him the good news, so I parked my car at the curb and walked toward the little house. The front door opened before I could reach it, but instead of Howard waiting to greet me on the small covered porch, rimmed with hanging baskets of bougainvillea, someone else stood there waiting for me in the shadows. For one crazy moment I considered running back to my car and driving away. Then I was suddenly terrified that something had happened to Howard, and the person standing in the doorway would deliver the devastating news. But when I got closer to the porch I knew at once. It was her.

All day I had imagined how happy Howard would be when I told him about our baby and how, surely, that would be the news that would convince him to finally leave his horrible wife and marry me. What happened instead was nothing I could have ever expected. Now my world has been turned upside down. In the morning I'll pack my suitcases and start the long drive back to Milwaukee. It's the last place on earth I want to be, but I'll keep the promise I made when I accepted the money, and stay out of his life, and hers, forever. Now he'll never know about our baby, only that he's about to have a second child with Victoria. She's known about Howard and me for nearly a year, but never said anything to let on she knew.

Last night she caught me in the ladies room throwing up between sets on the bandstand and recognized the changes in my body for what they were. Tonight, she confronted me. She told Howard about her pregnancy this afternoon, only hours before he was supposed to find out about mine. He'd packed the few things that he had at the bungalow and gone back to the house in Brentwood. I don't know what she threatened, or whether he ever intended to explain anything to me in person or not. Maybe he's planning to call me tomorrow, but I'll never know, because tomorrow I'll be gone, and I can never speak to him again. She promised me a thousand dollars a month for the rest of my life if I would just disappear and never have contact with Howard again.

And most importantly, she made me promise he would never find out about my baby. Victoria said that she was the wife. I was only the mistress. She said that she would never let him have a divorce and leave her children without a father, although it didn't seem to bother her in the least that my child would be left without one. Still, I wasn't going to go along with any of it, because I don't care a thing about her money. I'd be happy living in a trailer, as long as Howard and I could raise our child together. But then she said a really horrible thing, and that's what changed my mind. She said that if I didn't accept her offer, she would ruin him. Her parents would see to it that his career was destroyed. They have the connections to do it, too.

I won't be responsible for ruining Howard's career, even if it means I can never see him again. I know how important his career is to him, and I love him too much to let anything or anyone take that away. Victoria said I should make up a story to tell my family so they don't get any ideas about coming out here to find the man who's the father of my child. I don't know what I'll tell them, but I have more than two thousand miles to cover while I think about it. My life is ruined. My heart is broken. It's my fault, I know. I was wrong to get involved with him in the first place. I can't believe this is happening.

CHAPTER 5
Meredith

MY HANDS WERE SHAKING AS I closed the notebook and put it on the table next to the others. The sun had set while I was reading, and it was beginning to get dark in the house. I hadn't even noticed. At some point Blossom had crawled into my lap. When I put down the notebook she jumped down to the floor, leaving behind a chill in the place where her warm body had been.

As I moved through the house, turning lights on and pulling the curtains closed, my head was swimming with thoughts about my mother and I felt emotions ranging from anger to pity and everything in between, toward both of these women. I wondered if my mother had kept her promise all these years; or if she had broken down at some point and contacted him. After all, thirty years had gone by. It didn't seem as though my mother could have been a threat to my father's wife anymore. Her children would have been grown up just as I was, with lives of their own. Victoria's primary goal appeared to be making sure that her children didn't have to grow up without a father; that, and to avoid looking like a fool. It certainly didn't seem as though she loved him very much.

Then it hit me. I had spent my life as an only child, but in reality, I had at least two half-siblings, and one of them was a girl. I had at least one sister, an older one. How nice that would have been for me growing up. And I had a second sibling as well, one that was almost exactly the same age as me. They grew up with both their parents and lots of money. My siblings probably had everything they ever wanted. They didn't have to grow up feeling like the odd man out all the time because they only had one parent. And they probably didn't work from the time they were old enough to hold down a job, just so their mother could take a day off once in a while, or to help pay for groceries and the electric bill.

I realized I was becoming furious with these people I didn't even know. In turn I felt rage toward the woman who bullied my mother into leaving town without telling my father about me, and disappointment in my mother for getting knocked-up in the first place, and for failing to fight for the man she loved, thus robbing me of my father.

When Derek answered the phone, I hadn't been quite sure what I'd do next, but after talking to him I knew.

"Do you want me to go with you?" he asked.

"More than anything," I said. "But I can't ask you to drop everything and go on some wild goose chase across the country. I don't even know if these people are *in* California anymore, and she didn't tell me their last name, so I may not even be able to find them. I'm actually not sure that I want to, but I have to understand what this is all about. I'll never have any peace until I do."

"Look," he said. "What's the point in having my own business if I can't take some time off when I want to? My staff can keep things going while I'm away. I can check in by phone. Let me do this. What did your boss say?"

"She was great. I told her that I needed to take a leave of absence for at least eight weeks, starting immediately. It's amazing how easy it is to make a statement like that when you don't have to worry about money. The substitute they found for this week is available to continue as long as necessary, which was really lucky. Actually, she's thrilled to have the work. But it wouldn't have mattered how the people at school reacted, because I was prepared to just quit if they wouldn't go along with it. Maybe my boss heard that in my voice. Anyway, it's all taken care of. At first I felt a little weird about using any of the money that woman paid my mother off with, but I think she owes it to me. At least she owes me a trip to California to sort this out."

"So, according to your mother's journal, she took Route 66 from Chicago to L.A., just like in the song. Why don't we do the same thing? That sounds like a great trip to me. We could forget about all the airplane hassles and just take our time. Besides, I know you hate to fly."

"Derek, you're an amazing man. My grandmother even thinks so."

"Well, I don't know about amazing, but it's been a hell of a couple years for me, too, and I think we could both use a change of scenery."

"You've got that right," I said. "But most of that old highway is gone now."

"I know," he said. "We'll take the freeway most of the time, but we can make some detours along the way and check out some history. What do you say?"

I said yes. Three days later, my mother's house was on the market. The closets and cabinets were cleaned out, half the furniture had either been moved to storage or donated, and I was on my way back down to Chicago to pack more clothes and pick up Derek. A little more than a week after my mother's death, Derek and I were on our way to California in a rented convertible, stopping from time to time to visit what remained of historic Route 66, also known as the Will Rogers Highway, the Main Street of America, and the Mother Road. I thought the last was fitting. What lay ahead for us was a lot more than we had bargained for. Much more than just a change of scenery, the journey we had embarked upon would change us both more deeply and profoundly than we ever could have imagined.

We followed the same travel schedule as my mother had described in her first notebook, which meant five days on the road, and thought we'd drop in on my great-aunt Edie in Jefferson City, Missouri, as my mother had done on the first leg of her trip. My grandparents had said that would be a very nice gesture, which I thought was an odd way of putting it, until we discovered that her address was that of an extremely depressing nursing home. Great-Aunt Edie didn't remember my grandmother or my mother, much less me. It was a very awkward and brief visit. Rather than getting back on the road at that point, we decided to call it a day, have a nice dinner somewhere and check in to a hotel.

The next morning, we had a leisurely breakfast before getting on the road to Oklahoma City. We took a detour off of I-44 to see the Kansas Route 66 Historic District in East Galena, and explored some of the local history before getting back on the highway again just outside of Tulsa. Since we had made reservations at a hotel in Oklahoma City, only a hundred miles beyond, we stopped for lunch in Tulsa and took our time getting back on the highway to finish our day's journey.

When we reached our destination and checked in to our room, it was dusk, too early for dinner, but too late to do any sightseeing. So we settled in to our room, where Derek made a few phone calls, then I called my grandparents to fill them in on our trip so far. My grandmother apologized for not telling me what to expect with my great-aunt's condition. She had assumed that my mother kept me up to date on these things. Later, we ordered room service, enjoying the leisurely meal knowing we had no demands on our time for the rest of the evening.

"What shall we do now?" Derek asked. "It's too early to turn in. Maybe there's a good movie on TV."

"We should read the second notebook," I said.

"You haven't finished them all?"

"No," I said. "After the first one, I couldn't make myself continue yet. It's really painful to read her words so soon after losing her. Then we were so busy getting ready to leave town. I figured we'd have plenty of time."

"Sure," Derek said. "You could read it to me, that is, if you're comfortable sharing all of it."

"We're in this together, Derek. There's no reason to keep any of it a secret."

I supposed there wasn't a reason to keep the details of my mother's life a secret from the man I was in love with. He had shared many of the sordid details of his relationship with his wife, although he had never spoken much about his daughter's death. But I was sure that was because the whole story was too painful to talk about. I understood why he chose only to skim the surface, on those occasions when he spoke of it at all. I was sure that eventually he would tell me about it.

At the time, I believed that the details of my mother's life we uncovered on this journey together would simply round out the story of her. Fill in the blanks. It didn't seem as though it would affect the woman I was. After all, it was her life, not mine, we were prying open and peering into. And certainly, sharing my discoveries with Derek wouldn't change the way he felt about me. What I didn't realize though, was how much it had already begun to change the way I looked at him. While I was busy judging my mother for getting involved with a married man, I had been in a relationship with one of my own for nearly a year. The circumstances were different, sure. And, I had no intention of getting pregnant. They were separated, legally, but there was no hope for finalizing a divorce any time soon because of her instability.

So was what I was doing really any better than what my mother had done? Since learning this truth about her, I had begun to feel emotions that, up until then, had been foreign to me. I saw what a relationship with a married person looked like from the outside, and I didn't like the picture. My opinion of Derek had begun to deteriorate a bit, as I placed him in the same boat with my father, whoever he was. I had also begun to hate myself even more than I already did, for allowing our relationship to begin at all, or at least for not putting an end to it the moment I realized he was technically still married. Where had my righteous indignation been? Why hadn't I simply walked away?

Still, my relationship with Derek had begun casually, and it had never been about whether or not his wife understood him, or his trying to get a little something extra on the side. That's not who he is. If it were, we'd never even have been friends, much less anything else. Did I wish he had told me about Vanessa a little sooner? Sure. On the other hand, I didn't blame him for not divulging the sordid details of his wrecked marriage upon our first meeting either. Once he realized he'd begun to have feelings for me, he told me about her. Before that we talked about our work, and about books. We went to the theatre together, and the occasional baseball game.

After I knew the truth, I understood that he was a man in an unbearable situation, one with no satisfactory end in sight. But did that mean I was supposed to stop caring about him? We'd spent hours sitting in the coffee shop that marks the halfway point between Derek's building and mine, just talking. I knew all his history long before we ever slept together, and by then I was certain that his marriage was simply a technicality. I'm not a secret, nor is our relationship. It isn't the same as what my mother did. But in a black and white sense, it isn't right either.

Then I began to wonder how things might have been different if my father had ever learned about my mother's pregnancy. My mother had apparently been Howard's preference until his wife announced she was having a baby. Had he known that my mother was pregnant as well, there's a good chance he might have chosen her, and by extension, me. If we were to find my father, and if he was still alive, I could ask him. But with so much water under the bridge, I doubted it would make much difference, one way or the other. And then a horrible thought occurred to me. What if he knew about me all along? What if he knew I lived in Milwaukee with my mother and never attempted to contact me? I realized that given the choice between the two scenarios, I would prefer thinking that he was completely unaware.

"I wonder if they ever saw each other, my parents, on Mom's trips to California."

"It's possible," Derek said. "But it seems odd if they were in contact; that he wouldn't have known about you and wanted to see you. Do you think that your mother could have actually seen him over the years, and not mentioned you?"

"Or worse," I said, "that she did tell him and he still didn't want to acknowledge me. Up until two weeks ago, I believed my father was dead and had been for nearly my entire life. Now I don't know what's true and what's just more of my mother's lies. I loved my mother. We were close. At least I thought so. I don't want to be angry with her, but at the moment I'm having trouble avoiding it. I'll be glad when we get to the bottom of this mess and find out what really happened. Then maybe I can begin to forgive her, the way she asked me to in her letter."

I opened my suitcase and found the second notebook.

"This one begins in February of 1962, where the other one ended. I was born in August of that year, so she would have been about three months pregnant by then."

Derek sat in the small loveseat in the corner of our hotel room. I sat cross-legged on the bed with the spiral bound notebook in my hands. On the inside of the front cover were three photos affixed with yellowed and curling pieces of scotch tape. The first was the photo of my mother with Marilyn Monroe, the one that was taken that day in the wardrobe department. It was really Marilyn, and she was so beautiful. She had her arm around my mother, and my mom was looking up at her adoringly. In the center of the page was a picture of my parents in front of yet another hotel where I assumed the band had performed, because both of them were dressed in formal clothes. The photograph was very much like the one I had found in her cedar chest, but in this one her head was not thrown back in laughter, nor was my father smiling.

My mother was looking out toward the sun setting over the ocean, my father looking down at his shoes. Perhaps this had been taken when Howard had returned to his wife the first time, before their daughter was born. The third and final photo was of the outside of the bungalow where they had spent two months together, very likely the happiest days of my mother's life. It's funny how the happiest and saddest days of our lives are so often back-to-back.

CHAPTER 6
Anastasia

Driving away from Los Angeles this morning was the hardest thing I have ever done. As I headed back toward the entrance to Route 66, I remembered the day I arrived and saw the ocean for the first time, when I swore I would never, ever leave. It was supposed to be the place where my life would begin, and I was going to be near that ocean as an old woman. I wanted to walk along that beach with my husband and remember all the wonderful days of my life. We would have talked about our children and grandchildren.

Now, just two years later, I'm on my way back to Milwaukee, with the newness of Los Angeles still fresh in my mind. Two years ago I was filled to the top with hopes and dreams about how my life there would be, expecting that only good things would happen to me. And it *was* good, for a time. Then it was absolutely amazing for a little while. But my time in California was sort of like fireworks on the Fourth of July. They shoot up into the sky, burst into a beautiful explosion of sparkling color, and then quickly fade as they plummet toward the earth. Hitting the ground was painful.

I stopped twice to throw up my breakfast before I even left the city limits. The morning sickness has been better the past couple weeks and I thought I was just about over it. Maybe the morning sickness didn't have anything to do with the way I felt today, driving away from my life. I'm trying to be brave, but I haven't even called my parents yet to let them know I'm on my way home. Since I just spoke to them a few days ago, they won't be expecting a call for a while. Besides, the closer I am to home when I call, the less time they'll have to spend worrying about my being on the road alone, again. On the other hand, it would probably be better if someone in the world knew where I was, in case something goes wrong. I know something could, but the way I feel right now it's hard to imagine how things could get any worse.

I left Milwaukee a mostly innocent child. The worst thing that had happened to me by that point was that I had to have my tonsils out and spend one night in the hospital. Two years later, I'm heading right back where I came from, only minus the innocence. I have had an affair with a married man, and I'm carrying his child. I have also accepted a payoff from his wife, and promised never to have contact with him or his family for the rest of my life.

At the moment, I'm still having trouble reconciling any of that. Part of me acknowledges that Victoria is right. She's the wife. I was just the mistress. And all things considered, walking away seemed like the right thing to do. The other part of me hates what I did and thinks I'm a coward for being paid off and sent away so easily, without a fight. But Victoria has all the control, especially over Howard. She would have ruined him if I'd stayed. I couldn't live with myself if I had let that happen. Still, I can't help thinking that Howard would have chosen me, if I had only been given the opportunity to tell him about this baby I'm carrying. What's worse, I have agreed to deprive my child of its father. I suppose that's really the cruelest part of all.

I've made it as far as Flagstaff today, and I'm staying in the same motel as I did on the way out here. I figured I would make it as easy on myself as possible, and plan to stay in all the same places, except of course in Oklahoma City. I still have nightmares about that place. But I really liked Flagstaff, so at least for tonight I've managed to take a tiny bit of the misery out of this terrible process of returning home in shame, humiliated and a failure.

The young man who runs the place actually remembered me from the first time I was here. In fact, he said that if I could stay on a couple of days, there was an art festival of some sort coming up and he'd be happy to accompany me. He's sweet, and actually, pretty darn attractive. But if he knew the truth about me, he'd run screaming from the room, and I wouldn't blame him a bit.

Still, I've got plenty of money, thanks to the evil but wealthy Victoria, and I'm not in any rush to face my parents. So maybe I'll stay on a few days. I don't see the harm in that. I'll go next door to the diner and have something to eat. Then I'll get some sleep and see what things look like in the morning.

FEBRUARY 6, 1962

I had dinner last night with Tommy, the man who manages the motel. We didn't plan it, but he was outside the office when I passed by on my way to the diner, so I stopped to talk to him and he decided to join me. It turns out his parents own the place. He's been working here off and on since he was sixteen. When he graduated from college and his parents opened another place closer to Phoenix, they made him the manager and he's been here ever since. He'll inherit the property one day. Anyway, we had a really nice talk. He seems like a decent guy.

They're looking for a waitress over at the diner, so I think I might inquire about the position. There's still plenty of time before the baby arrives, and it won't be horribly obvious for another month or so anyway. I just can't bear the thought of telling my parents about it, at least not yet. Once their grandchild arrives, my parents will forget all about being mad at me, so the shorter the time between when I get home and when the baby arrives, the better.

Tommy and I have dinner plans again tonight. I'm actually looking forward to it. He's really nice to me and as long as he still doesn't know what a horrible person I really am, I'd like to spend some time with him. It's nice pretending to be a normal, single girl, who can have dinner with a normal guy without all the sordid truth of things getting in the way. I know it's only a matter of time before I have to tell him, or he'll figure it out for himself, but either way he probably won't want to have anything to do with me once he finds out what I've done. But for now, I think I'm going to just enjoy it. He's probably the last man on earth who will ever have the slightest interest in me. Anyone who could love me now isn't someone I'd want to be with. Soon it will be just me and my baby. And that's the way it will probably stay.

FEBRUARY 7, 1962

I just finished my first shift at the diner and my feet are killing me. But I think the job will help take my mind off my troubles, for a while anyway. Last night I spoke to Jill on the phone. That's still the number my parents have, since they don't know I've left California. They haven't called, thank goodness, and I asked her to lie for me. I hated doing it, but she understood. Jill has been a good friend to me. If they call, she's supposed to tell them that I'm in the shower, or at work, or out shopping, depending on what time it is, and then leave a message for me at the motel. Then I can call them right back and they'll assume I'm calling from Los Angeles.

Once a week I'll write a letter and send it to Jill to mail for me, so it will go through the L.A. post office. It's not like I'll be able to keep up this ruse for long, but for the time being I sort of like being in a secret place. I'm taking a little vacation from my real life so that by the time I'm forced to face it, maybe I'll be feeling a little stronger. But I know I'll need my parents' help once the baby arrives, and I sure don't need them to be any madder at me than they're already going to be, by finding out I've lied to them. It's not forever, just for a while.

FEBRUARY 14, 1962

If I hadn't been there to hear every word, I wouldn't believe it myself. Tommy took me out to a lovely Valentine's Day dinner.

Things were going along so nicely, but then I started to realize from the way he was talking that he has developed some really strong feelings for me, even after such a short time. And when he used the "L" word, I had to stop him. I knew that I had to tell him the truth right away, because obviously I had let things go too far. Tommy is a great guy, and I have feelings for him, too, which is why I did what I did.

I stopped him in the middle of a sentence, when he was talking about how I should consider staying in Flagstaff permanently. I couldn't let him go on thinking I was just an ordinary girl, who was free to plan a normal future with him. So I took a deep breath and said that I had something I needed to tell him. Once I started talking, I found it really hard to find a good stopping place. I ended up telling him my whole story from the time I arrived in Los Angeles until the day I pulled back into his motel a week and a half ago. Then I took a deep breath, sat back in my chair, and waited for him to start back pedaling. I wouldn't have blamed him, and I told him so.

But the most amazing thing happened. He said that none of it mattered. None of it! He went on to say that he wanted to marry me and that we would pretend the child was his and wouldn't ever look back again. I never dreamed he'd say something like that. Then he told me that his parents were coming to town next week and that he wanted to introduce me to them so we could tell them we were getting married. And, I agreed! It all happened so fast, but it's the solution to everything. We'll have a nice life together here. I can just tell that Tommy is going to be a great father. I've seen how he is with the children who come to the motel with their parents. He's great with them. He's funny and sweet, and so kind to me.

Best of all, he hasn't once tried to pressure me into having sex with him. He's the kind of guy who wants to wait until he's married to me, in spite of the fact that not only have I already had sex with someone, but with a married man whose child I was carrying. What are the odds of ever finding someone else like him? Very slim, I think. So it looks like I'll be meeting his family. After that, I'll break the news to my parents and we'll start planning a wedding. Quickly. I can hardly believe any of this, but I think it's the right thing to do. I'm getting married!

FEBRUARY 20, 1962

Tommy's parents will be here this afternoon. I'm so nervous! I couldn't decide what to wear, because all my clothes are getting so tight, even the really blousy ones I've been wearing to disguise my bulging belly. I have absolutely no waist anymore. Thank goodness for the cool weather and bulky clothes, or everyone would already know our secret. So this morning I went shopping and picked up a couple of things that will work for now. I've heard so much about Tommy's parents. They sound like really nice people. He told them he had someone he wanted them to meet, and that he had some important news. I wish I could have a look inside their heads right now! They're probably just as nervous as I am. I hope they'll like me, but Tommy loves me, so they will too, right? I'm actually going to have in-laws! His mother can tell me all about what he was like as a little boy, and teach me how to make all his favorite meals. It's going to be so wonderful!

Tommy and I talked about going to see the Justice of the Peace and getting married immediately, but he wants me to have the kind of wedding I always dreamed of, in the Episcopal Church in Milwaukee. He wants us to have both sets of parents there, with flowers, a three-tiered wedding cake and me in a long white dress. Imagine him still thinking of me as the kind of girl who was entitled to such a thing.

We talked about going to the Grand Canyon on our honeymoon when we get back to Arizona after the wedding. That sounds like so much fun, but wherever we go, I know it will be wonderful. I'm trying really hard not to think about Howard. I know he probably wonders where I am, and probably misses me. After what we've been to each other, in spite of how it turned out, I know he has to be missing me at least a little bit. In truth, I miss him a lot. I'm carrying his baby inside of my body! I know that I'll never be able to see him again. It's just going to take me a while to forget about him. But when I do think of him I feel guilty, not just because of Tommy, because of everything that happened.

When I'm with Tommy though, I feel like everything is going to be okay, and that I'm a good person. He sees me that way, and I so want it to be true. Maybe in time I'll begin to believe it. Meanwhile, I have to go get ready to meet my new family!

FEBRUARY 22, 1962

My life is a horror show. That's the only way to describe it. Tommy's parents were not at all the way I thought they would be. It's not like they're filthy rich or anything, but apparently they have made a good living with their motels. Tommy failed to mention that they own five of them. They pulled up in their fancy car, both of them dressed to the nines. Sure, Tommy had told his parents he wanted them to meet someone, but not the damn Queen of England for crying out loud. There I was in my new blouse and jumper with a beautiful new sweater, and I looked like a pauper in comparison. I felt like I should be cleaning the motel rooms instead of marrying their son, the way they looked at me.

We went to dinner together and they asked me all sorts of questions about my family and how I ended up in Flagstaff. I was getting so flustered and red in the face that Tommy interrupted them and said that none of those things were important. He said the important thing is that he loves me and that we're getting married. Then the worst thing of all happened. His mother said, "Is that right? Well then, please tell me whose baby she's carrying, because I'm sure we didn't raise a son who would be responsible for producing a child out of wedlock."

I don't know how they knew, or if they were just guessing, but I excused myself right then and went into the bathroom. His mother actually followed me in there! She said that while she feels sorry for any girl who gets herself in trouble like this, she is most certainly not going to allow her son to become responsible for a child that is not his. Then she just walked away and left me there. I didn't know what to do. I couldn't stay in the bathroom all day, and I didn't know if they were expecting me to come back to the table after that little exchange. As if! Eventually, I peeked out of the restroom door and saw Tommy sitting alone at the table. His parents had left the restaurant. Fortunately we had met them there, because otherwise I would have had to endure the car ride back to the motel with them, where they surely would have tried to dump me off alongside the road somewhere. It was all just so humiliating. Tommy was furious, of course, and told me we can just leave and go live somewhere else, even Milwaukee if I want to. He said he didn't care about inheriting the stupid motels one day. I even thought about it for a while, but in the end, I decided that I had already nearly torn apart one family. I wasn't about to tear apart another. So I came back here to my room at the motel and called my parents. They are not happy with me. Not one bit. But they're my parents and they love me. And as I had hoped, in spite of being furious at me, by the end of the conversation I'm pretty sure that they're already just a little bit excited about the idea of a grandchild. They told me that when all is said and done, I'm their daughter and they'll always be there for me. And, they will love my child and help us through whatever comes next.

So after a good night's sleep, I'll pack up my car and get on the road to Santa Fe. Four days from now I'll be back in Milwaukee. God help me.

CHAPTER 7
Meredith

I CLOSED THE NOTEBOOK AND TOSSED it on the bed. When I looked up, Derek was handing me a tissue. I hadn't realized I was crying. My mother had been so alone and humiliated, not just once, but twice in the span of a few weeks. I felt so sorry for her. Until you walk a mile in someone else's shoes, it's terribly unfair to judge the decisions they've made, because you have no idea about all the tiny details that figured into the equation. She loved my father, even though he wasn't free to be loved by her, and she made the very hard choice to leave Los Angeles because she wanted what was best for him. At least what she thought at the time was best. And painful as it was, she did it, because she loved him that much and wanted him to have the successful career he dreamed of. Victoria had every right to try to make my mother go away. She was the wife after all. But Tommy's parents had been cruel and she didn't deserve that.

"Are you okay?" Derek asked.

"Fine," I said. "Just trying to take it all in."

"There was some good information in those pages," he said. "For example, this friend of your mother's, Jill. It sounds like she knew how to contact your mom at the motel. If we can reach Jill, she may be able to lead us to Tommy."

"And then what," I asked. "Surely Tommy has moved on with his life by now. That was thirty years ago."

"Yes, but I'm sure he'd remember her. You don't forget about someone you proposed marriage to. She said that she told him everything, so maybe he has a name in L.A. Maybe he could lead us to your father."

"Maybe so. But I don't know who Jill is. I wouldn't have any idea how to find her."

"Your grandparents might. Jill and your mother were close in those days. They might have stayed in contact over the years. Even a Christmas card with an address would be all we need."

"Sure, but my grandparents clearly don't want to be involved in all this old business. I said I'd leave them out of it. My grandmother was in obvious physical distress at the mere mention of it."

"Was there anything else in the notebook after where you stopped reading, maybe tucked into the back?"

I picked up the notebook and flipped open the back cover. Sure enough, pasted to the inside of the back cover was the front page of a travel brochure with a drawing of the Thunderbird Motel in Flagstaff, Arizona. It had an address and a phone number, and below that it read, "Thomas Gallagher, Manager."

"Should we call the number?" Derek asked.

"No. We'll be there day after tomorrow. This isn't the kind of conversation I want to have over the telephone. If he's still there now, he'll still be there in a couple more days."

Then I remembered my mother. When I hadn't been able to reach her for our weekly phone conversation, I thought the same thing. We'll catch up in a couple of days. That's always what we think. How foolish we are.

The next morning we got up early, left Oklahoma City and headed toward New Mexico, where we already had a room reserved in a hotel in Santa Fe. As we drove along I tried to imagine what my mother must have felt like when she was heading through this same countryside, more or less, on her way to California. She had been so young, just twenty years old. It was all so new and exciting. She was brave to head out on her own that way, not knowing what was in store for her when she arrived. It was the adventure of a lifetime, though at that point in her life it should have been just one of many yet to come. Instead it seemed to be the first and the last.

As the miles passed, I found myself unable to stop thinking about my mother and how awful Tommy's parents had been.

"Would you like me to drive for a while?" I asked.

"That's okay," Derek said. "I'm fine. This countryside is so beautiful. I'm just enjoying the scenery."

"Sorry, sweetie," I said. "I've been lost in thought. Those people were so cruel to my mother. They didn't have to be so mean."

"You're right. They were pretty harsh. She was practically a child, obviously scared and confused. Your mother was doing her best to choose the next right thing to do and they didn't give her any credit at all. The good news is there's a decent chance they're dead by now."

"Derek," I said, "I don't wish them dead, although I have to admit I would like to see them suffer a little."

"They were just trying to do what was best for their son. Your mother was a stranger to them. But I agree with you, they certainly could have been kinder than they were. She was completely alone in a strange place."

"It's not only that," I said. "She had already been completely humiliated and had such a low opinion of herself, warranted or not. It's heartbreaking to think about someone kicking her when she was down like that."

"Do you think it was warranted?" he asked.

"Certainly," I said. "What she did was wrong. I know she was young and thought she was in love with my father, but he was married. She shouldn't have done it."

"But, Meredith, if she hadn't, there would be no you."

That stopped me for a moment, but still, what my mother had done was wrong. Sure, Victoria sounded like a bitter, angry woman, but who wouldn't be with a philandering husband?

"That's true enough, Derek, but how do you think it feels knowing that I'm the product of an adulterous relationship? Not really something I'm proud of."

"And what about us?" he asked. "Are you ashamed of our relationship?"

"Of course I am! I'm ashamed of what my mother did, and the truth is, I'm no better than she was. You're married to someone else. We should never have gotten involved in the first place. But by the time I found out about Vanessa, I was already in love with you, so what was I supposed to do? It's all just so damn frustrating. How can we have a future as long as you're married to Vanessa? And how can you divorce her when she's so unstable? The entire situation seems so hopeless."

I stopped and took a deep breath when I realized I was shouting. Derek and I were confined in a small space, not to mention the fact that we were going seventy-five miles an hour in the car.

"I'm sorry," I said. "It's all just too much. My mother is gone, and I didn't even know her. All of this has me a little off balance."

"I'm sorry too, Meredith. I know how hard it's been for you. Not just with your mother, but with me. You know that I want to divorce Vanessa. I'm certain that eventually she'll accept that our marriage is over and move on. I want to be with you. She knows that."

"But you loved her once," I said. "You and she had a life together, and the intimacy of marriage. All those tiny details you shared, and huge things too, like your daughter. That's a lot of history. We've only been together for a year or so, and haven't shared any of those things."

"We've shared lots of things, Meredith. And we'll share many more, including having children together. We'll have a good and happy life together, the kind that two healthy people can share. No alcoholism, drug addiction, or guilt. That would never be possible with Vanessa, no matter how much time goes by."

"There's guilt now," I said.

"I know, and I'm sorry to have put you in that position. But I promise you, it will be over soon and we'll be able to move forward with our life together. Please, Meredith, don't give up on me. Don't give up on us."

I didn't want to give up, nor did I want to lose Derek. But I simply couldn't reconcile it. In time, I was sure things would work themselves out somehow. Vanessa would eventually decide to get on with her life, although until she managed to control her substance abuse it was unlikely she would make changes that were positive ones. Meanwhile, it felt like a trap, my fingertips just inches away from opening the latch, but not quite close enough. I tried to imagine walking away from him, the way my mother had done, but couldn't do it. For better or for worse, I had decided to see it through to the end.

The miles passed slowly, and quietly, once my outburst was behind us. In spite of everything that was happening, I felt a strange kind of security in the car with Derek, just the two of us. As long as we were flying down the freeway in the car together, it was as if the rest of the world had fallen away. None of the nonsense could reach us as long as we kept moving. When we finished driving for the day, we decided to splurge on an elegant dinner. Still unaccustomed to being a person with a trust fund, I had usually suggested reasonably priced meals and modest accommodations. But in Santa Fe, we stayed in a beautiful old hotel that felt like it was inhabited by ghosts of the thousands of people who had stayed there over the years, in addition to the current living guests. The room was elegant and tastefully decorated, not the cookie cutter variety like most contemporary hotel chains where all the rooms are alike, right down to the placement of the soap and tiny bottles of shampoo and conditioner.

I felt a strange kind of optimism in that place, distant but palpable. With all the stress of my mother's death and the beginning of this journey of discovery, I had forgotten for a moment that I was travelling with the man I was in love with. He wasn't just my travel companion. As we settled in to the room, I began looking forward to a romantic dinner in the five-star restaurant where we had a table waiting for us, and then to coming back to the room where we would spend the rest of the night like the lovers we were and had been for a long time.

I didn't want to give up on him. But I didn't want to make the same mistakes my mother had.

As we drove to the restaurant, I noticed for the first time how lovely the city was. It was so different from Chicago. The architecture was low, with lots of stucco buildings, and there were cacti everywhere. It was like being on a strange new planet. The lights of the city seemed to sparkle more than they did at home, possibly because they weren't buried in snow. But it's as if I had been asleep for a time and I was suddenly awake again. I felt pretty in the sweater dress that hugged my body, and I was aware of the way my hair brushed against my face and shoulders.

Derek was driving and kept his eyes on the road, which gave me the chance to look at him. We had been in the car together for days already. How could I not have paid attention? He was so attractive, and he loved me. In spite of our difficult situation, him with his crazy wife, and me with my mysterious mother and father, we were experiencing all of it together. We were part of each other's life, and I realized how glad I was that he was with me there in Santa Fe. I knew that he would bolster me up, no matter what we found at the end of this journey, and I suddenly remembered that I loved him very, very much. More than anything, I needed to believe that it would all work out and we would eventually be together for real. We would both have to deal with our baggage, but in the end, it would be Derek and me.

"Why are you smiling?" Derek asked.

I hadn't realized I was.

"I'm just really glad you're here. I know it's a terrible time for you to be away from your office, in spite of what you say, but I'm glad you're with me anyway. I wouldn't want to have to deal with all this on my own. If I had to, I'm sure I probably could. But I don't want to and I'm glad you wouldn't let me. I love you, Derek."

"Love you too, Meredith. Don't ever forget that."

We ordered Champagne with dinner, and crème brulee for dessert. The food was exquisite, by far the best I had eaten in years, and Chicago is famous for its food, so that was quite some accomplishment. While we ate, we talked about anything but my family, and for the first time since my mother died, I had a glimpse of what my life had been like before this all came crashing down on my head. I knew it wasn't over, not by a long shot, but it was nice to have the brief respite.

When we got back to our room, Derek suggested that I change into something a lot more comfortable. I quickly and happily complied.

"While you change, I'm just going to check my messages. It won't take long. Then I'll meet you right here," he said, patting the center of the king-sized bed.

Derek sat down at the desk, dialed his office and entered the code to retrieve his messages. As I closed the bathroom door, I saw him making notes and then dialing again. I knew the routine. He had done this each night since we'd left town, first the office answering machine, then the one at home.

I put on the one nice nightgown I had packed at the last minute and brushed my teeth. Then I burst out of the bathroom and threw myself into the middle of the bed. Derek was still sitting at the desk. The phone had been replaced in its cradle, a pen was on the desk next to a small pad of notepaper and he didn't turn around.

"What's happened?" I asked, knowing from his posture that it was something awful.

"Vanessa is dead," he said, his voice low and flat. "She committed suicide last night. Opened the veins in both of her wrists, the long way. The way you do it when you mean to finish the job."

He just sat there, looking down at the desk and the notes he had scribbled. I got up from the bed and went to him, putting my arms around his shoulders and chest, my cheek next to his. He didn't turn around to face me, but I felt his body begin to shudder, his tears splashing onto the top of the desk. I held him like that until his body stopped shaking and he reached across the desk for a tissue.

"I have to go back," he finally said.

"Of course you do, Derek. We'll find the first fight to Chicago in the morning. I'll drive you to the airport."

"But I promised to go with you. You said you were so happy you didn't have to do this alone…"

"I'll be fine, Derek. Really. Vanessa was your wife. You have to go."

The words echoed in my head. She *was* his wife, and now she was dead.

"She left a note. According to Rachel, her closest girlfriend, Vanessa found out that I was travelling out west with you. She talked about it at dinner and seemed upset, but not out of control or anything. Rachel called her to make sure she had gotten home safely, because they'd both had quite a lot to drink. When Vanessa didn't answer, Rachel took a cab over to the house and found her in the tub. There was an empty bottle of Jack Daniel's on the bathroom counter, and an envelope propped up against it with my name on it. The note said something about not being able to handle my leaving for good on top of the guilt over our daughter's death. She had decided that I wasn't coming back. As if I would have just left town forever without saying anything. She knew me better than that, but she was drunk, as usual. Vanessa swore that she would kill herself if I ever tried to leave her for good. It's the only promise she ever kept."

I felt sick. I couldn't imagine how Derek must feel. The pragmatist in me knew that I couldn't control the actions of others, but right or wrong, I felt responsible for what she had done. It was a nightmare, one we would never fully wake up from.

By the time I made his flight reservation, Derek had made his phone calls to Rachel and, God help him, Vanessa's parents—it was nearly two in the morning. I knew there wouldn't be much sleep for either of us.

We both managed to drift into an interrupted and restless sleep for a couple of hours, and finally at seven o'clock we got up and showered. It was a fairly short drive to the airport, and since his flight didn't leave until ten thirty, we packed up the car and found a small restaurant where we drank coffee for an hour. The food we ordered was still on the table, untouched, when we left.

We tried several times to begin a conversation, but in truth, there wasn't a single relevant subject that wasn't simply too horrific to broach. I had so many questions, but I didn't feel that I could ask them. I wanted to know exactly what the note had said, and how her parents had reacted, if they blamed him, or understood how unstable she was. I couldn't help but imagine him facing her parents and going through the funeral, all the while Vanessa's family hating him, and hating me even more. Vanessa's death would change things for us, certainly. All of a sudden there were no more obstacles. But I was afraid that the final dose of guilt she had managed to heap upon his head would be too much for him to survive, much less allow him the freedom to be with me now.

In spite of it all, he still felt bad leaving me to continue travelling west alone, to face whatever I might find there. We were quite a pair. It didn't seem possible that so many things could conspire to rain misery down upon the two of us at the same time. It was really difficult to believe. But there we were, at the airport gate, saying goodbye. I still intended to drive to Flagstaff as planned, but waited at the gate until his airplane had taken off. In a few short hours he'd be landing in Chicago and it would all become very real indeed. I guessed that it would probably feel like the shortest flight he ever made. We'd talk on the phone at the end of the day to compare notes. But I was afraid that Vanessa's final blow would eventually separate him from me forever. And maybe that's what we deserved.

CHAPTER 8

AS I DROVE AWAY FROM THE airport, and the man who provided the only foothold I currently had to any kind of comfort or security, I imagined how my mother must have felt when she drove away from California. She left behind the only thing that gave meaning to her life at the time, looking toward a future that didn't appear very promising. I couldn't imagine a time when everything would be all right again. I think my mother must have felt the same way.

The miles between Santa Fe and Flagstaff passed by slowly. I tried to let myself be distracted by the scenery, but without much success. I was exhausted from the sleepless night, and had to stop frequently to get coffee and stretch my legs so I wouldn't drift off while I was driving. It seemed for a time that I would never reach my destination. The variety of emotions I experienced that day were difficult to endure, each in its own terrible way. I felt fear, sadness, guilt, and anger in a rotating sequence.

All those hours alone in the car were awful. I worried that Tommy would be dead, or at least no longer at the Thunderbird Motel. And I worried that I wouldn't be able to get in touch with Derek at the end of the day. I also considered that my involvement with Derek might have caused such a devastating blow to my karma that I would certainly face a painful and untimely death, probably from cancer. Vanessa was in so much pain, but I knew that only a small portion of it was actually my doing. Derek had left her long before he became involved with me, but they were still married nonetheless, and in spite of all the things he told me about her, their daughter, and their marriage, I'm sure there were many parts of their relationship that he kept from me.

They had been married for nearly ten years. Obviously there had been a time when they loved each other deeply. They had a child together, and probably shared lots of beautiful memories. He didn't talk to me too much about those things, because he didn't want to risk hurting my feelings, and I appreciated his sensitivity. I knew the truth, we both did. But it was easier if the things I knew about her were the ones he didn't like, rather than the ones he did. That made it possible for me to be in a relationship with him, in spite of the circumstances. I didn't want to know the good things about her, although I'm sure there were many, because then I might have liked her. And I didn't want to like her. Things couldn't work that way.

As I approached Flagstaff, I began to focus my attention on figuring out how I was going to approach Thomas Gallagher, Tommy, as my mother had called him. I wasn't sure how to open a conversation like that one. "So, Tommy, I'm the daughter of the woman your mother wouldn't let you marry because she was carrying someone else's child. Sorry she broke your heart and you never saw her again, but she's dead now." Okay, so my fatigue was really beginning to show. Best if I just check into the motel, call Derek, and get a good night's sleep. If Tommy were still running the motel, I'd talk to him in the morning.

When I drove into the parking lot I had a moment of panic, followed by another few minutes of disorientation. I was exhausted and overwhelmed. For a while I thought I might faint, but managed to pull myself together before anyone noticed me. There was an attractive, dark haired woman behind the desk when I went inside the motel lobby to check in. She appeared to be about my age, or maybe a little older. I asked for a room for one night, and as she was typing away at the computer, I noticed a couple of business card holders on the edge of the counter. One of them said, Tommy Gallagher, Manager. The other said, Mariel Gallagher, Assistant Manager.

Without thinking, I asked, "Are these your parents?"

The girl looked confused for a moment, and then realized I was looking at the business cards.

"Oh, no ma'am. I'm Mariel Gallagher. Tommy is my uncle. He stepped out to have dinner, but he'll be back."

"I see," I said, feeling kind of stupid. "Well it's nice to meet you, Mariel. I'm Meredith Springfield."

"I know," she said. "It says so right here on your credit card."

We both smiled then, and I had to laugh out loud at my ineptitude. I was an English teacher, for God's sake, charged with shaping the minds of young people, and I couldn't even carry on a conversation with an assistant motel manager. I needed sleep, no doubt, and I had already determined that the man I was looking for still worked at the motel. In the morning, I'd look him up and we would have a chat. Surely, I'd be capable of a more coherent conversation by then.

The moment she handed me the key, I hurried outside to move my car to the parking space in front of the door to my room, grateful to be away from Mariel, who must have thought I was a complete moron. My room was clean, and smelled fresh and smoke free as I had requested. But the motel was old. The bathroom looked like it still had some of the original fixtures. I brought in my suitcase and cosmetic bag, changed into some comfortable velour sweat pants with a matching sweatshirt, and pulled on some warm socks. Then I sat down on the bed, picked up the phone on the nightstand and called Derek. I held my breath until he answered.

"I'm so glad to hear your voice," I said. "How was your day? Has it been horrible?"

"Pretty horrible," he said. "It's good to hear your voice, too. I've actually been pacing the floor waiting for the damn phone to ring. I feel better now."

"Good. I miss you, Derek. The drive to Flagstaff took forever. I could barely stay awake to drive. But he's here. Tommy is here. I haven't spoken to him yet, but I met his niece. She told me he was out having dinner and that he'd be back later. So I'm going to find him in the morning when my head is clearer than it was when I spoke to Mariel. I couldn't put a whole sentence together."

I realized I was rambling, but I was just so glad to have Derek on the other end of the phone line.

"That's great, Meredith. You must be so relieved. I want you to call me tomorrow as soon as you talk to him, and tell me everything. I miss you too, honey. Something awful. This changes everything, you know. God help me, I never wished for something like this to happen to Vanessa, but she doesn't control our lives anymore. I shouldn't even be saying this out loud, and I'll probably be struck by lightning or worse, but…"

"It's okay, Derek. I had the same thought while I was driving this afternoon. Our situation has been so difficult, for all three of us. It seemed like there was no possible scenario where we all came out perfectly happy on the other side, but marriages end every day and people get on with their lives. It's difficult, and painful, but people get through it. What Vanessa did was her choice. It certainly wasn't the solution either of us would have chosen. She was sick and sad before your little girl died, and that piled on top of it all was just too much for her. It was obviously the only way she could be free of it, because she saw no life ahead of her that she could tolerate. She just made this her excuse to do something she very well might have done eventually anyway. The really insidious part of it though, is that she wanted to ruin your life in the process, and make sure you paid for something that wasn't your fault, Derek. This wasn't our fault."

"You're right," he said. "Of course, you're right. But now that we're free to be together, get married one day, and have children of our own. I want to be happy. Instead I just feel guilty."

"That was Vanessa's plan, Derek. She wanted you to be as guilty and sad and broken as she was. She played her ace yesterday, the one she's been holding over you for years. But the flaw in her thinking was that you were as responsible as she was for Lily's death. Vanessa was the parent who took her to the beach, got drunk, and failed to protect her. I'm sorry to be harsh, Derek, but that's on her, not you."

"Sure, technically speaking that's true. But I should have been there. She was my child, and I should have protected her from her mother. Instead, I let them go off on their own that day while I went to the office. I had work piled up sky high, and by then, work was much more inviting than spending the day with Vanessa, even with Lily as a buffer. We had an argument the night before. It had gotten fairly heated. It was nothing out of the ordinary, but there was still a lot of tension between us. We were barely speaking. She promised that she wouldn't drink, swearing that she would never put our child in danger, and rebuking me for even suggesting such a thing. And I chose to believe her.

"She made me feel like such a shit for not trusting her, so for a moment I remembered the girl she was before the drinking started to become a problem. In those days, she was sweet and funny. We were happy once, I'm sure you know that. So I made a choice. I told them to have fun at the beach, and I went to my office. But what had I been thinking? If I had a nickel for every time she promised she wouldn't drink, well, I should have known better. She had already broken that promise a thousand times. Why had I chosen that day to believe her?"

"It wasn't your fault, Derek," I said. "That wasn't your fault and neither was what happened yesterday. There must have been days when Vanessa and Lily went out for the day and Vanessa didn't drink. She couldn't have been drunk all the time, or she wouldn't have lasted this long. For most women, the most basic and strongest instinct we have is to protect our children from harm. You had no reason to think she wouldn't protect Lily."

"But I knew she was upset, and desperate," he said.

"What do you mean?"

"The argument we had the night before was about her drinking, yes. But I had given her an ultimatum then, too. That was the first time I told her that if she didn't stop drinking, I was going to leave her and take Lily with me. And I thought I had gotten through to her. Surely she wouldn't risk losing both of us. But I was wrong. Instead she must have felt so much fear, or pressure, or God knows what, that she couldn't help but drink."

"You couldn't have known, Derek," I said, but I don't think he heard me and I let him continue.

"When the police visited me at the office and told me what happened, I couldn't believe it. It was like a bad dream. I just knew that I would wake up soon thinking, wow, that was too horrible, but it was only a warning. From then on I'd never make that mistake again. I'd pack up Lily and we'd go away somewhere to start over, just the two of us.

Even when I arrived at the beach and saw her little car seat tipped over on its side with sand all over it, and Vanessa standing there in handcuffs, like a zombie, I still didn't believe it was really happening. Then the officer approached me and started asking questions. He explained what they believed had happened, and why Vanessa was in handcuffs. They had found her sitting in the car in the parking lot, passed out, with a bottle of Jack Daniel's in her lap. When they woke her up, she realized that Lily was alone on the beach and she panicked. And when she saw the empty car seat, she became so hysterical they had to restrain her. I'm not sure how long she had been passed out, but it was long enough for the tide to come in and my daughter to go…"

He was sobbing now, and I wondered if he had ever talked about this with anyone, the details of that horrific afternoon. My heart broke for him, having carried this around for nearly two years. He needed to work through it in order to begin healing, but now this with Vanessa. It was more than one person should have to go through all at once. I wanted to hold him, tell him it wasn't his fault, and let him cry until it was all out of him. But there were so many miles between us. I was helpless.

"They put her in jail, and after her lawyers performed some kind of magic, she ended up in a psychiatric hospital for six months. I told you about the hospital, but it wasn't like she volunteered to go in. It was either that or prison. I wish it had been the latter. It should have been."

"I'm so sorry you've been carrying this around for so long, Derek. And please, know that you can talk to me about it, whenever you need to. I think it will help to talk about it, if not with me, with someone. Also know that I will never hold you responsible, no matter how hard you try to convince me that you are. I just wish I could take away your pain. If things had been different, I mean, I couldn't have saved Lily, but if you hadn't been out here with me, Vanessa might…"

"No," Derek said. "Don't even say it. Not once. You're right. Vanessa was sick. She was sad, and she was broken. We were already separated when you and I met. She didn't have the right to threaten me when I wanted to move on with my life. Threatening suicide as a way of controlling someone is about as low as you can get. She let my daughter die, and she took her own life. I'm not about to let any of that craziness spill over on to you. Nor am I going to let it come between us."

I realized I was crying then. I did feel guilty, and had ever since I found out he was just separated and not divorced. It had been hanging over me like a cloud for nearly a year. I didn't wish Vanessa dead, but I did pretend that she didn't exist; that she was just some non-descript shadow in the corner of the room. Would things have ended up differently if Derek hadn't become involved with me? We would never know that. I just hoped that we would find a way to get through all this, and not lose each other in the process.

"What a mess," I said. "I wish I knew what the right next step is."

"The next step is for you to find out about your family. Those questions need to be answered before we can get on with our lives. We both have things to work through, Meredith. I just wish we could work through them together without half a country between us."

"I know," I said. "But we'll be back in Chicago together before you know it. Then we can begin planning our future together."

We exchanged our love, and hung up the phone. I turned out the light, crawled into bed, and pulled the covers all the way up to my nose, without bothering to change into pajamas. I was too exhausted to move, and fell asleep instantly. When I woke up the next morning, my last words to Derek were still ringing in my ears, and I hoped from the very bottom of my heart that they would prove to be true.

CHAPTER 9

MY FIRST MORNING IN FLAGSTAFF WAS crisp and bright. I woke up early feeling well rested, but a bit disoriented as all of the realities of my current existence came flooding back into my consciousness. After I showered, I walked down to the motel lobby to see if Tommy was there. My opening lines weren't completely prepared yet, but I took it on faith that when the time came I'd be able to express myself in a clear and coherent way. With luck, he wouldn't think I was a complete nut case and immediately call the authorities.

When I went inside, Mariel was behind the desk again. She was wearing different clothing, so I assumed she had gone home for the night at some point and someone else had taken over the responsibility. Maybe it had been her uncle. I had missed it the night before, but it looked as though there might be an apartment back behind the check-in desk and office area. There was a partially opened door, and I could see carpeting on the floor and the edge of a piece of upholstered furniture. Was that where Tommy lived?

"Good morning, Mariel," I said, in a voice that sounded way too chirpy for me.

"Good morning, Ms. Springfield," Mariel replied. "I hope you had a restful night. How can I help you?"

"It's actually your uncle who can help me. We have a mutual friend who I'd like to talk to him about. Is he here?"

"No, sorry. Not at the moment," Mariel said. "He'll be back shortly though. He just had to go into town to pick up some supplies and do the banking."

"I see," I said. "Then I'll just check back later. Also, I've decided I'd like to stay here another night. Is that possible, or are you booked solid?"

"That's no problem at all," she said. "I can't remember the last time we were booked completely solid. Probably shouldn't say that, I guess. I'll just change the register to show you're staying another night. Was your room okay? Should I ask the maid to leave extra towels or anything when she cleans up this morning?"

"Not necessary," I said. "Everything was just fine."

Once I had made the decision to stay an extra night, I felt more relaxed, knowing I didn't have to get back on the road any time that day. I needed a rest before I moved on. Normally, I would have kept to my schedule and pushed on, whether I felt up to it or not. But with everything that had happened, I decided to cut myself some slack. I wondered for a moment if the realization that I was a trust-fund baby was already making me lazy. This made me laugh. Lots of people who had trust funds worked very hard. I just hadn't come to terms with having all that money yet. In any case, I wasn't entirely sure I planned to keep it.

I walked out of the parking lot and down the street for a couple of blocks to a café I had noticed on my way in the day before. My stomach was growling, which reminded me that I hadn't eaten anything for dinner the night before. In fact, I had left my breakfast behind in Santa Fe, too. I was starving, and needed some coffee.

Flagstaff was lovely in its own unique way. Like Santa Fe, it was much different than what I was used to. Until a few days ago, I hadn't spent much time outside of Wisconsin and Illinois. I had never seen the Southwest. The landscape was so foreign, dry and brown. But at least there wasn't any snow. Then I remembered that I had been here before, in all of these places, but I was inside my mother's body at the time.

The café was nice, with its retro décor. A pretty young waitress with a dark brown ponytail, a pink dress, and a white apron showed me to a booth. The seats were upholstered with red leather in the old tuck and roll fashion. The tabletop was white with little silver squiggly lines all over it, and shiny chrome edges. It reminded me of a place in Milwaukee that my mother used to take me to for breakfast on special occasions. We didn't go out to eat very often when I was growing up, and going out to breakfast in particular was extremely rare. But when we did, my mother and I always went to the same place. Maybe it reminded her of this place, which had been restored, but had obviously been around a long time.

After I finished my breakfast and the dishes were cleared away, I lingered for another cup of coffee. I was in no hurry, after all, because it might be hours before Tommy got back. The last thing I wanted to do was get in the car and go exploring this strange territory all by myself. So I sat there, skimming through a newspaper that someone had left behind on one of the tables. The sun was shining through the window and the warmth felt nice on my face. I felt like a big fat house cat, and a little drowsy to boot.

Then I panicked for a minute. What about Blossom, my mother's cat? Who would feed her now that my mother was gone? But my panic quickly subsided as I remembered that she was with my grandparents, safe and sound until I could come back for her. Then she'd go to Chicago with me. I was wound up a little too tight, I realized. It wasn't like me, but all things considered, not all that surprising.

I heard the jingling of the short string of bells that announced each opening and closing of the door. A man in his late fifties, a rather handsome man actually, walked in and exchanged a few words with the cashier. Then he walked over to me and reached out to shake my hand.

"Miss Springfield?" he asked.

"Yes, I'm Meredith Springfield."

He took my hand and said, "I'm Tommy Gallagher. Mariel said you were looking for me."

"I am," I said. "Pleased to meet you. Will you join me?"

He sat down at the table, and before either of us could say a word, the dark-haired waitress appeared with a cup of coffee for Tommy and a refill for me.

"So, Miss Springfield," he said, "Mariel tells me we have a mutual friend. When she told me your name, I thought it might just be a really big coincidence. But I'd know you anywhere. You look just like her."

"You remember my mother?"

"Well, of course I do. She promised to let me meet you one of these days, although I thought she'd bring you to me herself. Either way, I'm just so pleased to finally meet you. Is your mother going to be joining you soon?"

Tommy had no idea my mother was dead, and I was going to have to be the one to tell him. I wanted to shrink into the upholstery and disappear. He and my mother must have gotten back in touch with each other after all these years and were planning some kind of reunion that included me. As I watched the smile fade from his eyes, I realized that he was responding to the look on my face. He was beginning to see that something was terribly wrong.

"My mother passed away two weeks ago." I said, softly. "It was a heart attack."

His face drained of color, and he whispered, "No, oh God, no. Not now."

Tommy's eyes filled with tears. He put his hands over his face, elbows on the table, doing his best to hide the emotion from me, but it was no good. I could see that he wanted to wail and smash his fists against the window until it shattered. This was not a man just recently reacquainted with an old girlfriend. This was much, much more.

"When did you see her last?" I asked.

After a moment, Tommy pulled some napkins out of the chrome dispenser, dried his eyes and blew his nose. He took a deep breath before speaking.

"You don't know, do you?" he said. "I saw her a few months ago. I've seen her twice a year since shortly after you were born."

I couldn't respond. All those trips to California. She hadn't been in California at all. She was coming here. This was the place that nobody knew about. I would have bet my trust fund that she never told my grandparents about Flagstaff, or Tommy. It was her secret place, where she lived her life in little pieces, twice a year. If my grandparents knew that my father was alive, they probably suspected she was visiting him in California. That's why my grandmother had been so ashamed to talk about it. My grandparents must have assumed she was carrying on an affair with a married man all these years.

"The last time I spoke to your mother," he said, "was a few weeks ago. I haven't been able to reach her by phone, but never once did it occur to me that something had happened to her. We wrote lots of letters, and it wasn't all that unusual to go a couple of weeks without talking on the phone. If we had talked as often as we wanted to, it would have been way too expensive. But I never imagined that God could be so cruel as to take her from me when your mother had finally agreed to marry me, after all these years."

My head was spinning. I remembered to take deep breaths, hoping it would calm my nerves and let me think straight.

"Wait," I said. "I would have seen the letters. I never saw any, and I picked up the mail every day on my way in from school. It was my responsibility."

"She had a post office box. Your mother didn't want you or your grandparents to know about me. She said our relationship was so precious to her that she wanted to keep it between the two of us, just for a while. But a while turned into years, and then decades. I brought it up now and then, but we had so little time together, I never wanted it to be spent arguing over the terms of our relationship. And over time, I just came to accept it. But wait a minute, if you didn't know about me, why are you here? And, how did you know how to find me?"

"It was all in her journals. Shortly after she died, a lawyer came to her house and handed over an envelope with some spiral note-books and a letter of apology for lying to me all these years. Her will stated that I was to spread her ashes in the Hollywood hills; that's why I'm here."

I could almost feel his stomach turn as he realized that I did have her with me, after all, so I quickly continued.

"I'm on my way to California. Along the way, I read about you, and in the back of one of the notebooks was a brochure for your motel. That's how I knew where to find you. I packed the notebooks in my suitcase and I've been reading them at night in my hotel rooms, a little at a time. It's very painful, Tommy, knowing my mother had a whole other life, one that I knew nothing about. And she lied to me, over and over. I feel foolish, and more than a little angry. At the same time, I miss her so much I can hardly stand it. All of this was so unexpected."

I lowered my voice when I realized that the people sitting on barstools at the end of the counter were beginning to stare at us.

"I know this is a shock to you, Tommy," I said. "I wish I didn't have to be the one to tell you about it. I had no idea how close you were to my mother after all these years. I haven't finished reading her journals yet. I'm taking it slow, and letting it sink in a little at a time. That's the only way I can stand it. Maybe she mentions more about you later. All I know is that she was here with you for a while, and the two of you were planning to get married, but your parents were awful to her and she went back to Milwaukee."

"My parents," he said, shaking his head. "They can be pretty awful, my mother in particular. My father just nods his head and says, 'Yes, dear.' But my mother is a tyrant, no doubt. You met Mariel, my niece? She's my younger sister's daughter. My sister, Carol, got pregnant when she was a senior in high school. Mother sent Carol away to a home for unwed mothers, and forced her to give her child up for adoption. She thought she'd controlled the situation, and avoided the imagined humiliation the family would have been forced to endure. But when Mariel turned eighteen, she came looking for her birth mother and they were reunited. My mother was fit to be tied, as you can probably imagine. Mariel lived with my sister until Carol died of breast cancer about ten years ago. That's when she came to work for me."

"How are you parents handling that?" I asked.

"They finally came around after a few years, when they realized the world didn't crumble because of her presence in our lives. Mariel was a big help to my sister throughout her illness, which meant my mother didn't have to be, so I guess they gave her some credit for that."

"She seems like a nice person," I said. "Sorry about your sister, though. My mother didn't mention you had one, just that your family's motels would be yours one day."

"My parents are old school I guess. They would never even consider leaving a business to their daughter, especially after what happened when she was in high school."

"People do strange things, Tommy," I said. "They lie and cheat and judge each other so harshly. It's truly exhausting. I don't know what to think anymore."

"I'm sorry, Meredith," he said. "For whatever part I played in this deception, I'm deeply sorry. I've loved you from a distance your whole life. And there wasn't a day that went by when I wouldn't have dropped everything to take care of both you and your mother. I have a scrapbook with all your school pictures, graduation announcements, and a variety of other things your mother sent to me over the years. And I always sent you presents for your birthday and for Christmas. You just didn't know they were from me."

There was an uncomfortable silence as his words sunk in. If I thought about it hard enough, I wondered if I could figure out which things came from him; something unusual, maybe, or not something I'd asked Santa Claus for.

"Did you send a purple and white blanket, with a southwestern-looking design and white fringe on both ends?"

Tommy laughed.

"I did."

"It was so unusual; different than anything in the rest of the house. But I loved it, and kept it on the end of my bed for years. I'd lay it across my feet in the winter when it was extra cold outside. It kept them toasty warm. So, thanks, Tommy. And thanks for everything else, too."

"You're welcome," he said.

He was smiling, but the tears were welling up in his eyes again.

"So what changed?" I asked. "You said she agreed to marry you."

"It was your father," he said.

"My father?"

"Yes. For all these years, she had lied to you about your father. She wanted to tell you, but she was afraid you might never forgive her. Your mother always said that she was afraid that if you ever met me, the truth about your father still being alive might slip out somehow. It was just too close for comfort."

My heart skipped a beat.

"So he's still alive then?" I asked, not sure which answer I would prefer.

"He is. What changed was that she finally let go of the idea he would come back to her one day. She loved me, yes, of that I'm quite sure. But Howard was the love of her life. I knew it, and accepted it. If he ever decided to go looking for her, I knew that would be the end of us. I just lived in the hope that would never happen. But last summer, after she visited you in Chicago, everything changed. I don't know what you said to her, but something made her decide to let go of him.

"She said that you were a grown woman, with a wonderful boyfriend and a solid career. She believed that you were old enough to understand the truth and felt sure you would understand why she did what she did, and made the choices she made. And the best part was that she chose me. She said that even if the two of us, Howard and I, were in the same room, both holding out a hand to her, that she would take mine."

There were tears pouring down his cheeks now, and he made no effort to hide them. I was furious with a God that could let something like this happen to such a nice man. He had loved my mother for more than thirty years. His dreams were finally about to come true when my mother's life was snuffed out just like that, for no good reason. I wanted to smash my fists against the window, too.

"Tommy, I'm so sorry. Really, I am. But I have so many questions. I know that this has come as a shock to you, and that my father is the last person you want to talk about right now. Still, I've come all this way, and day after tomorrow I'll be in Los Angeles. I need to know what I'm walking into and I don't have a clue how to find him. Can you help me? Could we have dinner or something later?"

"Sure, honey. Just give me a chance to pull myself together. I'll knock on your door at six o'clock and take you to the best restaurant in town. Then I'll tell you everything I know. I'll help you in any way I can. It'll be nice to spend some time getting to know you after all these years."

Tommy left the café first and I let him go on his own. I stayed behind, watching him through the window until I saw him round the corner to the motel. On my way out I stopped to pay the cashier, but it was already taken care of.

The day unfolded slowly. I was back in my room long before noon, wishing for the hours to pass quickly until six o'clock when I could get some answers about my father. Tommy was such a nice man, so obviously in love with my mother. She could have married him any time, and I like to think that I would have welcomed him into my life. Now, he was probably the closest connection to my mother that I had. He knew the truth about her life, so many things that I did not.

I left a phone message at Derek's office and at his home. When I got no answer either place, I wondered whether they had been able to pull together a funeral service already and if maybe that's where he was. Then I remembered my last words to him the night before. I told him that we would be back together before he knew it and we could begin planning our life together. Those could have been the very same last words my mother said to Tommy. Suddenly I was terrified. When I heard Derek's voice on the telephone a few minutes later, I was so happy I cried. This immediately terrified him, until I could manage to explain myself. Quite a pair, we were.

The funeral was arranged for first thing in the morning. Derek had been at the funeral home helping Vanessa's parents with the details. He was surprised to discover they were not angry with him, nor did they blame him for what happened. They were nice, normal people, free of the alcoholism that wracked their daughter's mind and body until she finally gave up. No one was sure how she ended up with such an addiction. These things run in families, her parents were told during one of the therapy sessions at the first rehab center. Vanessa's grandfather had died when she was just a little girl and he had been known to take a nip or two of his medicine, as he called it. But no one knew for sure why things turned out this way. Her parents had been exhausted down to their very bones. Derek had tried to make the whole terrible process even the tiniest bit easier for them.

I promised to call Derek after I had dinner with Tommy and fill him in on the details. He said he'd be home from the viewing by then and would be very happy to hear my voice. I could only imagine what a horrible evening he had ahead of him. She was so young, and had been very beautiful until the years of excessive alcohol and drugs had taken their toll on her.

When I hung up the phone, I immediately felt that emptiness and aloneness again. I put my shoes back on, grabbed my coat, and went for a walk. There were some little gift shops next to the café and the neighborhood felt very safe. So I ventured out in search of something to do. As luck would have it, I found a bookstore and spent a couple of hours browsing the aisles. When I finally headed back to the motel, I had two bags of books, both so heavy that my hands were sore from their handles by the time I dropped them onto the bed in my room.

I have always loved books, even as a child. But mostly I borrowed them from the library. I've always been a regular patron of whatever library I lived closest to. In the past, I would never have considered spending two hundred dollars on brand new books for no good reason. That day, however, I wasn't myself. And I began to wonder if I would ever be myself again, since the person I thought of as me for three decades felt like an illusion; like a bedtime story repeated so many times that it felt like the truth, but it wasn't.

I read for a while, took a nap, organized my suitcase for departure first thing in the morning, and got ready for dinner. Tommy knocked on my door at six sharp. He was wearing black, pleated slacks, a white button down shirt, and a nice black leather jacket. Although he was close to sixty years old, he was fit, and really quite attractive. He and my mother must have been a great looking couple. I wished that I could have seen them together.

He helped me into his truck and we drove to the restaurant without much conversation. It was only a ten-minute drive, thankfully, and we were seated in a booth near the back of the room, at his request. I understood why we were both quiet in the car on the drive over in spite of how much there was to talk about. I think that both of us wanted to be at our table in the restaurant before we started, so that once we did, we wouldn't have to stop while we got out of the truck and waited to be seated inside.

"So how are you, Tommy," I asked. "Are you holding up okay?"

"The truth, Meredith?" he asked. "I'll never be the same again. I've spent thirty years being in love with your mother and I don't know how to do anything else. Mariel said you haven't made a reservation for tomorrow night. Does that mean you're leaving in the morning?"

"Yes," I said. "I want to get finished with whatever business I have in L.A. and get home to Chicago."

"I understand," he said. "I just hope that you'll stay in touch with me, now that we've finally met. You're the only connection to Anastasia I have left now. I can't bear the idea of losing touch with you, too. You've been a part of my life for three decades and…"

"Tommy, it's okay," I said, seeing him start to break down again, "I promise we'll stay in touch. You're my connection to her, too, don't you see? That bonds us together. Besides, I like you very much. This afternoon, I was thinking about what it might have been like if we had become a family, the three of us, a long time ago. It would have been a good life, Tommy. I think you and I would have been the best of friends. There's no reason we can't start now."

"Good," he said, breathing a visible sigh of relief. "I'm really happy to hear that. Now, ask me your questions and I'll do my best to answer them for you. My knowledge of your father is limited, but I'll help in any way I can."

"Okay, let's start with his last name. I found my original birth certificate and the place where my father's name should have been is blank. So, was it really Springfield, or was that something my mother made up to make it look like she had actually been married?"

"No, it wasn't Springfield," he said. "And you're right, she had it legally changed before you were born. She told me that she had decided to do it when she was on her way back to Milwaukee in 1962. Before she left here, she called your grandparents and told them she was pregnant and that the man was married. I don't know how much of the rest she revealed to them over the years, but she never told them about me. She insisted that it had to be kept a secret, as I mentioned earlier. Her very own secret hiding place, where she started life over again. It sounds crazy, talking about it to you, but it was important to her and I loved her. I would have done anything she asked me to do.

"Anyway, changing her name was your grandparents' idea. One of her nights on the road as she made her way home, when she called to let them know she was safely checked in to a motel for the night, they suggested the idea to her. They helped her invent the whole story and they backed her up all these years. Your grandmother thought life would be easier for your mother, and for you, if you all pretended your father had been killed shortly after he and your mother were married. In those days, it was much better to be a widow than an unwed mother. So they told your mother to think about what your new last name should be. Then they went about finding an attorney to draw up the paperwork as soon as she got back to Milwaukee. No one ever questioned it."

"Unbelievable," I said. "Don't tell me, let me guess. She made her decision when she passed through Springfield, Missouri. Am I right?"

"You guessed it," he said.

We both chuckled, picturing a twenty-two year old Anastasia Burke trying to decide what she and her baby would be called from then on.

"Did she tell you my father's last name?"

"That's right, you asked me about his last name," Tommy said. "I'm sorry, Meredith, she didn't. And as far as I know, she never had contact with him or his family again."

I tried not to look too disappointed, but I was really hoping he could help me out with that one. I was running out of clues.

"What about her friend, Jill?" I asked. "They were roommates in California, at least part of the time. My mother wrote in her journal that Jill covered for her when she was here, if my grandparents called."

"Jill Parker. I haven't thought about her in years. But yes, I remember her. I never met her in person, but she was a good friend to help your mother like that. They had a whole scheme worked out depending on what time of day it was when your mother's parents called. Then Jill would call the motel and leave a message. Anastasia would call her parents back and no one was the wiser. That's what we believed, anyway. But I don't have a number for her, or an address. After all these years, I don't know how you'd go about finding her. Chances are she got married a long time ago and changed her last name. Sorry, honey, I'm just not much help, I guess."

I tried desperately to think of something else he might know about my mother's time in California, a clue that might lead me to my father. It occurred to me that Tommy was the closest thing I really had to a father at that point. If not for my mother's crazy fantasy that my father would come back for us one day, Tommy would have taken good care of us. And I would have grown up in a very different home. It would have been normal. For a moment I considered driving out to L.A., dumping the ashes as per my mother's request, and coming straight back here to Flagstaff for a while, until Tommy was feeling better. Then it hit me.

"Did she tell you she used to sing with my father's band?" I asked.

"Oh, yes," he said. "She loved to talk about that. It was among her proudest moments. I think she was really good. People would come back just to see her. Once in a while I'd catch her singing, but she'd always stop as soon as she realized I was listening. Your mother was really good at compartmentalizing things. I think that for her, the singing belonged in L.A., and although she freely talked about it with me, the actual music was something she shared with your father, and she protected the memory."

"Did she tell you the name of the hotel where they met?" I asked. "She worked there as a waitress when she first got to town. She mentions the place many times, but never by name. It's so frustrating!"

"If she did, I don't remember it," he said, and my heart sank. "But I do remember where it was. She said it was right across from the beach, in Santa Monica. It should be easy enough to find. Maybe someone there will remember her. They'll surely remember your father. From what your mother said, he was something of a local celebrity."

I was thrilled with this new information. For the first time since I'd left Chicago, I felt like I might actually be able to track my father down. And if that didn't work, maybe Derek would come up with something. After I had spoken to him that afternoon, I placed a call to my mother's attorney. I said I wanted to take him up on his offer to look into who was actually behind the monthly bank deposits on my behalf, and my mother's. If he found something, he was to contact Derek and tell him everything, since I'd be on the road and wasn't sure where I'd be staying.

Meanwhile, all I had to do was make my way to Santa Monica and look for the hotel in the old black and white photo with the welcoming front porch.

"So tell me about this long-distance romance you carried on with my mother," I said. "What was my mother really like?"

Tommy talked for two hours, while I listened. It was amazing how good my mother was at keeping secrets. I never had the slightest clue what she was up to. But she flew out to Flagstaff twice a year, and together they travelled all over the Southwest. He had pictures, lots of them, that he promised to make copies of and send to me. From his inside jacket pocket he produced a small stack of photos from their most recent visit. It was amazing. There was my mother, looking the same as she had the last time I saw her, with the man who was sitting across the table from me. His arm was around her shoulders, and her arm around his waist in most of them. They looked so happy.

"On your way back through town, after you take care of things in Los Angeles, I'll put you in the room your mother used to stay in when she was here. She left some of her things here so she didn't have to pack so much when she came to visit. But if you don't mind, I'd rather you didn't take them just yet. I'm not ready to…"

"It's okay, Tommy," I said. "I have the rental car, and not much room. Don't worry; there'll be plenty of time for all that."

I'd barely finished packing up my mother's house, and I didn't feel up to going through any more of her things just yet. I was relieved that Tommy didn't want me to. Maybe by the time I came back to Flagstaff I'd be ready.

When he walked me to my room, we hugged each other for a long time. I promised to say goodbye in the morning before I left town. He promised to find a picture of her that had been taken back in 1962 when she stayed for a while, enjoying her secret life, before heading home to Milwaukee to face the music. He thought the photo might be of some help to me in finding her. But mostly I think he wanted to find it, look at it, and show it to me. He needed to remember that twenty-two year-old girl whose life was already so complicated.

I told him that I wanted to promise that I'd see him again in a few days on my way back to Chicago, but that I had to wait and see what happened first. I didn't know how long I'd stay, and since Derek wasn't with me, I might just turn in the rental car and fly home. But I did promise to let him know what I decided. Either way, we'd see each other soon. And that was a promise I planned to keep.

I went inside my room and called Derek immediately. He had just returned from the viewing and said that he didn't want to talk about it; that it was horrific, sad, and terrible. But it was over and that was something. Tomorrow would be the funeral, which would be very difficult. Once that was behind him, he could begin the healing process. We both could. He said that Vanessa's parents had been very kind to him. They hoped that he could find happiness now and move on with his life completely. They even asked him to let them meet me one day, not for a while, but eventually.

We talked about what I'd learned from Tommy, and I told Derek that I couldn't wait for them to meet. He seemed happy that Tommy would be a part of our lives now, that it signaled the beginning of our family. There was no word from the attorney yet, but he'd let me know as soon as he heard anything. Neither of us was in a hurry to end the phone call. I was anxious about what the next days would be like, wishing more than anything that Derek was going to be with me. But he had his own dragons to slay. When we said good night, I took comfort in the secure knowledge that he would be there for me, no matter what. I'd be there for him, too.

I changed into my pajamas, put out my clothes for the next day, and packed up everything else for an early departure. Then I turned out all of the lights except the one on the nightstand, crawled into bed, and opened the third notebook. The year on the cover read 1982. The first entry inside was dated August 5th, my twentieth birthday. I had been about to start my third year of college. Taped inside the front cover of the spiral bound notebook was a picture of me, standing in the driveway of our house on Elderberry Lane, carrying an overburdened backpack full of books. I was the same age in the photo as she was when she got into her blue Ford Fairlane and headed out to find her future.

CHAPTER 10
Anastasia

IT'S HARD TO BELIEVE THAT MY baby girl is the same age I was when I left my parents' house in my powder blue car, bound for California. My how things have changed since then. You're out with friends, celebrating your birthday, and I'm feeling so nostalgic. I found two of my old journals that I plan to save for you. There's so much I've kept from you over the years. Your grandparents have been after me to either tell you, or write it down, because under no circumstances do they want to be responsible for telling you the truth about your mother.

So I agreed to assemble a written history for you, which I'll leave with my attorney for safekeeping. That way, if anything happens to me, my parents won't be the only ones who know the truth, nor will they feel responsible for passing the information along to you. The first journal is one that I kept during my trip out to California, and relates all of the unfortunate decisions I made while I was there.

That one spiral notebook contains secrets I've kept from you your whole life. Your father's last name wasn't Springfield, and we were never married. Well, he was. And he doesn't know you exist. Anyway, if you're reading this, then something terrible has happened to me, so I'll ask you to start at the beginning and read it yourself. It's too painful for me to repeat.

The second notebook was started the day I left California, un-married and pregnant with you. That one will tell you the story of how I met Tommy, the man I've been seeing since shortly after you were born. I never made any trips back to California. Twice a year when I said I was going there, I was actually going to Flag-staff, Arizona to see him. He loves me, Meredith, and I love him. He loves you too, and thinks of you as his daughter, even though he's never met you. We've talked many times over the years about getting married. I know he wants that more than anything. He tries not to pressure me, because we have so little time together, we just want to enjoy it.

But I can tell that every time he puts me back on the airplane his heart breaks all over again. I wish I could say yes to him, so we could live happily ever after. He's a good man, Meredith. I think you would learn to love him, too. The trouble is, he runs a motel in Flagstaff that he's going to inherit from his rotten parents one day, and you and I have built a life here. I have my business and this is your home. I would never want to take you so far away from your grandparents. But if I'm really honest, which at this point you probably think I am totally incapable of, the truth is that while I love Tommy, your father was "the one."

He was the love of my life. After him, it could never be the same with anyone else. I can't help thinking that one of these days he'll come looking for me. And if he did, in spite of the promise I made to his wife all those years ago, I would be with him. I'd follow him wherever he asked me to. But he knows where I am, and after nearly twenty-one years, he still hasn't come for me. I'm such a fool to keep waiting for him, but I just can't seem to let go of the dream.

Sometimes I think I'll go to Flagstaff for good, once you finish college. Of course, then I'd have to find the courage to tell you the truth about things. But then I think of Howard and tell my-self, just give it another year. Just another goddamn year, that's all. And then another…

CHAPTER 11
Meredith

THE REST OF THE PAGES IN the notebook were blank. I laid the book down on the bed beside me and switched off the light. She called him Howard, as Tommy had, but neither of them had provided a last name. Still, I thought it should be easy enough to find the hotel in the picture I carried in my purse; the one where my parents are happy and smiling, wrapped in each other's arms. I would get up in the morning, say goodbye to Tommy and head for Los Angeles. I couldn't share the contents of my mother's third journal with him, because I would not want him to know how broken and angry she was back then. It would break his heart in a million ways. I wasn't about to be part of that.

I wanted to talk to Derek so badly and share this latest information with him, but with the time difference I was sure he'd be in bed. And after the day he had, with what he was facing tomorrow, if he was actually managing to get some sleep, I did not want to disturb him. So I lay in my bed at the Thunderbird Motel in the dark, with my eyes wide open, making plans for the next day. She had kept her word all these years and not tried to contact my father, or at least up until a decade ago. I had no idea what had happened in the ten years since then.

I wondered how my father was going to feel about learning he had a thirty year-old daughter. What if he wasn't thrilled with the idea and didn't want anything to do with me? That would be horrible. And what about Victoria? She was definitely not going to be pleased to see me. But I thought it was about time people started telling the truth for a change. There had been way too many secrets for far too long.

Tommy was waiting outside the motel lobby when I went to check out. He tried to appear busy, sweeping the concrete just outside the entrance door, but I wouldn't be surprised if he had been there since way before dawn, wanting to be certain I wouldn't just drive away without saying goodbye. It wasn't necessary, of course. Tommy was like family to me now. But I didn't blame him for feeling insecure. He had waited for my mother for thirty years, knowing that another man could show up a snatch her away from him any minute. And now it had happened; not the way he thought it would, but she's gone forever, just the same.

"I wouldn't leave without saying goodbye, Tommy."

"Was I that obvious?" he asked.

I just smiled at him, and he smiled back.

"Here's the room key," I said, handing it over. "Do I need to go inside and check out with Mariel?"

"No, you're all set."

"Well, Tommy, I suppose I'd better get going. I have a long drive ahead of me, and a lot of questions to get answers to. But listen. If I decide to turn in the rental car and fly back to Chicago, I'll let you know. Otherwise, I'll see you on the return trip. Does that sound like a good plan?"

Tommy smiled at me again. He really was a very handsome man. He managed to keep his tears from spilling over onto his cheeks, and I hoped that what I saw in his eyes was relief, at least in some small part. I just let my tears fall.

When I hugged him goodbye, we both held on tight, neither of us ready to say goodbye yet. I felt safe and protected. I wondered if that was what it felt like to be in the arms of your father, the thing I had never known.

It was a beautiful morning when I left Flagstaff. I knew that the girl with the pink dress and dark ponytail would be serving breakfast. Mariel would be behind the desk at the motel. The bookstore probably wasn't open yet, but perhaps someone was in there anyway, stocking the shelves and putting change in the cash register. Then I realized that was the extent of what I knew about this place, but I also knew that I wanted to come back. Many times.

Somewhere a few hundred miles to the west, my biological father was waking up, although if he was still a musician working at night, he might be asleep for a few more hours. That was the first time I had thought of him that way, as a biological father. But maybe that was because now, after having met him not yet twenty-four hours ago, I had begun to think of Tommy as my dad. The only thing that had stood between us my whole life was simply a nod of my mother's head. If she'd let Tommy go back to Milwaukee with her in 1962, I might never have even known about my actual father. Tommy's name could have been on my birth certificate in the space that instead remained blank. But she chose to wait for Howard. I wondered if she would make the same choices if she had it to do over again.

The closer I got to Los Angeles, the warmer it got outside. By noon, when I stopped for gas, I decided that it was warm enough to put the top down on the convertible. I'd leave my coat on, of course. It was still early February after all. But I wanted to smell the ocean for the first time the moment I was within its range. I wanted to experience my first glimpses of the Pacific as my mother had so long ago, but with an unobstructed view.

I had picked up a map at the gas station and immediately longed for Derek to be there as my navigator. Life, I was coming to realize, was so much easier with a partner. Chicago is a big city, and I had been driving there for years. But Los Angeles was going to be something else. My goal was the ocean, and the hotel in the picture. Once I got close, it was likely that anyone on the street could tell me where it was. But there was still a lot of city between here and there, and as I approached Los Angeles, the traffic thickened until I was surrounded by what felt like millions of cars. At times I was at a full stop on the freeway, which I normally would have found irritating, but it provided the opportunity to check the map and make sure I was in the right place.

After sitting in heavy traffic for a while, I realized that all the coffee I'd been drinking was becoming a real problem. I had no idea where to pull off the freeway to find a clean, easily accessible restaurant where I could use the facilities, so I just took the first exit I came to. It may have been another fifteen minutes before I reached the next one, and I was already significantly uncomfortable. When I got to the end of the ramp, there were no restaurants at all. There was only one gas station and it did not look welcoming. But it had become something of an emergency, so I drove in to the gas station lot and pulled up next to the restroom doors on the outside of the building. The doors were covered with graffiti and I realized that with the top down on the car, everything inside of it would be vulnerable when I went into the restroom. But it would take way too long to put the top up, not having tried to do it yet. Then I noticed the dog. It was the biggest German Shepherd I had ever seen. The dog was restrained with a very long, heavy linked chain. I hoped against hope that it wasn't as long as the distance between him and me.

He was snarling, with his teeth bared. He was crouched down, ready to spring. When I stepped out of the car, the dog shot forward, practically strangling himself when he reached the end of the chain, which stopped him, thankfully, still a few yards from me. His barking continued, pausing only occasionally to let out a long, low, growl. Now I was about ready to wet my pants, or worse.

I quickly entered the restroom, where there was one stall with no door. My only viable option at that point was to simply get the job done and move on, with as little delay as possible. Naturally there was no toilet paper, but luckily I had a tissue in my pocket left over from my tearful goodbye with Tommy. Score one for me. I didn't even consider washing my hands. There was no soap and there were no paper towels, but I always carried wipes and hand sanitizer in the car for just this eventuality.

In my mind, I vaulted into the car without even opening the door, like they do in the movies, though I doubt I actually did it that way. The dog was still barking and straining so hard against his leash that he pulled himself up on his hind legs, clawing at the air with his huge front paws. Three men who had come out of the building were staring at me, probably wondering what the big hurry was. Or maybe they were thinking that I looked like easy prey. In either case, I didn't intend to stick around to find out.

I fired up the convertible and tore out of the parking lot as the men started walking toward me, and sent a spray of gravel in their direction. A few stress-filled minutes later, I was back in bumper-to-bumper traffic, breathing in the exhaust from all those cars, wishing I hadn't had the bright idea of putting the convertible top down. My mother had always cautioned me against stopping at rest areas, because she said they were too dangerous for young women traveling alone. I wondered if that was the result of an experience she had when she first arrived in L.A. If so, I hoped it hadn't been her first impression of the city as it had been for me.

I followed the signs to Santa Monica Beach. Once I'd found it, I spent fifteen minutes searching for a place to park. When I finally found a spot, I got out and closed the convertible top. It took a few minutes to figure out how to secure all the latches, but I eventually managed to get it right. I still felt like my luggage was vulnerable, even though it was locked in the trunk, but I wasn't about to haul it with me up and down the street looking for the hotel.

Eventually, I decided there wasn't anything in there that I couldn't replace and started to walk away. Except my mother's journals, I thought; and her earthly remains. So I went back, opened the trunk, took the three small notebooks out of my suit-case and stuffed them into my big leather shoulder bag. The urn that contained my mother's ashes was way too large to fit in the bag. I just had to hope that luck would be on my side this time and no one would steal the car, or break into it and take my luggage. What was wrong with me, I thought? I had never felt so unnerved before. But I had things to do and needed to get hold of myself.

I made my way to the sidewalk in front of the shops and hotels and started walking. I must have walked close to a mile, when suddenly all that was left was beach on one side and a road on the other. I still hadn't found the hotel. It wasn't there. It must be at a different beach, I thought, but I had no idea where, and not a clue where to start. It was getting to be late afternoon. The sun would set before long. I had planned to stay in the hotel in the photograph, and thought what I fool I was to have believed it would be that simple. I was starting to get a raging headache, when I realized I hadn't eaten since breakfast.

I headed back in the direction of my car and went inside the first restaurant I came to. It was a deli, and I ordered an egg salad sandwich with a cup of coffee. The food and the caffeine, combined with a couple of aspirin from my bag, would take care of my headache in a little while, but I still had to figure out what to do next. If only Derek had been there.

Although I hadn't found the one I was looking for, there were other hotels along that strip of beach, so I decided that I would check in to one of them, hopefully one with a parking garage for my rented car. Then I'd call Derek, who would help me figure out what to do next.

As I walked back down the sidewalk toward where my car was parked, the sun was low in the west, what looked like inches from the water. The sun setting over the Pacific Ocean was truly remarkable, just as my mother had described it. The sky looked like it was on fire, and I felt a sense of familiarity, as though I had been there before. Or, perhaps I had seen this particular view of the beach in a photograph.

Then I was stopped in my tracks. The beach was to my right, the sand a dull grey now, the enormous red sun working its way into the water. And to my left, the hotel with the welcoming front porch, where I could imagine a band playing while the sun went down, and my mother's voice in the cool night air. Then I began to smile. For an instant, I saw the sign next to the sidewalk, the one that spoke of my father's band, The Starlighters, with a special guest appearance by Anastasia Burke. I knew it wasn't really there now, but I also knew that once it had been.

What I hadn't been able to tell from the old black and white photograph was not only the name of the hotel, which I now knew was The Georgian, but also that the damn thing was blue! Once you knew that little detail, the hotel was impossible to miss. I stood on the sidewalk in front of the hotel and imagined my father there, his shiny saxophone reflecting the red sunset, and my mother in her beautiful sequined dress, the one that had been given to her by Marilyn Monroe.

As I walked inside, it felt like a dream, picturing my mother walking through the lobby, restaurant, and bar. She and my father had been there together often so many years ago; the father I had never known and who probably didn't know I existed. What a strange, awful, and wonderful life she'd had.

Later, when my luggage was safely deposited in my room and the rented car was valet parked somewhere; I freshened up and went down to the bar for a glass of wine to calm my nerves. I wanted to sit in the room where my mother had waited tables when she first arrived in L.A., and try to find the stage where she sang for an audience that loved her. While I drank my wine, I noticed the bartenders were changing shifts. A young man wearing black slacks, a white shirt, and shiny black satin vest, flipped up the hinged end of the bar and greeted the older man wearing the same clothes. They exchanged a few words, updates I supposed, on who had paid and who was running a tab, that sort of thing. When the older man came out from behind the bar and circled back behind me to leave, I quickly dropped some cash on the bar and followed him outside.

"Excuse me," I said. "Sir?"

He turned to look at me.

"Yes, ma'am?"

He had a low gravelly voice, and I imagined him having spent many years behind the bar, in the days when everyone smoked and you could barely see across the room.

"Can I ask you something?" I pulled the photo out of my bag and held it out to him. "Do you know who these people are?"

The man pulled a pair of glasses from his front shirt pocket and put them on. They were reading glasses, the kind that only have the bottom half, and he looked at the photo through the glasses, then back at me over the top of them. He did this a couple of times and seemed to be looking at me as intently as he looked at the photo in his hand.

"Oh, my God," he said. "You look just like her. That man is your father. I can see it. You're tall like him and you have his eyes, but you look so much like her. The resemblance is uncanny."

"Yes," I said. "That's what I'm told. Can you sit and talk with me for a few minutes?"

"Sure," he said. "Name's Oscar. And you?"

"Meredith."

We crossed the street to a bench on the beach side of the street and sat next to each other.

"Oscar? Please tell me you recognize the people in the photograph. I've come such a long way."

"Oh, sure I recognize them. It was so many years ago, but I loved listening to their music. Your father is one of the best sax players I ever heard, to this day, and your mother, well, she sang like an angel, with a little bit of devil thrown in. That's what your father used to say." Then he got quiet for a moment. "Is your mother still...?"

"No, she's not," I said. "She died very recently. I'm here to carry her ashes to the Hollywood hills like she wanted."

My voice caught in my throat. I had to take a deep breath and let Oscar carry the conversation for a while.

"I'm awful sorry to hear that," Oscar said. "Anastasia Burke. I remember it now. A beautiful name for a beautiful woman, I used to say. She was practically a child. Folks used to pack that bar when she was singing and your father was playin' his saxophone. 'Lotta people were sad when she went away, your father in particular. He was never quite the same after that. I could hear it in his music. A lovely girl, she was. The woman he married was nice too, but oh, the way he looked at your mother. She's the one he shoulda married."

"When was the last time you saw him?" I asked, heart in my throat.

"Well," he said, "I don't work the night shift anymore, so I can't remember the last time I actually saw him, but I do know that he still plays here from time to time. Seems to me he was here a few months ago. The group is mostly instrumental now. They don't usually have a singer, at least not one that lasts for very long. Oh they come and go, but I suspect your father doesn't want to hear anyone else's voice when he's on the bandstand. It was kind of magical when they were on stage together."

We sat there a while longer while I gathered my nerve. The next question would mean the difference between finding my father and being back at square one. I was afraid to ask it, but I had no choice except to follow it through.

"Oscar," I said, "I'm trying to locate my father. All my life I was told my father had died in an accident right after I was born, and that's why my mother went back to Milwaukee, where I grew up. She lied to everyone and said that she had been married to him. When she got back home, she even changed her name so it would look as though she had been. When my mother died, she left behind her journals so I could know the truth about my father. There's lots of information in them about their relationship, and why everything has had to be a secret all these years. But nowhere does she tell me what his full name is. I think she wanted me to know about him, but still wanted to prevent me from actually finding him. My mother promised my father's wife that she would leave town and never contact him again. As far as I know, she kept that promise. My father's name was Howard, I know that, but I don't have his last name. Can you help me, Oscar? Please say you can help me."

CHAPTER 12

"MY FATHER'S NAME IS HOWARD BRADSHAW!"

"That's fantastic news, Meredith," Derek said. "I'll call your mother's attorney right away and give him the information. It shouldn't take long for him to find some answers. When I checked in with him yesterday, he said they had a contact in L.A. who could help out. I'm sure they've already been in touch with him. They were going to visit the bank where the wire transfers originated to see if they could nail down a name and address. As an agent of your mother's lawyer, he should have no problem getting the information we're looking for. It won't be long now, honey."

"I wish you were here, Derek." I said. "I've always been so independent, but all of a sudden I feel, I don't know, like a girl."

Derek laughed. "You are a girl, Meredith. You're also a very strong and capable woman. You're just in some extremely stressful circumstances. That's all. I'm so sorry I can't be there with you, but I hope to catch up with you at some point on your way back to Chicago, if you decide to drive back."

"I do want to drive. This morning I promised Tommy I would stop there on my way home unless I decided to take a flight instead. But I really want to see him again. And I really want you to meet him."

"I'll do my best to get there," he said. "He's part of our family now, so if not this time, then definitely soon."

"Good," I said. "Now tell me about the funeral. Was it awful?"

"It was sad," he said, "but after the viewing last night and breaking the ice with her family, it wasn't as awful as I thought it would be. Once I knew that her relatives weren't going to lynch me, that made it a little easier." He paused for a moment then said, "It was really sad, but wasn't nearly as horrible as Lily's."

"Oh, Derek," I said. "I'm so sorry. What an ordeal this has been for you. I should be there."

"You will be," he said. "Soon, you will be."

My room in the hotel was elegant. It was old, like the motel in Flagstaff, but the furniture was antique and it was so beautiful. The fixtures in the bathroom were brass, polished to a brilliant shine. There were bright white tiles on the floor, alternating with shiny black ones. As I soaked in the white, claw-footed bathtub I felt some of the stress drain from my body.

Then I tried to imagine what the next day would bring. Until I heard from Derek, the lawyer or the investigator, I wasn't sure where I would start. I planned to order room service for breakfast and stay by the phone until one of them contacted me. Now that I was in L.A. with a hotel room and a phone number, I didn't feel so disconnected. While I had been in bumper-to-bumper traffic the day before, I noticed a lot of people talking on those huge, Motorola cellular phones. I saw them in Chicago, too, but not nearly as often.

It never occurred to me to actually consider purchasing one, but after travelling across the country by car, most of the time alone, I was beginning to think that a car phone would have really come in handy. Then I got to thinking that if there was a library nearby, maybe they would have a computer terminal where I could do some research. That would be my backup plan.

Between the wine and the bubble bath I was feeling relaxed and sleepy, the memory of the chained-up, snarling German shepherd beginning to fade. I was too tired to worry anymore, and as I drifted off to sleep I was thinking about Derek, hoping that he was able to put aside the horror of his past few days and get some rest himself. Soon we would be drifting off to sleep in the same bed once again, after all this drama was behind us.

In the morning, my room service tray held a small, old-fashioned silver coffee pot with a long, narrow, curving spout. It reminded me of the one they used to serve my hot chocolate in the dining car the time my mother and I had taken the train from Milwaukee to Chicago when I was eight years old. Besides the coffee, I had a bowl of oatmeal with fresh strawberries on the side, a glass of orange juice, and a bagel with low-fat cream cheese. The charge for the meal had been close to thirty dollars, but I wasn't worried about that sort of thing anymore. I had a trust fund.

I had finished my breakfast and was about to polish off the last cup of coffee when the phone rang. The timing was perfect.

"Derek," I said, picking up the phone.

"No, Meredith. It's Stephen Kensington, your mother's attorney."

"Oh, sorry," I said. "How are you, Mr. Kensington?"

"I'm fine. Thanks. Listen, I have some information for you. Do you have a minute?"

Did I have a minute? Really?

"Yes, please. What have you got for me?" I asked.

"To begin with, I have an address and a phone number. Grab a pencil."

I did as he asked and wrote down all the information.

"Wait," I said. "Did you say Elderberry Lane? I think that's a mistake. That's the street my mother's house is on."

"No mistake. Different Elderberry Lane," he said. "It's where your father and his wife have lived for more than thirty years. The address is in Brentwood."

I read all the information back to him to make sure I had it right. Then I thanked him and asked if there was anything else. There was.

"The deposits to your trust fund were made by Victoria Bradshaw's family lawyer, into an account that only she and her attorneys had access to. Same with the monthly payments to your mother."

"Victoria paid my mother to leave town, so it stands to reason she's the one behind the monthly payments. But you're saying she set up the trust fund, too? Why would she do that?"

"No idea," he said. "The only one who can answer that question is Victoria Bradshaw."

"Okay," I said. "What else?"

"You have a half-sister named Melody, who's a little older than you. She works as a photographer at a place called Shadow Box Gallery in Downey, a town about thirty miles from where you are. It should be easy enough to find the address in the Yellow Pages. There's a half-brother too, but I wasn't able to get much information about him, except that you're practically the same age. If you can find Melody, she can probably help you out with that."

It was strange, the idea of having siblings. Melody's arrival was the reason my father went back to Victoria the first time. Her younger brother was the reason my mother was sent away. They grew up in Brentwood, where the houses are big and expensive. And they must have had the best of everything their whole lives, while my mother and I struggled to make ends meet. It wasn't fair.

"There's one more thing," he said. "I have another of your mother's journals for you. She asked that I give you this last one if it looks like you intend to track down your father or his family. And now that you have their address, I assume that's what you plan to do. I mailed it after speaking with Derek this morning when I found out where you were staying. It should be there in a couple of days, so if you're not still in the hotel, please make arrangements to pick it up there or have it forwarded. And Meredith, are you okay? I mean, this is a lot to take in."

"I'm okay, mostly," I said. "It's all sort of surreal. But I'll be fine." And before we hung up I said, "My mother was a very sneaky person."

He laughed and said, "She had her secrets; that's for sure."

"This last journal, is that all of it? Please tell me that it's the last of her surprises. I'm getting a little bit tired of being manipulated like this."

"It's the last," he said. "I'm sure this information is all pretty overwhelming for you, especially on top of your mother's unexpected passing. I'm sorry to be the one putting you through it. I told your mother it would be better if she just told you the truth, whatever that was, so you could hear it from her, because I knew you'd have so many questions that I couldn't answer."

"Thanks for trying," I said. "My grandparents tried too; otherwise she might not have even left her journals for me. And maybe that would have been the best thing; just letting her secrets die with her. But I've already met one man that I was very happy to discover. So in the end, who knows? Maybe she knew exactly what she was doing."

When I hung up the phone, I dialed Derek's office number. His receptionist said he was at a lunch meeting and that she didn't expect him back for at least a couple of hours, if not more. I had forgotten about the time difference. I had just finished breakfast, so of course it would be about time for lunch in Chicago. So I left a message saying I'd heard from Mr. Kensington and that I would fill him in later that evening.

The place where Melody worked was only thirty miles away, but in traffic it might take well over an hour. I considered taking a taxi so I wouldn't have to bother finding a map and directions, but decided that might get pretty expensive. Besides, while a taxi was easy to get right outside my hotel, I had no idea what it would be like in Downey, and whether getting a taxi for the return trip would be as easy. So I decided to go ahead and drive. I called down to the front desk and asked to have the valet bring my car up. On my way out, I stopped at the information desk, used the yellow pages to look up Shadow Box Gallery, and found an ad that gave the address. Then I asked the concierge to help me find it on my map, and give me directions to get started.

When I pulled up in front of the building an hour and a half later, my breakfast was in a hard lump in my stomach. It was a dreary place that was not in the best area, but certainly not the worst I'd seen. At least there were no chained-up dogs, not that I could see anyway. As I parked my car at the curb two doors down from where I'd find Melody, again I struggled to find my words, and I realized that there was a good possibility she wouldn't even be there. But if she was, I wondered how you were supposed to approach someone and give them this kind of news. There was no easy way. But nothing that had happened in recent memory had been easy, so I decided I'd find my way though it somehow. When the time came, the words would come, too.

I went inside and asked the young man sitting behind the reception counter if Melody was in.

"Yeah, she's in back," he said. "I'll get her."

It's true what they say about a company's receptionist being the key to making a good first impression, and I hoped that the young man's presence behind the desk was merely a fluke, and not their idea of putting the best foot forward.

When she entered the room, I saw that she was tall, like me, with my father's blue eyes. But she had dark hair, and a hard face. She was also painfully thin, with bad skin and an angry look on her face. I don't know whom she was expecting, but they were obviously not welcome.

"I'm Melody Bradshaw," she said. "Are you looking for me?"

"Yes, I'm Meredith Springfield," I said, nervously. "Can we talk for a few minutes?"

"That depends," she replied. "What do you want?"

"I'm sorry, I don't want to be any trouble for you, but it's about your father." I paused. "And my mother."

There was a moment of dead silence as she processed my words. She looked me up and down, staring into my eyes with an intensity that made me uncomfortable. Then she got a rather slimy looking smile on her face.

"Oh, I see," she said. "Don't tell me, let me guess. We're related, right? Sisters maybe?"

"Yes," I said, surprised she'd figured that out so quickly. She didn't look like the brightest person I'd ever met, nor was she the friendliest, by a wide margin.

"I always knew this day would come," she said, laughing to herself. "My father has always had trouble keeping it in his pants. I have never understood why my mother didn't divorce his ass years ago."

I didn't know what to say. I wasn't sure what I had expected her to say, but it wasn't that.

"Could we have some coffee or something?" I asked. "I'd really like to talk to you, just for a few minutes. I don't want any trouble, I promise."

"Just wait there for a minute. I'll grab my purse and let them know I'm taking a break."

I did as she asked, while she disappeared through a swinging door, returning a few minutes later with her purse slung over her shoulder.

"There's a coffee shop next door," she said, walking out of the building ahead of me. She shoved the door open and let it fall back toward me as she walked through it. If my reflexes had been slower it would have flattened my nose. My half-sister may have grown up in a big house in Brentwood, but she sure hadn't learned any manners.

We took a seat at a small table where we were served coffee. Melody said "no thanks" to the menus the waitress offered. I had a feeling we wouldn't be there long.

"So what are you, twenty-seven, twenty-eight?" Melody asked, as she poured a third sugar packet into her coffee.

"I'm thirty," I said.

Melody thought about that for a moment.

"My younger brother, Elliott, is about to turn thirty," she said. "The old man must have been busy back then. He must have been so proud of himself."

"He didn't know," I said. "About me, I mean. Your mother threatened mine, and paid her to go away. Our father still doesn't know I exist."

"I see," she said. "Well, that's the way my mother operates. She controls all of us with her money. It's the only reason I have anything to do with her. She's an awful, angry woman. In fact she pays me to stay away. Dad doesn't like it when she gives me money, because he's afraid I'll spend it on drugs. I don't blame him, I suppose. For a long time, that's what I did with it. So when is he going to get the big surprise?"

"Soon," I said. "I want to talk to your mother first."

"I'd love to be a fly on the wall for that conversation," she said.

"I'm actually not looking forward to it, but there are some answers I want from her, and some things I need to say."

I didn't intend to tell my half-sister about the money. I didn't see any good coming from that. But I didn't want her to get on the phone and tell her mother I was coming. And the way she was talking, it sounded like she'd enjoy making her mother squirm. So I tried to make friends with her. In my heart, I think I really wanted to have a sister who could be part of my life. But this cold and miserable woman before me didn't seem to want the same thing. She obviously got a little thrill over the fact that her mother was going to be very unhappy to see me. Beyond that, there seemed to be very little interest in forming a relationship.

"So why are you here, Meredith?" she asked. "What do you want from me?"

"I don't want anything," I said. "Really. I just wanted to meet you. That's all. You see, my mother died recently, and I just found out my father was still alive. All my life, I thought he had been killed when I was an infant. I didn't realize I had any siblings. I'm just trying to put the pieces together. My mother kept a lot of secrets."

Her face softened, just a little. But she didn't ask any questions.

"I'm sorry about your mother," Melody said. "If you loved her, I guess that must really stink. Are you married?"

"No," I said. "But I'm in a serious relationship. You?"

"Divorced. No kids, thank God. I had some trouble with prescription drugs in the past. Mostly I'm better now, but my marriage fell apart because of it, and I ended up in rehab. It ruined my career, too. I was a photojournalist, actually won a couple of awards for my work. Now I'm lucky to have this stupid job taking family photos and wedding pictures. My parents give me an allowance, but it's not enough to live on. So this is my life, such as it is. At least I'm not dead, like a couple of the people I met in the hospital are now. That's something."

"I'm sorry," I said. "Really."

"Ah well, life is hard. Whatever."

She told me that my half-brother, born the same year as me, lived in Santa Barbara with his wife and two children. After talking about him for a while, she admitted that he was the kindest person in the family. He owned a small restaurant that his parents had bought for him after the car accident that left him with limited use of one of his legs. Even with his handicap, she said, he got around pretty well and the restaurant was very successful.

His relationship with my father and Victoria was obviously better than Melody's, but he didn't come home to visit very often. He always attributed that to the fact that he had a business to run and the kids had their activities, and so on. But I had the impression that the Bradshaw household had never been a very happy place. I think Melody sort of liked the idea of my showing up at their door, scaring the hell out of my father and potentially sending Victoria into a rage. Melody had said her mother was a very angry woman, which didn't surprise me. She had a lot to be angry about.

Melody finished her coffee, and reached for her wallet to pay.

"I have to get back to work. You seem like a decent person, Meredith. I hope you find what you're looking for."

She tossed a five-dollar bill on the table and walked out. My older half-sister was not a happy person.

When Melody went back to work, after promising not to reveal anything to her parents about our meeting, I returned to the hotel to regroup. I wanted the element of surprise on my side, and hoped I could get to Victoria before Melody alerted her that I was coming. But Brentwood was only a few miles from the hotel, and I hoped to be able to talk to Derek before heading over there. Melody had told me that her father always took a trip down to San Diego in early February, although she wasn't certain of the exact dates, so there was a good chance he wasn't even in town.

That disappointed me initially, because I wanted to take care of my business and go home. I didn't want to stay in L.A. any longer than I had to. There were parts of Los Angeles that were very beautiful. And the beaches were magnificent. But it wasn't my home. My home was in Chicago with Derek, and sometimes in Milwaukee with my grandparents.

Then it occurred to me that if my father really were out of town, it would leave Victoria home alone, a lucky break for me. I didn't want to see them together. The chances of her being alone were fairly good, in any case, because apparently he was still in the music business, which meant he probably spent some of his time on the road. Now that I had met Melody and the cat was out of the bag, I wanted to get to Victoria and then to my father quickly, before word got back to them. Melody had promised to keep her mouth shut, but I didn't trust her for a minute.

I returned to the hotel and tried Derek again, but he still hadn't come back to the office. So I studied the detailed map of Brentwood that I got from the hotel, and found Elderberry Lane. My mother was such a child, I thought. I bet that she picked the house I grew up in for no other reason than it was on a street with the same name as the one where my father's house was. Being sentimental was one thing, but my mother was out of her mind. With maps and directions from the concierge at the hotel tucked into my purse, I got back into my car and headed for Brentwood.

Marilyn Monroe had purchased her home in Brentwood in 1961, the year before she died. I thought about her as I began winding through the streets that would lead me to Elderberry Lane, and wondered if one of the houses I passed was hers. Then I remembered the photo of Marilyn with my mother in the wardrobe department that day. I tried to imagine how thrilling that must have been for her. I pictured Marilyn walking away from my mother, and turning back to smile and wink at her, and how that smile must have lingered in my mother's memory.

I found the address and parked the car, then sat inside looking up at the enormous mansion where my father lived with a woman he didn't like very much. It was a white stucco house with a sea of red tile roof. There was a circular driveway out front. Palm trees outlined the property on both sides and the front of the house. The black wrought iron gate that separated me from the house was closed, blocking the driveway. I nearly drove away right then, until I saw the black call box on one of the two brick pillars that flanked the driveway.

First I put on some lipstick and brushed my hair, as if it were important that I make a good impression. Then I got out of the car, on unsteady legs, to approach the call box.

When I pressed the button, a woman's voice responded. I thought it might be the maid or something, since it looked like a home that definitely had at least one.

So I said, "I'm looking for Victoria Bradshaw. Is she in?"

"Yes, who's calling please," came the reply.

I still wasn't sure whom I was speaking to, nor did I know what to say next, so I decided to go with the truth. Unlike my mother, I generally find that the best route to take.

"Meredith Springfield," I said.

No more response from the call box. After a few seconds had passed, the giant iron gates swung open. As I walked up the long, curving driveway, the heavy front doors parted, and I saw the woman who had forced my pregnant, twenty-two year old mother to leave town and never return. It was the woman who had deprived me of a father for my whole life, who tried to make up for that by giving me money. I wanted to kill her.

CHAPTER 13

"I ALWAYS WONDERED IF I'D MEET you one day, Meredith. You're a beautiful woman, just like your mother. My attorneys notified me of your mother's passing. I'm very sorry for your loss."

I couldn't make my voice work. Victoria, though she may have been attractive enough as a young woman, had not aged well. Her face was hard, like her daughter's, and her forehead bore the marks of the scowl that must have spent a good deal of time on her face. She was well groomed and polite, but difficult to look at.

"Thank you," I finally managed to say.

"I guess I always knew you'd come searching for your father evenutally," Victoria said. "But I also hoped that maybe your mother would outlive all of us, so there would be no one left to find." She stepped aside, clearing the doorway for me. "Please," she said. "Come inside."

The house's foyer was extravagant, yet tasteful. It instantly told of old money, blue blood, and the importance of appearances. It made me wonder how often any genuine human emotions were experienced inside those walls. Victoria led me to the formal living room, and as we passed an intercom, she called someone and asked that they bring coffee. We had only been seated for a moment on the beautiful loveseats that faced one another across a glass-topped table, when a plain-looking older woman appeared with a silver coffee service and two cups. She put them on the table, along with a crystal dish that held some sort of elaborate cookies of a kind I had never seen before.

Victoria didn't speak until the servant left the room, closing the tall double doors behind her. It occurred to me that she probably never employed young, attractive servants for fear that her husband would chase them around the house. Keeping him out of trouble had probably become her life's work, yet I doubted that she had been completely successful. What a life, I thought. I never wanted to be her.

"So, Meredith," she said, filling a cup of coffee and placing it in front of me. "Tell me about yourself. Are you married? Any children?"

I wasn't sure if these questions were her way of making small talk, or something deeper, something that was a prelude to how difficult it actually was being her.

"No to both," I said.

"I see. Well, I suppose it's your father you're really here to talk about. You have a half-sister, you know, and a half-brother as well."

"Yes, I know" I said, ready to thrust the first dagger. "I met Melody this afternoon."

"You what?" Her voice was sharp.

This did not please her, not at all. In turn, it pleased me very much.

"My mother's attorney told me about her and where I could find her. Melody told me about Elliott. You must be very proud of him for doing so well, especially after the accident."

Her eyes grew noticeably larger. I couldn't tell if it was surprise or anger.

"Melody is a very unkind and disappointing person," she said. "I suppose she told you all about the accident, and my part in it? That would be a very good way to embarrass me. I know how much she loves doing that."

"No," I said quickly. "She didn't give me any details, she just said that you and my father had bought him the restaurant after the accident and that Elliott was able to get around remarkably well, considering."

"I see. So it appears I've embarrassed myself then. Well, I might as well tell you, as long as we're getting all of our skeletons out of the closet, so to speak. It was my fault, the accident. My husband had been gone for several weeks. I had reason to believe he was being unfaithful to me, yet again. I had come to expect that behavior from him, of course, so it wasn't as though it was a surprise. Heaven knows our marriage has been devoid of that kind of relationship for many years. But Elliot was with me when my suspicions were confirmed, which was very sloppy on my part.

"I lost my temper and confronted your father while the three of us were having dinner in a restaurant, where he would be performing in the bar later that evening. I was humiliated in front of my son when your father made no effort to deny his infidelity and simply responded with an off-handed, 'So what.' I had already finished two glasses of wine, or I never would have allowed a conversation of that kind with Elliot present. And the third glass of wine is something I have regretted ever since. I'll regret it for the rest of my life."

"I'm sorry, Victoria," I said. What do you say to a story like that? "I'm sure you never intended to hurt your son."

"Nonetheless, he was hurt," she said. "And he remains hurt to this day, the result of his injuries a constant reminder of what happened, and why."

"I'm sorry," I said, again.

"Your mother was only the first infidelity; the first of a long line of them. But none that followed meant a single thing to him. I suppose that's why I've been able to live with it all these years. It's only about the sex, nothing more. The women never last very long, and he's usually fairly discreet about it, so I just let him be. I only intervene when rumors of his behavior get back to me.

"Your mother was different though. He loved her. I suppose he loved me, too, in his own way, at least at the beginning, but he was never in love with me. I could give him opportunities and an extravagant lifestyle while he struggled to make a name for himself. Besides, I was the mother of his first child by then, so that elevated me significantly in his opinion. But we fought constantly. He'd stay away for weeks or sometimes even months at a time.

In those days it was no good being divorced with a child. I didn't want to face that humiliation, so I always let him come back.

"I know you don't understand why I did what I did to your mother, but I felt it was the only choice I had. I knew if your father had found out she was pregnant, he'd leave me for good. So I told him I was pregnant before she had a chance to. Then I paid your mother to go away. Howard came home, and before he could discover I'd lied about it, I actually was pregnant. But ever since, I've lived in fear of that lie coming back to haunt me. And now you're here. You must hate me."

Before I walked through the front door of her house, I wanted her dead. I did hate her at first. She had everything, including my father, all these years. But the truth was that I was really beginning to feel more pity toward her than hatred. Her life had been empty, sad, and pathetic. She'd spent more than thirty years with a man who didn't love her, and never really had. Still she had paid my mother off, and while Victoria knew how difficult it would be as a single mother in those days, it didn't bother her at all to subject my mother to it. She was controlling and manipulative. She had lied about being pregnant and changed the course of history as a result. She was kind of a monster.

"I don't hate you," I said. "It's all just such a mess."

"That it is," she said.

"I just came here because I wanted to tell you that I'm not going to keep the money. I can't accept it from you. It was your guilt that made you do it, because as manipulative as you are, I still think there's a decent heart beating inside of you somewhere. You felt so bad about depriving my mother of my father, and vice versa, that you thought you could make things better by giving me money. But it doesn't work that way, Victoria. Your actions have consequences."

"Please, Meredith. I hope you'll reconsider. You're an innocent victim in all this. You have a right to be angry with me for what I did, and I've had to live with it for thirty years. At first, I would lay awake at night next to your father and consider the cost of having him there, how many lives I'd interfered with by insisting I get my way. It made me sick.

"I saw our children growing up with everything money could buy, while you and your mother were probably struggling. When Elliott was born, I thought of how I had lied to your father about the pregnancy, and the extremes I had gone to in order to make it so. I followed him all over the place, dragging Melody along with us. I insisted that a family should be together, and we travelled with him just long enough for me to get pregnant. Then we never travelled with him again, not on business, or any other way.

"But after Elliott came along, I decided that if I didn't do something decent, God would probably either strike me dead, or take one of my children from me. That's when I started making deposits into your account. Every time I did something for Elliott, I did something for you. When he got braces on his teeth, I deposited an equivalent amount into your account. The money piled up quickly when he went to college, as you can imagine. So please, Meredith, I beg of you, reconsider what that money means to me. Please don't throw it back in my face. I'm not sure I could live with that."

"I'll think about it," I said. "So where is my father now? I've come all this way to spread my mother's ashes and talk to my father. After that, I want to go home. I have a life in Chicago, without all this drama. I want to get out of here. But first, I have a few questions for him."

"I know you do," she said. "Of course it will mean the end of my marriage, once he realizes I've kept you from him all these years. But I suppose I deserve that. I was beautiful once, you know. Not as beautiful as your mother. But I had plenty of other suitors when your father came along. I suppose I should look some of them up to see if they're still alive and single. After all, I'm only fifty-eight years old. And I still have lots of money. Not a bad bargain for one of them."

I felt sick, and needed to leave that house as soon as possible, but I intended to get what I had come for.

"Where is he?" I demanded.

"Tell me where you're staying and I'll send him to you tomorrow morning. He'll be back from San Diego late this evening, and I'll confess everything, all my sins. But let me be the one to tell him. Please."

"Fine," I said. "But I promise you if he doesn't make an appearance by lunch time, I'll be back at your door."

"I know, Meredith," she said. "He'll be there. Where are you staying?"

When I told her where, she lowered her head, shaking it from side to side, and smiling, but not in a happy way.

"Of course," she said.

It was going to be a very long night.

I had dinner at the hotel and was finally able to talk to Derek on the phone that evening. After we filled each other in on the events of our day, we said goodnight. I was still much too wound up after my encounter with Victoria. Her words kept repeating in my head. I wasn't anywhere near ready to try sleeping. So just for fun, I pulled the phone book out of the drawer of the nightstand and started flipping through the pages.

There were three Jill Parkers listed. Before I could lose my nerve, I dialed the first number and held my breath waiting for an answer. The number had been disconnected. When I dialed the second number I got an answering machine and the Jill Parker who recorded the message sounded about sixteen years old, at the most. So I dialed the last Jill Parker in the phone book and waited for someone to answer.

"Hello?" a bright cheery voice said.

"Hello," I said. "May I speak to Jill Parker, please?"

"Speaking," she said.

"My name is Meredith Springfield. I'm looking for the Jill Parker that had a roommate named Anastasia Burke between 1960 and 1962. Is that you?"

There was a pause, during which I waited for her to either tell me I had the wrong number or just hang up on me.

"Oh, my God," she said. "I can't believe it. How do you know Anastasia? I haven't thought of her in years."

"She was my mother."

"Was?" she asked, clearly deflated after only just now hearing of her long lost friend.

"Yes, I'm afraid so," I said. "Sorry to spring it on you like that. I gather I've found the right Jill Parker."

"You have. How did you find me?"

"Remember Tommy Gallagher, in Flagstaff, Arizona?"

"Yes, of course!" she said. "That's the guy she met on her way back home, and I had to cover for her because her parents thought she was still in L.A. He gave you my name?"

"He did. I was with him yesterday."

"I haven't seen your mother or heard anything about her for just about thirty years. And how old are you, anyway, if you don't mind my asking."

"Just about thirty years," I said, and waited for it to sink in.

"No," she said. "Was Anastasia pregnant with you when she left here? Is that why she left L.A.?"

"Yes, she was," I said. "And it's a very long and frustrating story, but basically yes, that's why she left."

"I had no idea," Jill said.

"I wondered if you knew," I said. "I only just found out about any of this myself in the past couple of weeks. I'm in Santa Monica, at the Georgian Hotel. I hope to meet my father tomorrow."

"Of course," she said. "That's the hotel where your mother used to sing with Howard…"

"Yes, that's the place," I said.

"Does that mean that Howard Bradshaw is your father?" she asked.

"That's right," I said.

"Oh, God," she said. "He was so handsome. And your mother was so in love with him. That wife of his was so mean spirited. She didn't love him, not really, but she didn't want anyone else to have him either. I don't know, I guess you can never tell for sure what goes on in a marriage, but everyone thought that your mother and Howard would end up together. Then she just disappeared one day while I was at work. The next thing I knew she was calling me from Flagstaff asking me to cover for her with her parents. But I had no idea she was pregnant. As far as I know, I was her closest girlfriend back then, but she never breathed a word of it to me."

By the time Jill and I said good night it was well after midnight. I had told her all about my mother and me, and our life in Milwaukee. And I even told her about Derek, in a general sort of way. She told me about the two years that she and my mother spent as best friends, and filled in some of the details for me that weren't included in my mother's journals. Not only had Anastasia Burke been a very popular entertainer, she had caught the attention of a talent scout right before she left town. He had come to Jill's apartment trying to locate her to discuss a recording contract. When Jill told my mother about it on the phone, she just said that part of her life was over now and to tell the man thank you anyway, if he should ever come around looking for her again.

The conversation with Jill was a little awkward at first, but eventually it was as if we were old friends who just hadn't spoken for a really long time. Once we had established our connection with my mother, we fell into a comfortable conversation as if we'd known each other for years. I was so glad I had taken the chance and called her, because the details she shared would have been lost to me forever if I hadn't. We exchanged addresses, and I gave her my number at the hotel and at home in Chicago. We promised to stay in touch, and she said that if I was comfortable with it, and it wasn't too much of an intrusion, she would love to be present when I scattered my mother's ashes. As she said it I thought, yes, my mother would have liked that idea very much. And, I would very much enjoy meeting Jill in person.

I got up early the next morning, picked up a to-go coffee from the smaller, more casual restaurant in the lobby, and took it across the street to the beach. I slipped off my shoes and felt the cool sand between my toes as I walked all the way down to the water. Seagulls left their pointy footprints in the wet sand at the water's edge, then flew away, squawking, when I got too close.

The breeze was cool, but the sun felt warm on my face, and I thought about how long it would be before I felt the same thing back home in Chicago. I might have grown up here, if not for Victoria. And Melody might have been an only child like I was. I thought about how amazing it was; the ripples that one big lie and the stroke of a pen in a checkbook could create in the lives of so many people.

Tommy might have met a nice young girl in Flagstaff, gotten married and had a happy, normal life. I could have had two parents, instead of being that poor little girl who had to grow up on Elderberry Lane without a father. My mother and I never felt sorry for ourselves, but other people felt sorry for us.

Even Victoria could have had a decent life if she had just dumped my father before it was too late to catch one of the other suitors she talked about. Elliot would never have been born, but Melody might have been raised in a happy household and not grown up to be a drug-addicted hard ass. So much wasted time, and so much unhappiness. Things didn't have to turn out this way.

At first, when I realized my father's family was going about their lives, oblivious to my very existence, most of them anyway, I was angry at all of them. I was angry because it seemed like they had everything. But I'd come to realize that I had so much more. My mother and grandparents devoted their lives to making sure I was happy and well taken care of. They made sure I grew up to be self-reliant, strong, and independent.

In the end, the poor little girl on Elderberry Lane actually had it better that anyone else in this crazy drama. My mother saw to that. Victoria provided money that probably eased my mother's worries a great deal. But it was out of guilt that she provided it, not out of kindness.

As I crossed the beach on my way back to the hotel where I'd meet my father soon, for the very first time, I wondered if we would ever become friends, or if we would remain the same strangers tomorrow that we'd been all my life. And then I considered, for the first time, that perhaps Victoria hadn't said anything to him at all and there would be no meeting today. For a moment I thought, maybe that would be the best thing.

So I went up to my room and waited to find out. It was still very early, not nine o'clock yet, so I called downstairs and ordered breakfast from room service again. Not two full minutes after I hung up the phone, there was a knock at the door. That was fast, I thought, as I answered the door.

But it wasn't breakfast, nor was it my father. It was Victoria.

"What are you doing here?" I asked. "When is my father coming?"

"I just couldn't do it," she said. "I couldn't bring myself to say the words."

She came in and flopped down on the loveseat, dropping her bag on the floor.

"I was thinking," she said. "Maybe your father doesn't have to find out. What if you just get in your car, drive back to Chicago, and forget all of this. I could make it worth your while, you know. My pockets are really quite deep."

That's it, I thought. I'd had just about enough of this woman.

"Listen to me, Victoria. I've had enough of this crap. I don't know who you think you are, that you can just throw your money around and ruin people's lives! You are the most self-centered, manipulative, not to mention crazy person I have ever met. You've caused enough trouble for one lifetime. If you think I will be bought off as easily as my mother was, you are very sadly mistaken. She was a scared, pregnant, twenty-two year old, and you bullied her into leaving town. I, on the other hand, am a full-grown woman who has had quite enough of your bullshit! Tell me, right this minute, where I can find my father. You have kept him from me my whole life and we are finished with that. Where is he?"

Victoria slumped in her chair. The fine and well-bred posture I witnessed yesterday was completely gone. She was finished, and she knew it.

"Oh, all right," she said, sounding dejected. "You can't blame me for trying. Your father will be playing at the Hyatt Santa Barbara tonight. You'll find him there around seven, in the bar."

"Thank you, Victoria," I said. "You should really go now. And by the way, I've decided to keep the money after all. I've earned it."

She picked up her bag, stood up, and walked out the door without another word. After she was gone, I called the hotel in Santa Barbara and made a reservation for the night. It was only an hour or so away, but I decided to keep my room at the Georgian as well, in case something went wrong in Santa Barbara. And, I still had some business to take care of in Los Angeles. The package would arrive from my mother's attorney tomorrow or the next day, I would scatter her ashes on my way out of town on Monday, and I would never come back here again.

I called Derek's office and filled him in. It was important to me that we weren't out of touch, even though we were thousands of miles apart. I was alone, a long way from home, and I needed to know that at least one sane person knew where I was. I consolidated some of my clothes and all my cosmetics in the smaller of my bags and loaded them in the car. Then I put down the convertible top and headed for Santa Barbara. But not before popping in to the corner coffee shop for a last-minute pit stop. I was not about to let that happen again.

An hour and a half later, I was checked into my room, talking on the phone with Derek and letting him know I had arrived safely. When we hung up, I took one of my new books out onto my balcony and read while I waited for the sun to set. That would be my signal that it was time to go downstairs and meet my father. This time, I was sure of it.

CHAPTER 14

WHEN THE SUN FINALLY FINISHED LOWERING into the Pacific Ocean, I went back inside to change clothes for dinner. I had only packed two dresses for the trip. One of them was black, in anticipation of the event that would be as close to a funeral for my mother as I was going to get. The other was red. It was devoid of sequins, but it was red, and very flattering to my tall, slim frame. I wore my long blonde hair that I'd kept in a ponytail for most of the trip, loose around my shoulders, and used the curling iron to add some soft waves. It was Saturday night, after all, and the people downstairs in the bar of this moderately expensive hotel would be dressed up. I wanted to fit in, of course, but I also wanted to stand out.

Both Tommy and Victoria commented on how much I looked like my mother, even though I hadn't ever really seen it, but I planned to put it to the test. Since I could not, despite my best efforts, come up with a good way to open a conversation with my father, especially as a complete stranger, I decided to let him come to me. If I looked as much like her as people said, he should recognize me at once. If not, I'd have to approach him and just find the words.

The bar was already beginning to fill up, but the band had yet to make an appearance. I found a table near the back of the room and ordered a glass of wine to calm my nerves, and a plate of cheese and crackers to prevent the wine from going to my head. I've never been much of a drinker, much to Derek's relief.

It was getting close to eight o'clock and still no sign of the band. Then it occurred to me that maybe Victoria had lied to me again. There was a sign in the lobby advertising "live jazz," but the name of the group didn't mean anything to me. It could have been anyone. That lying, manipulative bitch had done it to me again. Maybe I really would kill her, I thought, and then just sighed and took another sip of my wine. If only I were a violent person, but alas, I was not. But I was definitely going to give her a piece of my mind. She was a complete nut job...

But my thoughts were interrupted by a flurry of activity at the door when five men carrying instruments and brief cases that probably contained sheet music or electronic cables for their amplifiers walked into the bar. I was in the back of the room and they were making their way to the front, so I couldn't see their faces. The room was quite crowded by then and people were milling around in front of me. All their voices seemed to combine into one chaotic conversation with the clinking of bottles and glasses behind the bar.

I watched the men from across the room as they set up their equipment and then moved to the bar for a drink before getting started. Their backs were to me again, so I still couldn't see their faces, and from where I was sitting all I could tell was that there were five men in all, only three of them white. One of those three men could be my father. With only a couple of faded photographs from thirty years ago, it would probably be difficult to pick him out, even if the three of them were standing right in front of me.

And then the room grew quieter, as a tall, handsome black man approached the microphone. All five men were on stage now and I could see each face clearly. None of them looked like the younger man in the photo, not even close. My heart sank, and my rage toward Victoria was bubbling up again, when a sixth man joined the others on the stage. His back was to me as he took an instrument out of its case. When he turned to face the crowd, he was holding a sparkling silver saxophone. The room erupted in applause. It was my father, no doubt, and apparently we were *all* there to see him.

The man at the microphone welcomed the crowd and they launched into their first song. He called it "Harlem Nocturne." If ever there was a song that could make a person fall in love with the saxophone that was the one. The crowd went silent, while the saxophone wailed and moaned, and I felt my father's heartbreak with every note. The drummer's slow bum, bumpa, bum, with his brushes on a snare, evoked the dark, smoky room jazz feeling of fifty years past. It was haunting and beautiful. I will never forget that moment.

When the song finished, there were whistles, yells, and exuberant applause that only quieted when the next song began. The second song was another I didn't recognize. My mother always played jazz records while I was growing up, and I had grown familiar with many of the songs, but not with their names. At the time, I had no idea what that music must have meant to her. She was playing her favorite style of music, but for thirty years, every time she listened to it she was remembering the man with the saxophone and the hotel on the beach where she stood beside him on the bandstand. My heart ached for her, for both of them.

Sometime during the second song, as my father was scanning the crowd, his eyes went right past me, then stopped and returned to mine. I think that he actually lost his breath for a second or two, because he missed a couple of notes. Throughout the remainder of the first set, his eyes kept returning to me. It was so strange. I wanted to know what he was thinking, and felt a sudden urgency about clearing up the mystery for him, because it seemed to be killing him. He was having trouble focusing on his own music.

Finally, the other man returned to the microphone and announced a twenty-minute break. My heart started pounding so hard I could feel it in my temples. When my father stepped down from the stage and began walking toward me, I thought it would explode right out of my chest. As he stood before me, I held my breath, anticipating my father's first words to me. How fitting that he should begin with an apology.

"Hi," he said. "I'm Howard Bradshaw. I'm sorry if I kept staring at you, but you bear a striking resemblance to someone I knew a long, long time ago."

"Anastasia?" I asked.

The friendly smile that had been on his still handsome face was replaced with shock, confusion, and something else. Love, I think.

"Yes," he choked. "But how did you..."

"I'm her daughter," I said, watching his face for the realization, "and yours."

He was quiet for a long moment, taking it all in. He didn't know about me, and never suspected. Of that I had no doubt. My father pulled out a chair and sat down across from me at the table.

"My name is Meredith Springfield," I said.

"So she married then," he said.

"No, actually," I said. "She never did. She had her name changed when she returned to Milwaukee, pregnant with me, so everyone would think she had. My whole life, I believed my father had been killed in a car accident and that was why we came back to live in Milwaukee. But she told me I was born here, in California. I only found out the truth a few weeks ago."

I could see he was processing this information, running through the possible scenarios, trying to figure it all out. By the look on his face, and the mist in his eyes, I could see that all the roads his mind was traveling down caused him pain. He had loved my mother. Of that I had no doubt. And now before him was a daughter that, for whatever reason, had been kept from him all these years. I wondered if he was picturing the three of us together, if only in fleeting glimpses as he sat across the table from me, or if he had already considered that Victoria might have had a hand in making my mother disappear.

"How did you find me?" he asked. "And why did she choose to tell you everything now, after all these years?"

Then I remembered he had no idea she was dead. I was going to have to deliver the news of my mother's death to yet another man and watch that news destroy him. Her death had broken so many hearts, beginning with mine. My grandparents, Tommy, Victoria, and now my father would all soon be feeling the loss of her and the impact of her secrets and lies.

"You have no idea how sorry I am to tell you this," I said, and his face began to crumble, "but my mother died a few weeks ago. It was a heart attack."

He was struggling not to break down. I wanted to take him away from the noisy bar to a quiet place where we could talk, so I could tell him the whole story, at least as much of it as I knew, and have a chance to hear his side of things. It must have felt like a nightmare, knowing he would have to return to the stage for the band's second set in just a few more minutes.

"How long will you be here? Will you wait until I'm finished, just one more set, so we can go somewhere and talk?" he asked. "Goddamn it! If I could leave right now I would, but they hired a six-piece band and unless there are six musicians at the end of the night, nobody gets paid. Besides, lots of these people are here just to see me. And I need them to keep showing up."

"I understand," I said. "Sure, I'll wait. I'm staying at the hotel tonight, so I'm not going anywhere."

"Good," he said. "Now if you'll excuse me, I really need a drink before we start again. I'll see you again in an hour. Promise you'll wait."

"I promise," I said.

In my entire life, I can't recall an hour that passed as slowly. I ordered what I intended to be my final glass of wine for the night; certain that it would take just a little more liquid courage to get through what would come next. Most of the songs in the first set had been unfamiliar to me. They were wonderful, but I was sure I hadn't heard them before. The second set, however, held one song after the other that I not only recognized, but I knew every word of them. There was no singer on stage, but the words in my head were my mother's. I was sure he was hearing the same voice, a clear, pure sound that was breathy, yet strong. These were the songs they had performed together, that bound them together across the miles and the years. It was beautiful and horrible at the same time. My father's eyes were shiny and he made little attempt to hide it. Maybe the other band members thought it was just the alcohol, but I imagined that some of them knew the truth.

When the set was finally over, he quickly packed up his saxophone, grabbed his coat, and returned to my table to get me. He paid my bar tab and we went to the hotel desk, where he asked them to keep his things. After a moment, the desk clerk returned with two beach towels, a bottle of wine, a corkscrew and two glasses, all packed neatly into a tote bag. We walked through the lobby and out into the courtyard. My father hoisted the strap of the bag over his right shoulder, offering his left arm to steady me as we crossed the street to the beach. He spread the towels over the cool beach sand, where we would sit in the moonlight while the gentle waves kissed the shore, and talk about a lifetime of secrets.

"I saw your mother, you know," he said. "Just last year. She was wearing dark glasses, and she didn't know I had seen her. But I had. After all these years, she was still just as beautiful as the last time I saw her; before she left, without a word to anyone."

"Do you have any idea why she did that?" I asked.

"I figured Victoria or her family had something to do with it. But I had no idea about you. If I had, I would have found you."

"Where did you see her last year?"

"It was at the beach, outside a hotel in Santa Monica. I was unloading my equipment and getting ready to go inside and warm up with the guys before our gig. Victoria was there, although I have no idea why she chose that night to insist on coming with me. She hadn't come to see me perform in years. I saw your mother across the street in what she probably thought was a very good disguise, but I recognized her at once. If Victoria hadn't been there, I could have gone after her, but there she stood, in front of the car, watching me like a prison guard would a convict. I wanted to get in the car and drive straight over her, so I could go after your mother. When one of the guys walked up, I turned to say hello, and when I looked back to where your mother had been standing, she was gone. Just like before, she left without a saying a word."

Poor Victoria, I thought. It seems I wasn't the only one who wished her dead recently.

"I feel sorry for Victoria," I said. "After all, she was the real victim in all this. She was your wife, and you were unfaithful to her. The rest of it is all just collateral damage."

"That's pretty harsh, Meredith. She may have been the first victim, and don't think for one single day of my life she has ever let me forget that. But life is not just black and white, good guys or bad guys. How do you think I felt when I finally realized that the love of my life had been standing right in front of me for months, and I had just married someone else? Why was the universe so goddamn cruel? And why should I have been forced to sacrifice my one chance at happiness, just because the timing was all wrong?"

Then I thought of Derek, and the night when he admitted to me that he was separated, but not divorced. I had decided that what I wanted was more important than what his wife may have wanted. Then I had disregarded her role in his life as though she were inconsequential in the grand scheme of things. Maybe I had to give my father a break, and begin to understand the grey area between what's right and what our hearts desire.

"My mother left her journals with her attorney, along with instructions to deliver them to me immediately upon her death. Several days after she died, he arrived at my doorstep with a manila envelope that contained a letter of apology for thirty years of lies, and three small spiral-bound notebooks. The first is a record of her trip to California, when she had her whole life ahead of her and she couldn't wait for it to begin. She wrote about her early days in L.A., and about you. That first journal recounts the reasons for the choices she made, and the person who forced her into them."

"Tell me what she did," he said. "Victoria."

"The night before she left L.A., my mother had gone to meet you at the bungalow, planning to tell you that she was pregnant. She was sure you'd be thrilled, and you would finally end your marriage so that the three of us would be together forever. But when she arrived, Victoria was waiting for her. Your wife offered my mother some money and a promise of an ongoing stream of payments in exchange for my mother's promise to leave town and never contact you again. Ever. In the end, my mother accepted the money, because she would need it for me, but that wasn't why she agreed to leave. Victoria said that if my mother didn't go, she, Victoria, would see to it that your career was ruined. And apparently her threats held water. She had money, contacts, and a well-connected, powerful family. My mother couldn't let that happen to you. So she left the next day, without a word to anyone, or the opportunity to let you know she was carrying your child. Although, Victoria had already told you about her own pregnancy."

I could see that my father was seething. If Victoria had appeared that moment, I'm sure, without a doubt, that he would have ended her, right then and there.

"Elliott," he said.

"Yes," I said. "But it gets worse."

"I can't imagine how," he said, his teeth clenched so tightly in his jaw that it was a miracle they didn't crumble and fall out of his mouth with his next words.

"Victoria wasn't pregnant yet," I said. "She…"

"What?" he asked, his voice much louder now. "That lying bitch! That controlling, manipulative, lying bitch! I felt responsible for my children, and I knew that if I tried to leave her with a second baby on the way, her family would destroy me. So I had to go through the motions; all the while your mother was getting further and further away from me, and out of my life forever. I had to endure Victoria's insistence that the family travel together, even though I knew she didn't want to be there any more than I wanted to…"

"That's right," I said. "I'll bet she insisted on having more sex with you on the road than she ever had before or since."

He was too angry to speak, but I knew it was only a matter of time before he asked me the question, and I was dreading it.

"Wait," he said. "Your mother couldn't have known that, so it wouldn't have been in her journals. How do you know these things?"

"Because I spoke to Victoria yesterday," I said. "And this morning."

"Where?" he asked. "How?"

"My mother's attorney handed me a check for over half a million dollars along with her journals. He followed the money trail and found Victoria at the end of it. Then he told me where you live. Apparently Victoria, through her own sense of guilt, or more likely, mental illness, had been putting away money into a trust fund for me for years. This, in addition to the monthly annuity she sent my mother. I always thought that the payments my mother received were from a life insurance policy, because that's what she told me. Anyway, yesterday I confronted her at your house on Elderberry Lane. I'll bet you didn't know that my mother and I also lived in a house on Elderberry Lane."

He smiled then, and nodded his head.

"That's one of the many things I loved about your mother. She was so sentimental, and so innocent. I never heard her say an unkind word to anyone. She was pure goodness, in spite of what that venomous woman who owns my life probably said about her."

"Actually," I said, "the only thing she said about my mother was that she was beautiful, and you were in love with her. That's what made her such a threat."

"What else?" he asked.

"She told me about the accident that caused Elliot's injury, and about her part in it."

"Why would she tell you that?" he asked. "Of all things."

"When she found out I had talked to Melody…"

"You met Melody, too?"

"Yes, and when I told Victoria, she assumed that Melody had told me about it already. She said that Melody was an angry person, who enjoyed hurting her mother."

"Well, she was right about that. We have quite the family. Dysfunctional behavior at its finest. What about Elliot? Did you talk to him, too?"

"No," I said. "But I understand he lives here in Santa Barbara and owns a restaurant that was a gift from his parents, after the accident."

"Yes. Elliot is a fine man. Hard working. He's turned that restaurant into a real moneymaker. Gets that from his mother's side of the family. But I'm proud of him anyway."

My father smiled. I was relieved, and would have bet money that Elliot had been the only bright spot in his life.

"You said that you saw her this morning, too."

"Yes," I said. "You'll love this. When I saw her yesterday, she promised to tell you I was in L.A., and where to find me. And when I opened the door to my hotel room this morning expecting to see you on the other side, Victoria was standing there instead. In the end, she couldn't bring herself to tell you about me. But here's the best part. She actually offered to make it worth my while, if I would just get in my car and go back to Chicago and pretend none of this ever happened."

"Obviously you said no."

"Not just no," I said. "Hell no."

My father laughed again, with bitterness toward his wife, but not toward me.

"Good for you," he said.

"I also told her I was pretty damn sick and tired of her trying to pay people off, and that I wouldn't stand for any more of her bullshit."

"Excellent!" he said, bumping his shoulder against mine.

My father was proud of me. That felt nice.

"Her head was hanging pretty low when she left my hotel room. She tried, but she knew she was beaten. She said something about looking up one of her old suitors, because she was certain you would be finished with her once and for all when I told you the truth about what she did to my mother."

"You've got that right," he said. "Are you hungry, Meredith? I haven't had anything since breakfast."

"Starving," I said.

"Well, how about you let your old man buy you a late dinner?"

"Can't think of anything I'd rather do."

We returned to the hotel, after shaking the sand out of our shoes, and were seated in the restaurant. Everyone we encountered was on a first name basis with my father. It was clear he had many friends there. I imagined that this had been a regular destination for him over the years, and I wondered if it was one of the places Victoria and their daughter had accompanied him, while she was on her mission to produce Elliot in order to cover her lie.

While we shared our first meal together, my father told me about Melody, how happy she had been as a small child, until her mother's coldness and bitterness had begun to wear off on her. By the time she reached high school, Melody was already taking anti-depressants, which seemed to work for a while, once they found the right mixture of prescriptions. But eventually she had decided that alcohol and cocaine were a better combination. It was all downhill from there. He said that Melody hated both her parents, and just as she had told me, the only time they ever heard from her was when she needed money.

My father said that he was against giving her money, because she would only spend it on drugs. But her mother, out of some sense of guilt or responsibility, insisted on doing it. And it wasn't as if he had a choice, in any case, because Victoria held the purse strings and did as she pleased.

Elliott and his family were the only real source of joy in my father's life, as I had imagined. My father told me that he enjoyed spending time with Elliott's family. When I asked, he seemed delighted to show me the photos of them that filled his wallet. He was a proud grandfather, which tugged at my heart a little, until I realized that now, maybe he could be proud of my children one day, too. My father admitted that he was never a good husband to Victoria, even before he met my mother, because he didn't love her. And for his part in that, he accepted much of the garbage she laid upon his head over the years. But he always loved his children, and while his relationship with Melody was extremely limited, he had a very good relationship with his son.

"Do you want to meet him? Elliott?" my father asked. "He doesn't live far from here. Maybe in the morning before…"

"I don't know," I said. "I'll think about it. Okay?"

"Sure," he said. "I'm sorry, I know this is a lot to take in all at once."

"It's just that my plans aren't set yet. That's all. My mother sent me on this trip, courtesy of her last will and testament, to scatter her ashes in the Hollywood hills. I still have a room at the Georgian Hotel in L.A.…."

"I should have known you'd be staying there," he said.

"I know there's a lot of history in that place," I said. "But I'm thinking I'll drive back down there tomorrow, take care of her ashes on Monday, and then head back to Chicago. So much has happened, and I need to spend some time in Milwaukee with my grandparents, too. I lost my mother, but they lost their daughter, and all this intrigue on top of that has been really hard on them. They've always been there for me, and I want to be there for them now. Also, there's a very important man in my life. His name is Derek. He's had a recent tragedy as well, and I really should be with him. No, I want to be with him."

My father looked sad, and it occurred to me that he had just had a tragedy of his own. He had just received the news that the love of his life was dead. And then I thought about Tommy, too.

"I'm sorry," I said. "All of a sudden there are so many people in my life who are hurting. I wish I could make it stop, for all of you."

"What about Meredith?" he asked. "How are you doing? You seem to want to comfort everyone else. But what about you, how are you holding up?"

"I'm okay," I said. "Grandma tells me I'm a very stoic person, good at bottling up my feelings. But to tell you the truth, I think I might be reaching my limit. My head is beginning to throb from all the emotion. Frankly, I could use a time out. But life has its ups and downs, and I'm sure that eventually things will lighten up in my world. I certainly hope they will."

"I hope it's soon, honey," he said. "So tell me about this man in your life, Derek. It sounds like he has problems of his own to deal with, but is he there for you as well?"

I smiled, sitting there with my actual father, while he asked about my boyfriend, and whether or not he was treating me properly. All of my friends had probably experienced similar conversations, beginning in their early teens, yet there I was having my first one at thirty. It was nice, though. We'd only known each other for a couple of hours, but already he was my knight in shining armor, ready to protect me from anyone who didn't have my best interest at heart.

"He's been wonderful," I said. "I don't know how I could have managed any of this without him. He was with me when I got the news about my mother, and travelled half way to California with me before he had to go back to deal with his own problems. But we talk every day, at least once, and that's what has kept me going. I think you'll like him"

I hadn't intended to tell my father much about Derek, but once I started talking, it all came pouring out, including the fact that he was still married up until Vanessa's suicide just a few days before. And I told him about Lily. We talked about the things our hearts tell us to do, and the choices that we make. And in the end, there was plenty of guilt to go around, for all of us. At thirty years old, I had met my father for the first time, and now that we were finally together, I didn't want to leave him. But he had things to work out in Los Angeles, and I had things to work out in Chicago. It wouldn't take long, though. And once things were settled down, and some of the shock wore off, we'd find a way to build a relationship. Now that we knew the truth, we weren't about to lose each other again.

"I'm not sure it's legal," he said, "spreading someone's ashes up there."

"I don't intend to ask permission," I said.

"My daughter is such a rebel," he said.

We laughed, as we had done many times that night, in spite of the rage he must have felt toward Victoria.

"I want you to know something, Meredith," he began, "If I had known the truth, that your mother was pregnant, even if they both actually were, had I been given the opportunity to choose, I would have chosen Anastasia immediately. She was the love of my life, the only woman I have ever loved. I allowed that wretched woman to control me all these years and keep me away from your mother. For that I will never forgive myself. But I always believed that one day I'd figure out a way to be with her; to find some leverage I could use to disarm Victoria and get her out of my life forever. The truth is that I always knew exactly where your mother was. Her friend, Jill Parker, gave me your grandparents' phone number. But Jill didn't know anything about you, and when I spoke to your mother, just that one time, she didn't tell me.

"You spoke to her?" I asked.

"Just once, many years ago. You must have just been an infant. She wouldn't talk to me about anything. She just kept telling me over and over, that I should never try to contact her again. Your mother must have been afraid of Victoria and her family. I always suspected they were behind her sudden disappearance, but I couldn't prove it. When I tried again the next day, the number was disconnected, so I called directory assistance and they told me the new number was unlisted. I had no address, so short of getting on a plane and hiring a detective to help me find her, I didn't know what else to do. Besides, Elliott was about to be born any day, so I couldn't just leave."

"But what about after that? Why didn't you get on a plane later?"

"Because of what your mother said to me on the phone."

"What?" I asked. "What could she have said to keep you away if you loved her that much?"

"Don't you see? It was because I loved her that much. She said that if I ever loved her, I could prove it by never trying to contact her, and never coming to look for her."

He was crying now, openly.

"She told me that I was the only man she would ever love in her entire lifetime, but what we did was wrong and she wanted me to do the right thing. She told me that if I didn't, I was not the man she thought I was. She didn't want to have to go through life without me, knowing that I wasn't. Because going through life without me was going to be the hardest thing she ever had to do. But she intended to do it."

I took my father's hand and let him cry. He was so broken, had been for such a long time, but there was nothing in the world to be done about it. My mother was gone, permanently this time, and his memories of her would be all he had to hold on to.

Victoria must have been terrified of what the following day would bring. Not that he would really do her physical harm. He wasn't that kind of man, though he would certainly never forgive her. But if he left her and tore apart their family for good, in spite of how dysfunctional they were, it would all have been for nothing. In a way, I was furious with my mother for allowing herself to be run off like that, without ever seeing to it that my father knew about my existence. Because the result of that was that nobody ended up with what they really wanted, and I missed out on the first thirty years with my father.

I wanted to talk to Derek. As the hours passed, I knew that it was unlikely I'd get the chance. With the time difference, he had already probably been asleep for hours.

"I need to go now, Dad," I said, feeling awkward as the words came out, but liking the sound of them just the same. "Will you be all right?"

"Yes," he said. "I'm staying at the hotel, but I have to leave very early. I need to be back in L.A. for an appointment with my booking agent. I've been doing some recording, not head-liner stuff, just background, but I have to be there by ten. With weekend traffic, I'll need a good head start."

I thought about the traffic, which reminded me of the gas station with the snarling dog, and how I pictured myself vaulting over the convertible's door and into the seat. I started to laugh. And I kept laughing until the tears were rolling down my face. I couldn't stop. My father was laughing by that point, too, and he didn't even know why. It was contagious I supposed, but once he realized I was hysterical, and not in a very good way, he came over to my side of the booth and wrapped me in his arms.

"I'm sorry, Daddy," I choked, "A funny picture just popped into my head, and I'll tell you about it sometime, I'm just so exhausted, and…"

"It's okay honey," he said. "Everything is going to be okay."

These were the words I had waited for my whole life, and until recently, I believed the man I wanted to deliver them was lost to me forever. I felt a wave of gratitude wash over me, knowing that I would never look at my life the same way again.

Eventually my sobs subsided, and my breath settled into a normal rhythm. My father paid our dinner bill, and he walked me to the elevator.

"How can I just walk away from you, Meredith," he asked, "without knowing when I'll ever see you again, or how to contact you. I don't want to lose you, not ever again."

"Don't worry, Dad," I said. "There is absolutely no chance of that. I promise."

I reached into my bag and pulled out two business cards. On the back of one, I printed my home address and phone number, and on the back of the other, Derek's name, address, and phone number. And at the last minute, I pulled out a third, and printed my grandparents' names, address, and phone number.

"Whatever you do, don't lose these!" I said.

"Kind of bossy, aren't you," he said, smiling. "I won't lose them. In fact, I'll guard them with my very life. And here," he said, handing me one of his. "It's got all the information you'll need to contact me."

"So what do you think about Monday morning?" I asked. "Will you be there? Jill suggested that the Hollywood Bowl Overlook was probably the best location, and closest to what my mom probably had in mind, without getting us arrested."

"I'll be there," he said. "Ten o'clock sharp. Don't start without me."

"Oh, good!" I exclaimed, and hugged him again. "Now I'll be able to sleep, knowing I'll see you again before I go back to Chicago. This time."

My father smiled at me as he turned to leave. I stood there watching him until he was completely out of sight.

When I got back to the room, my message light was blinking. I called the front desk and they read it to me. Derek had called at ten o'clock West Coast time, when it was already midnight in Chicago. It was after one a.m. my time when I got the message, but he had said to call when I got in, no matter what time it was. I'll bet he had started pacing the floor hours ago, wondering about my night, dying to hear how it all worked out. By now he would surely be sound asleep, but he'd said to call, and I wanted more than anything to hear his voice.

"Meredith?" a gravelly, sleepy voice said from thousands of miles away.

"Hi, Derek," I said. "I'm so sorry to wake you. I just wanted to say goodnight, and tell you how much I love you."

"I love you too, honey," he said. "Did you meet your father? Was it wonderful? Tell me everything."

I could tell he was forcing himself to wake up and be enthusiastic, and I loved him more than ever.

"Oh, Derek. Yes, I met him, and it was wonderful. I'll tell you everything in the morning before I head back down to Los Angeles. We're going to scatter her ashes at ten o'clock Monday morning, and then I'm going home."

"That's such good news, Meredith."

"Yes, it is," I said. "Now try to go back to sleep before you're wide awake. I just wanted to let you know that I'm fine. Everything is going to be fine."

I got ready for bed as quickly as I could, while the voices of the men in my life were still in the air, the shadow of my father's smile such a vivid memory. And as I drifted off to sleep, I pictured us together, all of us, and knew that my life was full to bursting with all of the things I had ever dreamed of.

CHAPTER 15

WHEN I RETURNED TO THE HOTEL in L.A. Sunday morning, I stopped at the front desk to see if my package had arrived from my mother's attorney in Milwaukee. It wasn't there yet, but I would check again later in the afternoon. Since I was leaving town the next day, I hoped it would make an appearance. Otherwise, it would have to make a round-trip. There was, however, a message from Derek saying that he would be out most of the day, but would talk to me that evening. I had so much to tell him, it was going to be difficult to keep it to myself all day, but I knew we'd talk at some point.

When I got to my room, it was so quiet that I had to turn on the television for company, as had always been my custom in hotel rooms. I sat on the bed for a few minutes staring at the local news, which was terrifying, so I switched the channel. But I was restless and needed to do something or talk to another human being. Then I remembered my conversation with Jill Parker. I realized I should call her again, to confirm that I planned to spread my mother's ashes the following morning, and let her know that I looked forward to seeing her at the Hollywood Bowl Overlook at ten o'clock.

When I reached Jill, she promised to be there, but was on her way out of the house and didn't have time to talk. Our brief conversation, though it provided the relief of knowing for sure that she'd join us Monday morning for support, did not satisfy my need to talk to another human being. There were simply too many things going on in my head. I hadn't spoken to my grandparents since I called to let them know I had arrived in L.A. safely, but I decided that the details of what I had learned were best saved for a conversation once I was home. Besides, I wasn't sure how much they already knew but just didn't want to talk about. It would take time to work through it all. We eventually would, but not long distance.

Since I would be leaving the next day, I decided to do some sightseeing. But when I looked at the massive expanse of Los Angeles on the map, I couldn't even begin to imagine where to start. I had almost decided to just spend the day on the beach, when it hit me. I knew exactly where I wanted to go.

A few minutes later I was on the highway, heading toward Westwood. Traffic wasn't too hideous since it was a Sunday afternoon, although I had begun to believe that in L.A, rush hour never really ended. I found Wilshire Boulevard, then Glendon Avenue, and pulled in to the Westwood Village Memorial Park Cemetery. Although old, it was beautiful and perfectly maintained. There were huge ancient trees whose root balls were partially exposed as though they were being launched out of the soil, the nearby markers disrupted out of their many flat rows. This was perhaps the result of earthquakes over the years, I decided.

As I walked along the blacktop, I passed the acres of green grass, dotted with flat headstones and a scattering of flowers in tiny pots on the ground. In the distance I saw the crypt, the place where the earthly remains of Miss Marilyn Monroe were kept. I had a physical response to seeing it, like an internal shock wave, remembering the thoughts I'd had as a child once I learned that I came into the world on the exact same day that Marilyn left it.

There were marble benches, with carefully manicured and sculptured hedges in the grassy corner formed by the L-shaped marble structure. I quickly found the rectangular bronze plate on the pink marble face, with the words: MARILYN MONROE, and below it, 1926—1962, in raised lettering; second up from the ground, and second to the right from the corner. Many of the crypts had narrow vases attached to them, meant to hold flowers. On that day, only Marilyn's vase had flowers in it. Red roses. I'd read that for more than twenty years after her death, Joe DiMaggio had arranged to have fresh red roses placed in that same vase twice a week for the woman who had once been his wife, and whom he planned to marry again. But instead of remarrying her on August 8th, he had attended her funeral. As I looked at the roses in the small vase, I wondered who had brought them.

I stood before the crypt, with some of my mother's ashes in the tiny urn I carried in my shoulder bag. No, I did not intend to leave them there. I was pretty sure that would be illegal, and it wasn't what my mother had asked me to do. Besides, that tiny urn was for me. The reason I brought them with me, was that I felt she would have appreciated one last chance to be near the woman who had provided such a cherished memory.

There were other visitors when I arrived, so I waited patiently for them to leave, hoping I might have a chance for a minute or two alone with Marilyn once they left. After they'd gone, I stood close to where she lay resting for all of eternity, and spoke to her very quietly, keeping a lookout for other visitors, lest they think I had gone mad and were compelled to call the police to take me away. The tiny urn was safely wrapped in both of my hands, and held close to my heart.

"Marilyn," I said, "you don't know me, but you knew my mother, Anastasia Burke. I should say, for a brief moment my mother was in your presence, but what you did for her had a great impact on her life. You gave her some beautiful dresses that she wore when she sang on stage as a very young woman, during what was without a doubt the happiest time of her life, brief though it was. My mother made the mistake of falling in love with the wrong man. He was actually the right man in every sense except that he was someone else's husband. I know that you understand what it was like for her, and that you won't judge her too harshly. They were both so young. The universe simply conspired against my parents by bringing them together at the wrong time. But their hearts were broken for the rest of their lives because of it.

"I didn't even know my father was alive until a couple of days ago. It was hard, growing up without a father, and I know you can relate to that as well. My mother did the best she could to make sure I had everything I needed, but sometimes the empty space where my father should have been was very large indeed. She was so beautiful, my mother, and left this earth way too soon, just like you. But because she was so beautiful, other women felt threatened by her, especially married women. So as a result, she didn't have many girlfriends, and as a single parent back in the sixties, it wasn't easy for her. She must have felt so alone.

"Tomorrow we're going to scatter her ashes at the Hollywood Bowl Overlook up on Mulholland Drive. My father will be there, and my mother's old friend from years ago, Jill, will be there, too. I wish my boyfriend, Derek, was going to be there, but he had a sudden tragedy in his life right after my mom died, so he's back home in Chicago. He'll be there in spirit though, I'm sure of that. Derek belonged to someone else too, technically, until a few days ago. He and his wife were separated, but not divorced. So I guess I'm not in a position to judge anyone either. She died last week; took her own life. Depending on whom you listen to, it's possible you might know something about that as well, although it looks like we'll never know for sure. Frankly, I don't believe that nonsense. I think some powerful people felt threatened by you, and were trying to protect themselves. But someone knows the truth, and maybe it will come out one day.

"Anyway, now there's nothing to keep Derek and me from moving forward with our lives together. I want to feel like it's all right to do that, I just feel so guilty. She thought he had left town with me for good, and that's why she did it. At least that's what it said in the note. So I can't help feeling that it's my fault, and if I hadn't gotten involved with Derek she'd still be alive. But she's the one who got drunk and let their baby girl get swept out into Lake Michigan and drown, so between the three of us, there's plenty of guilt to go around. But what can we do? Will walking away from each other now make any of it right? It doesn't seem like it. I wish you could talk to me, and tell me what to do. I've always felt a connection to you. It is because of the kindness you showed my mother, but before that, it was because you died on the same day I was born. Until a few weeks ago, I thought I was born right here in L.A., when in fact I was born in Milwaukee. It's kind of silly when I hear myself say it out loud. It was really just the product of a child's imagination; a little girl trying to make sense of who she was, and what made her different from everyone else.

"Well, Marilyn, it looks like you have some more visitors coming, so I'll stop talking now before they get out the butterfly nets, but I just wanted to say thank you for being so kind to my mother, and for helping me to grow up. I'm going to think that you would approve of my relationship with Derek, and that I should grab hold of my chance at love, and let the past go. If you could talk to me, I think that's what you would say."

Before I turned away, a single, red rose petal fell onto my hands that were still curled around the tiny urn that held my mother's ashes. I considered that a confirmation. Just before the newcomers approached the crypt, I kissed my fingertips and pressed them to the bronze plate that carried her name and said, "Goodbye, Marilyn, and thanks."

As I drove back to the hotel, I thought about Marilyn Monroe, how beautiful she was, and yet how sad. Marilyn thought she belonged to everyone, and that left nothing of her for herself. From a fatherless child, living in poverty or passed from one foster home to another, to a person who will be remembered forever by millions as the epitome of glamour and sex appeal, Marilyn reached a pinnacle of success few women ever achieve. She became a cultural icon, but still, she never found the lasting happiness she deserved. That made me sad, and I thought of my parents, how happy they might have been together if only they had been given the chance.

That's when I decided that I was going to spend the rest of my life with Derek; that we were going to be the two happiest people on the planet. We were going to have some children who would grow up with two parents that loved each other. It was time to break the cycle of unhappiness that was the trademark of my family tree.

When I returned to the hotel, I checked at the front desk again and found that my package had finally arrived. They handed it across the counter, and when I turned around, Derek was there waiting for me, with a dozen red roses, and a smile on his face that brought tears to my eyes. He was as thrilled to see me, as I was to see him. Our relationship began anew, standing in the lobby of the Georgian Hotel. We would leave all of the guilt and pain behind us and start over again, with nothing standing in our way.

We went up to my room and greeted each other as though we'd been separated for months instead of days, and it was like being together for the first time. There were no longer any obstacles between us. And I had proof of that; the sparkling diamond ring he'd placed on my left hand the moment we entered the room.

Later, as we lay in each other's arms, while the sun set into the Pacific Ocean, we read my mother's final words to me. This would be the last of the secrets, and in their telling we would put my mother to rest, with a clearer understanding of who she was and what she planned to do with her life, if only there had been more time.

CHAPTER 16
Anastasia

NOVEMBER 1991

My Dearest Meredith,

I'm writing this now, as I've finally made some grownup decisions about my life. My friend, Marty, who lives next door would call this a "dead letter." He writes them all the time, just in case something were to happen to him. That way nothing in his heart would remain unsaid. It actually makes perfect sense when you think about it. It would be just my luck to drop dead now that I've finally made the decision I've been struggling with for thirty years. So I'm writing this to let you know what my plans are, just in case something should happen before I see you next and have the chance to tell you about it in person.

You'll probably think this is an incredibly creepy and superstitious thing to do. But actually, after my last visit to the sawbones, it's not an entirely impossible set of circumstances. He told me that I have some problems with my heart. I have some arteries that are slightly blocked, and I'll need surgery soon to clean them up. I also need to make some major changes in my lifestyle, including diet and exercise, or I'm at serious risk of a heart attack or stroke. It's sad that someone as young as I am should have to worry about such things, but it really got me to thinking about my life, and my future.

Now, if you're actually reading this, my life is over, and if my lawyer did as I instructed, you've already read about my past and all the secrets I've kept from you your whole life. You know about Howard, and about Tommy, my dear, patient Tommy. You also know that my trips to California were really to Arizona to see him. I made quite a mess of things; I'll give you that. And I'm deeply sorry for all the lies I've told. But in my own way, I really was trying to do the right thing for all of us.

Anyway, what you don't know is that the last time I went out west to see Tommy I went to Los Angeles first. I wanted to see your father one last time, and I was prepared to see Victoria, too. I saw both of them, although in the end neither of them saw me. I wore dark glasses and a hat pulled low on my face so I was sure they wouldn't recognize me. Maybe if Victoria hadn't been there I would have approached him. I wanted to say goodbye. Now I'm sure that sounds strange to you, but in truth, we'd never had the opportunity to say goodbye. Victoria had handed me a check, and I hit the road the next morning. That was part of the deal; that I would have no more contact with Howard, not ever.

He did call me once, when you were just a baby, but I told him not to try contacting me again. Still, I always wished we'd had a chance to say goodbye in person, and talk everything through. It all seemed so incomplete. Although, all things considered, there really wasn't much more to say. In truth, in my most secret heart, I always hoped that something would happen that would free your father to come and find us, and we could finally be together as a family. But the reason I chose that particular time to take one last look, is that I have finally said yes to Tommy, after all these many years, and agreed to move to Flagstaff and marry him.

I needed closure with Howard, because after thirty years of waiting for him to come for me, I'm finally ready to move on with my life.

They both looked so unhappy, Howard and Victoria, and she seemed downright miserable. She stood there watching him unload his equipment at the curb outside the hotel where I used to sing with his band, as if she were a soldier guarding the border. It was as if she knew I was there somewhere, although I couldn't imagine how she'd know. Maybe she's had people watching me all these years to make sure I didn't slip up and break the terms of our agreement. I don't know, or care. It just made me sad for both of them.

Anyway, I've put all that to rest, finally. It wasn't easy, but I know that until I let go of Howard, I'll never be able to be happy, and I've made Tommy wait long enough. With any luck, you'll meet him soon. I've agreed to let him come to Milwaukee so he can get to know you, and then in a few months, I'm going out to Arizona to stay. The doctor says the warm weather will be good for me, and it will be a nice place to recuperate after the surgery. He has given me a referral for a doctor out in Flagstaff with a very good reputation. I'm going to give up the salon, sell the house, and become a woman of leisure. I think I've earned it.

You'll love Tommy, I'm sure of that. He's a wonderful man, and he's been so kind to me all these years. But if you're actually reading this "dead letter," then you have to promise me that you'll look in on Tommy once in a while, because his heart will be broken, no doubt about that.

Tommy knows all about your father, in fact, he even knows that your father is the reason I haven't been able to make a commitment to him. Still, he has remained faithful, and determined to wait for me, for all this time. After my visit to L.A., when I went to Flagstaff, I told Tommy I was finally ready to marry him. You should have seen his face. He was beaming; all the while tears were running down his face. He was happier than I've ever seen him, and that made me happy, too. I can't wait to get there. I'll miss you, Meredith, but we'll visit each other as much as possible.

One thing, though… while Tommy knows just about everything about your father, Howard doesn't know anything about Tommy. If possible, I'd appreciate it if you could try and keep it that way. This is for Tommy's sake, more than your father's. I think Tommy would feel bad if Howard knew that he'd been able to keep Tommy and me on hold for all these years. I never want anything to hurt Tommy again. I'm going to give this letter to my lawyer to keep with the other papers, just in case something happens to me. His instructions are to send this last one to you if you seem to be looking for your father while delivering my ashes, so you don't accidentally tell him about Tommy, not knowing my wishes on this subject.

So now that I've written it all down, I can relax, knowing that if something were to happen to me, you would know what I was thinking. I'm done with secrets, honey, and I'm ready to move forward. With any luck, I'll be able to tell you all of this in person before long, and I hope you'll be happy for me. I think you will. And assuming we have the chance to talk about it in person, I also plan to tell you everything, about your father, Victoria, all of it; all the secrets I've kept from you all these years because I was afraid you wouldn't forgive me. It's time for me to stand up and take responsibility for my actions, and you deserve to know the truth.

Talk to you soon, Meredith.

Love, Mom

CHAPTER 17
Meredith

MY MOTHER HAD WRITTEN THAT LETTER to me less than two months before she died. So she had known her health wasn't perfect, she just hadn't bothered to share that information with me. I wondered how much of it she had shared with her parents. They had mentioned the doctor wanting to put her on some medicine she wasn't interested in taking, but still, I wondered if they had known how serious her condition really was. If they had, they probably would have insisted she have the surgery immediately.

I understood her wanting to protect Tommy's ego. I had done that instinctively, not having mentioned him to my father at all. It pleased me that she had planned to clear up all her lies, finally, and tell me everything. And I believe she would have done that, if she'd been able to. I had seen her at Christmas time and she had plenty of time to talk to me then. But, we had been with my grandparents most of the time. In fact we'd both slept at their house throughout my short visit. I guess she just figured there'd be plenty of time after the holidays. Maybe she'd planned to come to Chicago and talk to me there, but now I'll never know.

I was exhausted with all of it, the speculation, revelations, and the two men who had been strangers to me, yet were so important to my mother. I hoped the surprises were over, and I felt pretty sure that for the most part they were. My mother had woven a very intricate pattern of secrets and lies. It may be years before they are all known to me, if they ever are.

We woke up early, Derek and I, together at last. We checked out of the hotel and loaded our luggage into the trunk of the convertible. My mother's ashes were in the backseat, in a duffel bag on the floor behind me. It was a perfect Los Angeles morning, with minimal smog, a warm breeze, and bright sunshine.

As we wound up Mulholland Drive toward the Hollywood Bowl Overlook, with the convertible top down, I understood what it was that drew so many people to this place. There were more sunny days, in proportion to most places, and the weather was rarely what anyone would call cold. The palm trees and desert terrain, so different from where I had grown up, were beautiful. It really did seem like a place where dreams could come true. That's what my mother had thought, all those years ago. I supposed there were plenty of sad things in this place, in fact I already knew about some of them, but with all that sunshine, it seemed hard to believe that anyone could be sad for long.

"Pull in right there," Derek said.

We passed through the iron gates to a very small parking lot, with an immense view. It was spectacular. The Hollywood Bowl Overlook offered the most incredible vista I'd ever seen. It was an enormous valley, with green and brown hills surrounding it. Directly across the valley from the tiny parking lot, I saw the Hollywood sign up on the side of the hill. I'd seen that sign a million times, on television, in movies, and in magazines. It was something everyone in America would recognize. But there was something truly magical about seeing it in person, across so much open space, with a California breeze blowing through my hair. It was another moment I'd never forget.

There was a tour bus parked near the fence and one other car in the lot. The car was an aquamarine late model Mercedes sedan. As we parked beside it, my father got out. I greeted him with a hug. I could tell he was uncomfortable, sad, and had very likely had no sleep the night before.

"Derek," I said, "I'd like you to meet my father, Howard Bradshaw."

He smiled at this, liking the way that sounded as much as I did.

"Pleased to meet you, Derek," my father said. "I've heard a lot about you."

They shook hands, with the thought, "I've heard a lot about you, too," lingering in the air, yet thankfully left unsaid.

"Jill is going to meet us up here, too," I said.

"I hope she gets here soon," Derek said. "As soon as that tour bus leaves, we should probably do what we came to do before anyone else shows up. I'm not actually sure what we're doing is legal."

"Again," I said, "I don't plan to ask permission."

My father and I laughed, but Derek didn't know why.

"My dad said the same thing," I said. "Maybe it's true what they say, that girls want to marry a man just like their father."

That's when I held out my hand to show my father the engagement ring Derek had given me the night before.

"Congratulations," he said. "I'm very happy for you both."

"Thank you, sir," Derek said. "I probably should have asked you first, but it sort of hit me all at once and I had to do it immediately. Hope you'll forgive me."

"Nonsense," he said. "A man should go after the things he wants, and never let anything stand in his way. I learned that the hard way."

Jill Parker pulled into the tiny parking lot then, looking a bit frazzled, and jumped out of her car to join us.

"So sorry I'm late," she said. "I was held up at work so I got a late start, and then traffic…"

"Good to see you again, Jill," my father said. "It's been a while."

"Howard Bradshaw," she said. "It sure has been. I've got to say that you are just as handsome as ever."

"The years have been very kind to you as well, Jill. How's life been treating you?"

"Good, Howard. But I think we need to take care of business, because that bus full of tourists that just left will be back in exactly twenty minutes. Plus, I'm not actually sure what we're doing is legal."

We all smiled.

"What?" Jill asked.

"Nothing," I said. "It's just that everyone but me seems to be worried about the same thing, so you're right. We best get on with it."

So I gathered up the urn that held my mother's earthly remains, and the four of us walked outside the iron fence that encircled the parking lot. We climbed down the hill just a little, trying to get out of sight in case the tour bus returned ahead of schedule, but not far enough to be risking our lives in the process. With Derek on one side of me, my father on the other, and Jill beside him, I started to open the urn, but my father stopped me. He obviously had something on his mind, but didn't say anything. And then I saw it in his eyes and I knew. He couldn't bear the thought of having her gone forever, with nothing tangible for him to hold onto. I tightened the lid on the urn and handed it to Derek. Then I reached into the bag the urn had been in, and pulled out a tiny ceramic container with a small amount of my mother's ashes in it.

"It's okay, Dad," I said. "Here, this is for you."

I placed the tiny urn into his hands, and hugged his neck.

"But you should…"

"It's fine. I have one just like it, and so do my grandparents. This is for you to keep."

Tears were filling his eyes now, and he nodded at me. It was time.

Derek, always the practical one, held up a finger to test the direction of the wind, and I was grateful that he had. It hadn't occurred to me how hideous it would be if we dumped my mother's ashes and they were blown right back in our faces. We allowed him to realign us, out of danger, before we continued.

"You were a good friend, Anastasia, and I'll miss you," Jill managed.

"I'll take good care of Meredith, I promise. I'm sorry we didn't have more time together," Derek said. "You would have been a fantastic mother-in-law."

We all looked at my father. He sighed heavily, and took a deep breath.

"You were the love of my life, my darling Anastasia," my father said. "I'm sorry, for everything…"

My father was sobbing, and had no more words, at least not that the rest of us would hear. He had his own private thoughts for my mother. I could see that his heart was torn in a thousand pieces. The time had come, and there could be no more delay.

"Well, Mom, you had a lot of secrets, that's for sure," I said. "I don't understand why you couldn't confide in me, once I was all grown up, but you had your reasons and I'll accept that. Just know that I don't hold any of it against you. And thank you, for finally giving me my father. I miss you."

My hands shook while I struggled to open the container. As we looked across the valley to the Hollywood sign, with the wind at our backs, Derek and my father each with an arm around my waist, we scattered my mother's ashes to the wind.

CHAPTER 18

AS DEREK AND I DROVE AWAY, putting Los Angeles in our rear-view mirror, I remembered my mother's words from her journal, written on the day she headed toward Flagstaff as we were doing now. She was so sad and dejected, scared and alone. My mother had been pregnant with me, wondering how she would face her parents, and she had just left the love of her life behind in California. I tried to imagine how she must have felt, and it made me want to weep for her. My father's time in her life had been so short, yet it had changed her forever. She had spent the next thirty years waiting for him. I wished that she had at least known that he longed for her, too. I still didn't understand how, if he loved her as much as he said, he could have stayed away from her. There should have been nothing in the world to keep them apart, both feeling the way they did about each other.

When my mother crossed these same miles toward Flagstaff, she had no idea she was about to become involved with a man who would, in turn, spend thirty years waiting for her. So much pain was caused by the relationship between my mother and father. Their joining was a disaster of epic proportions, and I was its living legacy.

It was after nine that evening when we arrived in Flagstaff. We'd called Tommy from the road, and he was waiting for us outside the motel lobby when we drove in. Standing there alone, he looked like a man whose life was over. I believed that my mother was his reason for living, and already knew that without her, his life would rapidly wind down to its end. Waiting for my mother had given him a reason to get up in the morning, with the hope that one day he'd wake up to find her next to him for good. And perhaps the same thing had happened to my mother, without even realizing it, when she finally decided to stop waiting for Howard.

"Tommy," I said, and could say no more.

He held me as we cried together, our own version of my mother's nonexistent funeral service on the day I had returned her to California for good.

"This is Derek," I said. "The man I told you about."

"A pleasure to meet you, Derek," Tommy said. "I'm glad to have the chance to get to know you."

"Same here," Derek said. "Meredith has told me lots of wonderful things about you."

"Well, our Meredith is quite a girl," Tommy said. "In many ways, she's so much like her…"

He took a handkerchief from his pocket, one I was sure he'd kept there since I had broken the news to him about my mother.

"You'll have to excuse me," he said. "Can't seem to pull myself together yet. I have your room all ready for you. It's the one your mother used when she was here. She kept some of her clothes and pictures and things in there, like I mentioned before you left last week. I guess you could say it's where she kept her secrets."

Tommy carried my suitcase as he walked ahead of us down to the last unit of the stucco building. Pale pink lace curtains were at the window, with what looked like a roll up shade at half-mast that could be pulled all the way down for privacy. The rest of the units had standard heavy motel stock curtains, the kind that didn't quite meet all the way from top to bottom. He unlocked the room and set my suitcase down on the little wooden luggage rack just inside the door. Derek set his bags down beside it, and stood next to Tommy as I walked into the center of the room and lost my breath.

The walls were covered with the same tiny flower patterned paper as her bedroom in Milwaukee, the same bedspread, and matching throw pillows. There were framed photographs of me hanging on the wall, a chronological history of my entire life.

On the dresser were pictures of Tommy and her together, also spanning thirty years. They appeared on the deck of a cruise ship in one, and at a campsite in what looked like Utah, in Bryce Canyon, or Zion National Park. Beaches, mountains, cities, countryside, they had been everywhere together. They were so young in some of the photos, possibly taken on her first visit to Flagstaff. Through the pictures I could watch my mother grow older, until she looked just as she had a handful of months ago when she had been here for the last time.

When I walked into the tiny bathroom to wash the tears off of my face, I found all of my mother's cosmetics on the shelf, the same familiar brands she always used, and a shower curtain that matched the one in her home. That feeling of being transported to a parallel universe, the one that had started to become all too familiar, was back again. Everything looked similar, but not quite accurate. For a moment I felt like I was going to faint, until I realized I'd been holding my breath.

I heard Tommy and Derek talking quietly in the other room, their voices muffled by the closed bathroom door between us. I dried my face and joined them just in time to see Tommy heading out of the motel room.

"Where are you going?" I asked.

"I'll just let you two get settled in. I'm sure you're tired from the long drive," Tommy said. "Just come by the office in the morning and we'll go have breakfast, okay?"

"Sure, Tommy," I said. "I'm sorry, but this is all so unexpected. It caught me off guard."

"I know, Meredith," he said. "It's a lot to take in. The closet is filled with your mother's things, too. We'll have to talk about what to do with them I suppose. Everything, actually."

Tommy turned away and wiped at his eyes.

"It's okay, Tommy," Derek said. "There's plenty of time for that. Let's all just get a good night's sleep and we'll talk about it in the morning."

"Good idea," I said. "Mom always used to say that things would look better in the morning. She was usually right."

"I remember that about her," Tommy said. "The eternal optimist, she was."

"Maybe you'll show us around Flagstaff tomorrow," I said. "It's such a beautiful town. I'd like you to take us to some of my mother's favorite places. She must have loved it here."

"Done," he said. "We'll start with her favorite breakfast place. Just come to the office when you're ready."

Derek shook Tommy's hand and patted him on the back as he turned to say good night to me. I hugged him tight, and as I stepped back, I saw that his cheeks were damp. I would mourn my mother's death for years to come, but I'd had a few weeks for it to settle in. For Tommy it was still so fresh and raw. He'd been inches away from the happiness he had waited three decades for, and it had been ripped from his grasp with just a few words from my mouth. I think Tommy died along with her. It just took a while for his flesh to catch up.

"It's hard to watch, isn't it," Derek said.

"I know. He must have loved her so much, enough to wait for her for all these years. I'm worried about him," I said. "I don't know how he's going to survive this."

"I know what you mean," Derek said. "Maybe he'll come to Chicago and stay with us for a while. The change of scenery would do him good. The distraction might help."

"Maybe," I said. "Let's talk to him about it tomorrow."

I began settling in to the room, putting my purse on the desk, my cosmetics in the bathroom, and was about to put a stack of clothes from my suitcase into one of the dresser drawers, when I found it was full. All the drawers were filled with my mother's clothes. The smaller drawers held her lingerie, the medium sized drawers held lightweight summer shirts, and the larger bottom drawers held jeans, shorts, and several sweatshirts bearing the names of vacation spots, including the Grand Canyon and Disneyland. I took one of the sweatshirts from the drawer and held it to my face. I was instantly surrounded by the smell of my mother, the perfume she always wore still lingering in the soft cotton cloth. As I sank to the floor and fell back against the foot of the bed, the sweatshirt clutched tightly in my hands, I began to sob.

"I just miss her so much, Derek."

"I know," he said, as he sat down next to me on the floor and wrapped me in his arms.

Between the dresser and the desk, there was a small refrigerator that I hadn't noticed before. I opened it, and surprised myself by laughing. It was a miniature version of her fridge at home, vitamins and special cosmetic concoctions in the door, Diet Cokes and Hershey bars on the top shelf, two bottles of Chardonnay and a carton of French Vanilla coffee creamer on the bottom. A bag of fresh ground coffee was tucked in to the tiny drawer under the top shelf. I checked the date on the coffee creamer. It was fresh. I wondered if he had stocked the fridge especially for us, or if he kept it this way for her. Then I wondered how many nights he sat alone in this room, looking at photos of the two of them, and maybe talking to her on the phone over on the nightstand. Quite a few, I decided. I thought about opening one of the Diet Cokes, then stopped myself and thought maybe it would be a crime against Tommy to disrupt anything in this shrine he'd built for her. And just as if he'd heard my thoughts, we found the note tucked inside the door next to the vitamins.

"Didn't know what you'd like, but these are the things I used to keep in here for your mother, so I hope it's okay. Wasn't sure if you two were coffee drinkers, but if so, you'll find everything you need in the cabinet next to the television. Water bottles and extra soft drinks are in the closet. Just call if you need anything, Tommy."

"Great," I said, relieved. "I'll put some water in the fridge. Want one?"

"Yes please," Derek said as I picked myself up off the floor and walked over to the closet. "I was afraid to touch anything in there. It was like—"

I stood, frozen, in front of the open closet door, the knob still in my hand.

"What is it, Meredith?"

"Oh my God," I said.

The closet was packed from floor to ceiling. The top shelf was lined with scrapbooks and photo albums, and a wicker basket filled with loose photos. The album at the end next to the basket was still wrapped in its plastic covering, obviously the next one she would have filled if only she'd made it back here.

Against the right side of the closet was the folding ironing board found in most motel rooms, but the hanging rod was packed full of clothing. Many of the things I recognized, some of them I had even given to her, but what caught my eye were the two clear plastic zippered garment bags hanging on the far left end.

"I can't believe this," I whispered.

"What?" Derek asked.

"Look." I said, carefully removing the garment bags from the closet and laying them out side by side on the bed.

I gently lowered the zipper on the first bag. Tears filled my eyes as I looked in awe upon the red sequined evening gown that had once been worn by Marilyn Monroe. It was stunning. I was afraid to take it out of the bag for fear it would dissolve in my hands, but I had to see it. So I ever so carefully removed the dress and held it up to show Derek.

"You know," he said, "that dress is probably worth over a million dollars."

"You're right, I suppose. But there's not enough money on the face of the earth to make me let go of this dress. I can't believe I'm touching it."

"Let's see the other one," he said. "In her journals she said that Marilyn gave her two dresses. I'll bet that's the other one."

"You're probably right," I said, unzipping the second bag. "Wasn't the other one silver, or beaded, something like that—"

I sat down on the bed in the space between the two garment bags, and for a moment I felt sick.

"What is it?" Derek asked.

"It was going to be my mother's wedding dress."

There was no mistaking it. The ivory dress was full-length and subtle, appropriate for a woman her age but definitely a wedding dress. It was elegant, with beautiful beadwork and touches of lace. And if there had been any doubt, it would have been erased by what I found in the bottom of the bag. There was a pair of ivory pumps and a small beaded ivory handbag, but most telling was the ivory pillbox hat with chin-length lace that fell down over the front with a scattering of the tiniest ivory sequins.

"I need some air," I said.

"I'll come with you. You're as white as that dress."

We stepped outside the motel room and crossed into the courtyard. Two pairs of wrought iron benches were placed on either side of a small fountain. It was surrounded by tiny colored lights that pointed up from the ground, and reflected off the splashing water, the result of which looked like a strange kind of fireworks. Between each of the pairs of benches stood a giant potted cactus. As we sat quietly on one of the benches, listening to the water falling into the fountain, I began to fully realize how much my life had changed in the past few weeks.

It seemed as though it had been a year since Derek and I had sat watching television on the familiar sofa in my condo and done other normal things, like grading papers and preparing lesson plans, grocery shopping and dusting. I was both amazed and overwhelmed by how much had happened, and I longed to feel normal again. But I had experienced so many major changes to my life since the night my grandmother called to tell me my mom had died, not the least of which was the fact that I'd become engaged to Derek. It was a lot to take in, and I found myself desperately wanting to go home.

"Derek, let's just stay here a couple of days and then head back to Chicago, okay?"

"Whatever you want, Meredith," he said. "I'll stay here as long as you want, or drive away tonight if that makes you happy. But home sounds pretty good to me, too. Speaking of which, in all the excitement we haven't even talked about where we're going to live. Your place or mine?"

"I vote for a third option, something completely different. Let's buy a new house and make a fresh start. What do you say?"

"Done," Derek said. "We'll start looking as soon as we get back. Let's find something with a few extra bedrooms and a nice backyard, just in case. You know? Maybe we can even get a dog."

"Yes, let's do all those things. I love you, Derek."

"I love you too, sweetie. Are you feeling better? You're getting some color back, I think."

"I do feel better. Talking about home has helped, and looking forward. All this looking back has been hard. I'm so sleepy all of a sudden, more exhausted than I've ever been."

We went back to the room and I fell asleep the moment my head hit the pillow beside Derek's, safe in the arms of my future husband, and surrounded by memories of my mother.

In the morning, Tommy was waiting for us outside the motel lobby, sweeping off the sidewalk, as he had been the last time I was there.

We had a lovely breakfast at what had been my mother's favorite café where they made world-class eggs benedict, and Tommy drove us all over town in his truck, showing us the places she loved the best. As it turned out, many of my mother's favorite places were restaurants, and before we went back to the motel for the night, we'd been out for lunch and dinner as well.

When we finally returned to the Thunderbird Motel, we invited Tommy to our room so he could tell us all about the places he and my mother had travelled together. We went through all the photo albums and scrapbooks, and I learned a few things about my mother that I hadn't known before. It turns out she was a deadeye shot with a rifle; and in her youth had enjoyed white-water rafting. They had gone deep-sea fishing and between the two of them had landed a marlin. Anastasia and fishing were two things I'd never thought of in tandem before.

She was full of surprises, my mother. They had planned to be married in the spring or early summer, but hadn't decided where yet. She'd found the dress on their last trip to Napa Valley, in an eclectic little shop they'd been browsing through. Tommy said she told him she simply had to get it; that it was exactly what she had pictured getting married to him in, and he'd bought it for her at once.

"You're a little taller than your mother was, and slimmer," Tommy said. "But maybe the dress can be altered in some way so that you can wear it instead."

I hadn't even begun to think about a wedding dress, but immediately decided that I would do just that. Besides, between eating all my meals in restaurants for the past couple of weeks, and sitting in the car much of the time, I was sure I'd gained some weight since leaving Chicago. The dress might not need to be taken in that much after all, and adding some lace to the bottom would take care of the length. It was poetic, all things considered, and it would be as if a part of her were there with me on our wedding day.

"You'll probably want to take her things with you," Tommy said. "But I hope you'll leave some of the photos for me. The memories are all…"

"Of course, Tommy," I said.

"I can send you copies of anything you want," he said. "You do know about the red dress though, right? That thing is probably worth over a million dollars. You'll want to take good care of it. In fact, you probably shouldn't tell anyone you have it."

I laughed.

"Derek said the same thing. But I'll tell you what I told him. First it was Marilyn's, and then it was my mother's. No price tag is high enough for me to let it go."

"Good," he said. "That's exactly what she said."

We spent the next two days packing up my mother's things and getting them ready to ship back to Chicago. The dress and some of the scrapbooks were packed in the trunk of the convertible. I left most of the photos with Tommy, with his promise to have copies made for me. The framed photos were left on the walls, and the bedspread and throw pillows that matched the ones that had been in my mother's house in Milwaukee were left where they were. On the surface, the room looked unchanged, and that made me feel better. The idea of stripping it all away and leaving Tommy with an empty motel room was just too sad to bear.

After four nights in Flagstaff, we said our goodbyes, loaded our luggage into the rented convertible, and hit the road for Chicago. We left the mild temperature of Arizona and headed toward the harsh Midwest winter that awaited us at home. But home was where we wanted to be, nonetheless. It wouldn't be long before spring would arrive, and our city would transform itself from a snow-covered and colorless landscape, to a beautiful place on Lake Michigan where you could walk out onto the pier in sandals and eat ice cream.

As we drove away, Tommy stood in the parking lot of the motel waving at us until we were out of sight. It was heartbreaking to see him standing there all alone, so broken and sad. We had promised we'd see each other again soon. He would come to the wedding, meet my grandparents, and one day he would meet our children. But I think I knew in my heart, even then, that we would never see Tommy again.

It was twenty-three degrees in Chicago when Derek dropped me off at my condo and headed to his office to work for a couple of hours before we had dinner. When he came back, he'd bring Chinese take-out. After so many days on the road, eating in restaurants and sleeping in beds that countless people before me had slept in, I wanted to eat at my own dining room table, take a hot shower in my very own bathroom, and best of all, sleep in my own bed. If I'd had the energy to cook the food myself, I would have done that, too.

I was exhausted in every way possible, except of course, financially. Then it occurred to me for the first time, that I didn't have to go back to work for a very long time if I didn't want to. I had told the school administrator that I needed at least eight weeks, and although I was home much sooner than that, it didn't mean I had to go straight back to work. In fact, I thought, I could take the summer off and not return to teaching until fall. After all, I did have a wedding to plan. I also had a house to sell in Milwaukee, which reminded me that I had to go right back down there and pick up my mother's cat, Blossom. By now, if my grandfather's cat allergies were real and not just a ruse to keep them out of his house, he'd be a sniffling mess.

Our road trip back from California had been far less meandering than the trip out. We stayed on the highways, made no stops to see tourist attractions, not even the world's largest catsup bottle in Collinsville, Illinois, and made the trip from Flagstaff to Chicago in three days, instead of four. But we used all that time in the car to begin making plans for our future. We settled on a May wedding date, because late spring in the Midwest is not only beautiful, but a stark and welcome sign of renewal after a long hard winter. And God knows, it had been a hard one.

As promised, I called Tommy to let him know we were home safe and sound. He sounded good, and we managed an entire conversation without tears, at least until after we had hung up the phone. My heart ached for Tommy. I wished that there were something I could do to ease his suffering. Sometimes the world can be so cold and cruel. This was a man who had never intentionally hurt another person in his whole life, probably not even unintentionally.

It was so unfair the way things had turned out for him. He and my mother shared a lot of good times, but Tommy spent thirty years living just shy of his dreams, almost there, but not quite. The threat of losing her to another man must always have been on the edge of his awareness. That kind of patience and devotion should have been rewarded with a more satisfying outcome.

I called my grandparents next, promising to drive up on Saturday morning. I'd go without Derek, while he stayed in Chicago to catch up on his work. My grandparents and I had a lot to talk about. Grandma said that several people had looked at the house on Elderberry Lane while I was away. According to the real estate agent, the salon in the basement was a big selling point, with its outside entrance, for anyone who ran a home-based business. But she thought it would likely be spring before anyone made an offer, so they could see what the house looked like when it wasn't buried in snow. I didn't tell Grandma what else was on the horizon for that spring. I wanted to do that in person.

After I finished talking to my grandparents I thought about calling my father, and for a panicky moment I wondered if I hadn't just imagined the whole thing. But then I took his business card out of my purse and looked at it for a long time. He didn't keep regular business hours, and I certainly wasn't going to call him at home, so I decided to wait until he called me in the next day or two as promised. A part of me really needed to find out whether he'd keep his promise.

CHAPTER 19

"WHY ON EARTH WOULD YOUR MOTHER have let us go on thinking that all these years she'd been carrying on an affair with a married man out in California?"

"I don't know, Grandma," I said. "Did she ever actually say that's what she was doing?"

My grandparents both got quiet for a moment, obviously replaying some of their conversations with my mother. This went on for a good while as I watched their expressions change from frustration to puzzlement and finally to resignation.

"Well, not in so many words," my grandfather said. "But when we got after her about it, she never denied that's what she was doing. She made us look pretty foolish, I guess, for all those years."

"I'm sure that wasn't her intention," I said. "My mother just wanted to have a special place in Arizona with Tommy that no one knew about, so no one would question her about it or try to force her into making another decision she wasn't ready to make. If you had known about Tommy, what would you have said to her about it?"

"We would have encouraged her to bring him here to meet us," Grandma said. "And if he was as nice a man as you say he is, we would have urged her to marry him and make a proper home for you."

"Exactly," I said. "She knew that. And as much as she really seemed to love Tommy, she wasn't ready to let my father go yet."

"Let him go?" my grandfather asked, his temper beginning to rise. "She never had him! Your father was another woman's husband!"

"I know, Grandpa, but wrong as that was, she loved him," I said. "In her heart, she always believed that he would come for her one day, to make things right. I know you don't want to hear this, but sometimes these situations have a happy ending."

"Not for everyone," my grandmother said.

Point taken, I thought. My mother always told me that when there are three people in a relationship, whether they're children or adults, someone always ends up being the odd man out. It's human nature. I just hadn't realized the extent of her experience in that area. Things were going to work out for Derek and me, but in our case, the odd man out was dead. Otherwise, we might never have been able to get on with our lives.

"You're right, Grandma," I said. "You're both right. But this family has had way too many secrets, and I think it's time we put an end to that once and for all."

My grandparents had liked Derek. I didn't want to ruin that, especially when I was about to tell them we were getting married. The secrets my mother kept, whether to protect me, her parents, or herself, resulted in broken hearts all the way around. Life is messy. There's no point in denying it.

"I have some news," I said.

I slipped the diamond ring out of the pocket of my jeans and put it back on my finger, holding it out for my grandparents to see. Grandma gasped and put her hand to her mouth. Grandpa smiled, and it lit up his whole face. It may have been the first time I'd seen him smile since my mother died.

"Congratulations, honey," my grandmother said. "We're both so happy for you. Derek is a wonderful man."

"Do you really think so?" I asked.

"Well, of course, Meredith," my grandfather said. "Don't you?"

"Yes, I do. And I love him with all my heart. But I want you both to remember what you've just said, because I have something else to tell you about Derek and me, and you're probably not going to like it."

I took a deep breath and launched into the story of how Derek and I met. I told them about Vanessa, her addiction to alcohol and drugs, and her failed attempts at rehab. Then I told them about Lily's death, the breakdown of the marriage that followed, and the eventual separation. Throughout all this, my grandparents were both very quiet. Having come this far, I knew it was time to get the rest of it out in the open, no matter how ugly it was, so I pushed on.

"While we were on our way to California," I said, "the second night on the road, Derek called to check his messages and learned that Vanessa had committed suicide. He flew home the next morning to be with her family and help with the arrangements. After the funeral, he came back to California to be with me. He proposed to me that night. When you look at it from a distance, it's not a very romantic story. But for us, it was the chance to finally be together for real, the chance to have a happy life. It wasn't Derek's fault that his wife was an alcoholic, and it wasn't his fault that she took their daughter to the beach and let her drown. He gave her many chances to clean herself up before they finally separated. I don't think he should have been sentenced to a life of misery. Whatever mistakes Derek and I made along the way, in the end, we do deserve to be happy, don't we?"

Neither of them spoke right away, and I wasn't sure I wanted them to. When they finally did, I was surprised by what they said. It's not easy for people to change their minds about beliefs they've held for a lifetime.

"Of course you do, Meredith," my grandfather said. "Both of you do. Your grandmother and I judged your mother very harshly throughout her whole adult life. Sure, we supported her and tried to help her raise you so that you wouldn't feel such a void where your father should have been. But we didn't approve of her choices, and we never let her forget that. Because of it, she felt that she needed to hide her life from us. I don't want to do the same thing to you."

"It's hard to change your way of thinking once you've reached our age," my grandmother said. "But I'll try to give your mother the benefit of the doubt from now on, and try to understand why she did what she did. Besides, if you're getting married in the spring, I'll probably have to meet that father of yours, God help me, and I'm going to have to be nice to him."

"Will Tommy be there, too?" my grandfather asked.

"Yes. He said he would come. That will be interesting," I said. "Tommy knows about Howard, but not the other way around."

"It's okay," Grandma said. "They're both grown men, and your mother is gone. No sense in worrying about that."

Right, I thought. They are both grown men, who have been in love with the same woman for thirty years. What could go wrong?

By mid-afternoon on Sunday, my car was packed, and Miss Apple Blossom was set to ride shotgun in her cat carrier. My grandmother, never comfortable that I was eating enough, had packed a bag full of snacks for a drive that would take less than two hours.

My father had kept his promise and called me before I'd left Chicago for the weekend with my grandparents. He had been on the road since we said goodbye in L.A. and hadn't been home yet. Elliott told him that Victoria was planning to leave on a cruise for three weeks, so my father was going to move out of the house while she was gone. I suggested it might be a good idea to stay in the house until she returned and they could discuss their future, or lack thereof, but to my surprise he said that he didn't care what she did. It no longer mattered. If she planned to follow through with her threats to ruin him, so be it. He was finished with being controlled by her, ashamed that he'd allowed it to go on for so long.

I asked him to reserve the second Saturday in May, to come to Chicago and walk me down the aisle. He said he wouldn't miss it for the world. My whole life I assumed my grandfather would have to do that job in his absence, and while I would have been perfectly fine with that, I was thrilled to know that my very own father would be there to give me away. He even offered to put a band together for the reception, with friends who had been part of the Chicago jazz scene for many years.

As I drove back down I-94 toward Chicago, it occurred to me that my mother had wanted her relationship with Tommy to remain a secret from my father. I started thinking about how I could honor her wishes and still have Tommy in our lives. When he agreed to come to the wedding, he must have known there was a possibility my father would be there. In all the confusion and emotional turmoil, none of us had thought about that. But I decided that things would just have to work themselves out in their own way. We allow our secrets to cast a very large shadow over our lives. So much effort is wasted on keeping them, when in the end the secrets themselves hide nothing but an imagined drama, which is usually not nearly as compelling as we think it will be.

Monday morning I called the school and told them I would be taking an extended leave of absence through the summer, but would return to work in the fall. I didn't know whether I actually would, I only knew that I needed some time to sort things out. Not only did I have my mother's business to attend to, I had a wedding to plan, a new house to buy, and another project I didn't even realize I'd begun.

Yet another thing I didn't realize was how soon I'd be heading back to the airport to catch a plane out west. Several days later, while Derek and I were eating dinner at my place, I received a phone call from Mariel Gallagher.

"What is it?" Derek asked when I hung up the phone. "What's wrong?"

"It's Tommy," I said. "I can't believe it. He's dead."

"What happened?"

"It was a car accident," I said, shaken. "At least they think it was an accident."

Derek took my hands in his, and looked into my eyes.

"Tell me what happened."

"Mariel said that he'd taken a couple of days off to go up to his cabin on the property he owned near the Coconino National

Forest on Historic Route 66. When he didn't come back after the third day, Mariel drove out there to see if he was okay. She saw the police cars, ambulance and wrecker before she saw his truck, but said that she wasn't surprised to find that it was her uncle."

"Why would she say that?" Derek asked.

"She said that she'd been worried about him, ever since we left Flagstaff. He wasn't eating, and several nights she found him sitting out on the benches by the fountain where you and I sat that night when we were there. Mariel said that his truck hit a tree. There were no other vehicles on the road, unless they left the scene, but they couldn't find any evidence that there had been another car involved. The way the front of the truck was flattened, practically all the way to the cargo area in back..."

"Okay," Derek said. "Just breathe for a minute."

The image in my mind was so vivid it was as if I had been there. And hadn't I known when we left that day that something like this might happen? No one would ever convince me it was an accident.

"The police told Mariel that the gas pedal was stuck all the way down, but they weren't sure if that was a result of the accident or the cause. In any case, they're not looking into it any further."

"The funeral?" Derek asked.

"Sunday. His parents will be there."

"I assumed they were dead."

"Me, too," I said. "But apparently those terrible people are alive and well, and you and I will have the pleasure of making their acquaintance in just a few days."

"So we're going, then?" he asked.

"Oh, yes," I said.

Saturday morning we took a flight out of O'Hare, and with the time difference, we arrived in Flagstaff in the early afternoon. We didn't intend to stay at Tommy's motel, because we were sure his parents were going to be there, but we planned to pay a visit in order to collect the rest of my mother's things. Mariel had promised to start boxing up the photographs and other things we'd left behind for Tommy so we could load up the rental car and be gone before his parents arrived that evening.

Derek and I would find a UPS office and ship her things back to Chicago on Monday morning on our way back to the airport. We were just loading the last of the boxes into the car when a Cadillac, carrying two of the people who had endeavored to ruin my mother's life, pulled into the parking lot. I had been furious with them when I read my mother's journal and learned how cruel they had been to her when she was so young and vulnerable. In the days before we headed to Arizona yet again, I had been so angry that I couldn't wait to confront them, tell them what a mess they had made of their son's life, my mother's, and mine. But by the time we were on the airplane, some of that anger had been diffused. I had come to realize that these were just a couple of old people who had lost their son. If I confronted them and vented my rage all over them, what kind of person would I be? So I had resigned myself to quietly packing up my mother's things, attending the funeral, and keeping my distance from Mr. and Mrs. Gallagher to whatever extent that was possible. But then I actually met them.

A younger man in a black suit got out of the front seat of the Cadillac and opened one of the back doors. He leaned in to help a woman who appeared to be in her mid-eighties out of the back seat, while a similarly aged man stepped out of the other side. The woman wore a fur coat, which immediately pissed me off, and so much jewelry it was almost comical. They were the epitome of conspicuous consumption, and they carried themselves as if they were royalty, expecting everyone to bow down to them. It only took a moment for them to notice us, packing boxes into our rented car that was parked in front of the end unit. Surely, after all these years, they knew whose things were stored in that room. Mrs. Gallagher immediately started walking toward us. As she approached, her posture changed in such a way that by the time she reached us it seemed as though she planned to tackle us both to the ground.

"What do you people think you're doing?" Mrs. Gallagher barked.

"Excuse me?" I said.

"Why are you taking boxes out of that room? Who are you?"

"Who do you think?" I asked. "I'm Anastasia's daughter, Meredith?"

"Anastasia who?" she asked. "That's my niece Mariel's room. What do you think you're doing with her things?

"Anastasia Burke. That was her name when you met her." I said. "Those aren't Mariel's things, they belonged to my mother, the woman that Tommy has been in love with for the past thirty years. The woman he would have been married to all those years if you hadn't been such a horrible monster!"

Derek took my hand, as if to prevent me from jumping the old woman and beating her to death. My heart was pounding. A part of me really wanted to smack her a good one.

Mariel was approaching now, along with Mr. Gallagher and the driver. Mrs. Gallagher just stood there with her mouth open, looking befuddled.

"She's right," Mariel said.

"I am not a horrible monster, Mariel! Why would you say that to me?"

"That's not what I mean," she said. "They're telling the truth. Those aren't my things. They're Anastasia's. She used to visit here for two weeks, twice every year since ages ago. She kept lots of her things in there, and Uncle Tommy had the room fixed up just the way Anastasia liked it. I only stayed in that room when you came to visit. Mine is on the other end, by the office."

"I'm so confused," Mrs. Gallagher said. "Robert, get me my bag and a glass of water. I need another pill."

"She was really nice," Mariel said. "I liked her a lot. We used to go shopping together every time Anastasia came to visit. Uncle Tommy was in love with her, and they were going to be married soon."

"That's not true!" Mrs. Gallagher wailed. "I told Thomas that he was not to see that girl ever again. She was pregnant with someone else's child, for God's sake."

"It is true," Mariel said, turning to look at me. "Meredith is Anastasia's daughter. We just met her in February. Uncle Tommy was so happy that she came to see him."

Mrs. Gallagher finally began to put the pieces together. I could watch the various stages of recognition washing over her face. I couldn't be sure, but I might have even seen a bit of embarrassment in the mix, at recalling her mean-spirited dismissal of my mother so many years ago.

"So that's why he never married," Mrs. Gallagher said. "I was beginning to think he was interested in men. He could have married a nice woman, but she kept him from it by coming back here when I specifically forbid it. Where is your mother now? I want to have a word with her."

Sometimes in life we encounter situations when we must choose between allowing ourselves to become engaged in a brutal exchange of words that can never be unsaid, and taking the high road. In my experience the high road has usually been the better choice. Not this time.

"My mother is dead, Mrs. Gallagher. Tommy couldn't live without her, and that's why he's gone, too. Now, they're finally together forever, and there's absolutely nothing you can do about it."

"What are you talking about?" she asked. "My son was killed in a car accident. I don't appreciate your insinuation. His death had nothing to do with your mother, or any such nonsense."

"You just keep telling yourself that, Mrs. Gallagher," I said.

Derek and I both hugged Mariel, and thanked her for her kindness to my mother. Then we got into the rental car and drove away. Mr. Gallagher hadn't said a single word. He just stood there looking confused and a little embarrassed. I had the feeling he spent a good deal of his time that way, as he watched his battle-axe of a wife blasting people everywhere they went.

The next day at the funeral, Derek and I tried to stay in the background to avoid another confrontation with Tommy's mother. The service was very sad, but surprisingly well attended. I should have realized that although his life with my mother was spent in two-week increments, six months apart, he must have had other people in his life the rest of the time.

Tommy had lots of friends. He was deeply involved in his community, and he sat on a variety of boards and committees. An impressive number of people stood up to eulogize him at the service. They told such wonderful stories about all the good things he had done in his life, and all the people he helped. It's funny; I had focused so much on what he'd been deprived of that I failed to realize how much he really had. In the brief time I'd known him, Tommy showed himself to be a kind, generous, and loving man, in spite of being raised by wolves. I sincerely wish we'd had more time together.

I wondered what would happen to Mariel, now that Tommy was gone. His parents had never considered leaving their businesses in the hands of their daughter. So there probably wasn't much chance they'd leave the Thunderbird Motel in Mariel's hands, even though she was their granddaughter. I had the feeling they only tolerated her presence because Tommy had insisted upon it. Now that he was gone, she'd probably be unemployed and homeless, if the Gallaghers had anything to say about it. But knowing Tommy, if only for a short time, I liked to think that he had made arrangements for Mariel to be taken care of, whether his death had been accidental or not. He had loved his sister, and his niece. But I made her promise to stay in touch, and let me know if she needed anything.

I felt a pang of regret for being so cruel to Tommy's parents, in spite of the way they had treated my mother. It only made me as small a person as they were, but at the time, I felt it was the least I could do. As it turns out, revenge only tastes sweet for a short time. After that, it's just embarrassing.

CHAPTER 20

SPRING FINALLY ARRIVED, JUST WHEN WE had begun to think that the snow would continue to fall on us forever. My mother's house had sold in April, and the last of her furniture was distributed between my grandparents' house and the new house Derek and I bought in Lake Forest. We finished moving in a week before the wedding, and had a guest room all prepared for my father when he arrived a couple of days later. I didn't know how long he'd stay, but he'd given the impression he wasn't in a rush to return to L.A., which was perfectly fine with us.

We told him he was welcome to stay at the house while we went on our honeymoon in Italy. Having a trust fund comes in handy sometimes. Since tax season was behind us by then, Derek and I planned to spend three weeks exploring Europe before coming back to Chicago to begin the next chapter in our lives. After all the surprises, losses, and changes we'd experienced since the year began, we were ready for a fresh start.

We'd have my father all to ourselves for one night, and my grandparents would arrive the next day. Then, everyone would be under one roof, and if any drama was going to unfold between my father and my grandparents, we hoped that it would all take place well in advance of our actual wedding day. By then, I wanted only peace, tranquility, and happiness throughout my family. For better or for worse, it was going to be an interesting time.

The night my father arrived, we took him into the city and visited three different jazz clubs. To my surprise, he knew people in two of them. So much I had yet to learn about my dad. By the time we headed for home, he had already made plans to get together with a few local musicians to play in a club downtown. I had been worried about what my father would do all alone in Chicago while we were vacationing in Europe, but as it turned out, my father was perfectly capable of entertaining himself, not to mention roomfuls of other people. He was accustomed to traveling and being alone among strangers. And he was completely uninhibited about sharing his musical talents. My father was also rather charming, and really knew how to work a room. He would be fine while we were away.

The next morning, I made us all a big breakfast. My father was impressed. Afterward, we sat at the table drinking coffee and reading the paper while we waited for my grandparents to arrive.

"Your grandfather isn't a violent man, is he?" my father asked.

"Of course not," I said. "He's a very nice man. I told you, they're looking forward to meeting you."

"Don't worry, Howard," Derek said. "I've got your back."

"All right, you two," I said. "They're going to be here any minute. I actually am a little nervous. I've got butterflies in my stomach."

"It's all that wonderful food you made for breakfast," my father said. "I hope you guys don't eat like that all the time. I've got to watch my figure."

Just as I was about to pour a warm up into Derek's coffee cup, my grandparents arrived.

"Well," I said. "Here we go."

My father got up and began pacing around the kitchen. I couldn't imagine what was going through his mind, but I'm certain that he had imagined this moment many times during the course of his life. The fact that he was a grown man in his fifties didn't seem to make it any easier. He was still meeting his girlfriend's parents for the first time, and they knew he'd misbehaved in a very big way.

My grandparents appeared at the kitchen door, their arms laden with packages. Grandma never goes anywhere without bringing food, no matter how many times I tell her it isn't necessary. But I could see that some of the packages contained gifts, with silver wrapping and white, lace bows.

"Here, let me help you with those," Derek said, jumping up from the table.

"You're a fine young man, Derek," my grandpa said. "Good to see you."

"Good to see you both. Martha, you look lovely as always."

"You're very kind, Derek," she said. "Now would someone please introduce me to this handsome man standing there next to your future wife?"

"Hello, Mr. and Mrs. Burke," my father said. "I'm Howard Bradshaw. It's a pleasure to meet you both."

My vision had started getting a little fuzzy around the edges the moment my grandparents started up the walk, and now my stomach was beginning to clench. The butterflies had turned into something much less lovely.

"Meredith," Grandma said. "Are you all right, honey? You're looking kind of green around the gills."

And with that, I sprinted to the hall bathroom and threw up. But this time, I understood why, and so did Derek. By the time I was able to pull myself together and get my stomach under control, everyone was settled in at the breakfast table and talking up a storm. I had been so worried about what would happen when they were finally in the same room together, but all that worry had been for nothing, which is so often the case. After all, these were just ordinary people, in spite of the enormous cloud of drama that had mushroomed out of my mother's secret past. These people all had my mother in common, and they had me. It was my wedding we were all there to celebrate, and no one was about to ruin that by arguing over water so long under the bridge.

"Should I tell them, Derek?" I asked.

"Yes, I think so."

"You're about to become a grandfather, again," I said, looking at my father. "And great-grandparents for the first time," I said, as my grandmother's eyes grew wet.

We'll never know for certain whether our little Marilyn was conceived that night in Los Angeles when Derek came back to finish the journey with me, but we like to think so. We like to think that we live in the kind of world where it's possible for something so beautiful to be born out of all that pain and turmoil, because we deserved to be happy. And we were very happy.

The week before, my doctor had pronounced our child to be both female and in possession of all her appendages. In the midst of all that sadness and loss, Derek and I had created a whole new human being. I only wished my mother and Tommy could have been here to meet her when she arrived.

My father rode in the limo with me on the way downtown to The Four Seasons Hotel where the wedding and reception were being held, and my grandparents went with Derek, earlier in the day, to make sure everything was in order. We splurged, and got my grandparents a suite at the hotel, with a second bedroom for my father. My grandma nearly fainted when she discovered how much the room had cost. She said that she could buy groceries for two months for that amount of money. But I told her that her granddaughter was only getting married once, so she might as well enjoy it.

Derek and I would leave for the airport the following day, and Grandma and Grandpa would drop my dad off at our house in Lake Forest on their way back up north to Milwaukee. Dad would take care of Miss Apple Blossom until we returned three weeks later. The way the two of them had bonded, I was beginning to think they had some cosmic connection between them. When he held her on his lap and looked into those mismatched blue and green eyes, it was as if the two of them knew something the rest of us didn't.

I hoped that I could hold the morning sickness in abeyance, at least during the actual ceremony, if not for the whole day. Although the wedding was purposely scheduled late in the afternoon, typically the time of day when I felt the least nauseous, my morning sickness had a tendency to appear at any time of the day. But this was just one of so many things I had no control over, so I simply decided not to worry about it. Someone once told me that life is a lot easier if you ride the horse in the direction it's going. Since taking that to heart, I've found that I'm a much happier person. Any sense of control we have over our lives is mostly an illusion.

By the time I was ready to make the alterations, my mother's wedding dress didn't need to be taken in at all. I had grown into it, and then some. The seamstress had worked her magic with lace and beadwork at the hemline. When she had finished, the dress reached all the way to the floor. She managed to loosen it a bit around the waist so I could breathe, but if we'd waited much longer after that final fitting, it would have been no good at all.

On my wedding day, I wore my mother's dress, her shoes and her pillbox hat with the whisper of a veil in front. I also carried the small ivory clutch. Inside were the old photo of my mother with Marilyn, the keys to my new home, and a pretty blue handkerchief that I borrowed from my grandmother. The house keys were a stretch, I thought, because the keys themselves weren't new, but they were new to me, as was the house. So, I figured I had it covered. But my father had been way ahead of me. As the limo worked its way through the traffic, he handed me two small boxes. I untied the bow, and opened one of the boxes.

"That one's from Elliott," he said.

Inside the box was a sapphire necklace on a fine gold chain. It was delicate, understated.

"I don't know what to say."

"He and his wife wanted you to have something that was your grandmother's. It's old, and it's blue. The other box has something new. You're on your own for something borrowed."

"It's so amazing, but it's a family heirloom!"

"They wanted you to have it. They really wished they could have been here, but one of these days they'll meet you," he said. "Open the other one."

The other box contained a small satin bag that held a beautiful strand of pearls. I held them to my neck and let my father fasten the clasp.

"They're stunning, Daddy, thank you," I sobbed. "My makeup is going to be a mess."

"You look beautiful, Meredith. So much like your mother. I'm really proud of you."

"Thanks, Dad," I said. "I'm really proud of you, too."

"Why?" he asked.

"Because you're getting on with your life. I really hope you'll decide to stay here for a while. Your family in California has had you long enough. It's my turn. Is that an awful thing for me to say?"

"Of course it isn't. I feel the same way. Listen, Melody has decided to move to Denver with her latest boyfriend, not that I saw much of her anyway. And Elliot has his family and the restaurant. Besides, he's the only one his mother actually likes, so she can keep him company. And as for Victoria, well, I'd be happy if I never laid eyes on her again."

"Aren't you afraid of what she'll do to your career? She's been threatening to ruin you for three decades now."

"You know what I finally figured out? If she really thought she could ruin me, chances are she would have done it years ago. I don't think there are any bullets left in that gun. In truth, maybe there never were. She'll end up with her curmudgeonly old parents living with her, and then she'll inherit all their cash. Victoria will have all the money in the world, but it won't make a bit of difference, because it won't bring her any joy. All these years I let her control me, out of guilt. When the lawyers get through with the paperwork, if I end up without a cent to my name, it won't bother me in the slightest."

"You don't have to worry about that. I've got a whole bunch of your money stashed away. Remember?"

"You're a good daughter, Meredith, but that money is for you and your family. I can take care of myself, in spite of what Victoria thinks. But I do want to be near you and Derek, and greet my new granddaughter when she arrives. By the time you get back from Europe, I'll have found a place of my own, right here in Chicago. Meanwhile I'll take good care of Blossom. I didn't know your mother liked cats, but the two of us have already become quite close. She slept on the empty pillow next to mine last night. I think we're going to get along just fine. It'll give me a chance to tell my side of the story."

"Oh, thank you, Dad. I'm so glad you'll be staying here. That's the best wedding present I could ask for. Of course the jewelry is nice, too."

We both laughed, and I put my grandmother's blue hankie to good use fixing my makeup before we arrived at the hotel.

"Glad you approve," he said. "Maybe Elliot and the family will come out for a visit sometime. I'd like for you to know him. He's really a very good man."

"I'd like that too."

As we pulled up in front of the hotel in the shiny black limousine, with my father at my side, and a wonderful man waiting just inside, who wanted to spend the rest of his life with me, I knew without a doubt that I was the luckiest person on earth. And soon we would be blessed with the arrival of our baby girl. I couldn't possibly have asked for anything more. My mother had managed just fine on Elderberry Lane, even without a husband in the house. She worked hard, and made sure I always had what I needed. We had a good life, and between she and my grandparents they taught me to be independent and strong. They gave me the courage to find out the truth about my life, instead of closing the door on it.

All my mother asked me to do was deliver her ashes to California. I could have flown out there, done as she asked, and turned right around and come home. Instead, I took a chance and sought out my father. He might have refused to acknowledge me, but instead he welcomed me with open arms. Now the father I'd thought for my whole life was lost to me forever, was about to walk me down the aisle. Imagine that.

Most people, for some duration of their lives, however brief, have the opportunity to experience their parents simultaneously, even if they're living under separate roofs. Families break apart sometimes, and children spend years being shuttled back and forth between their parents like little tennis balls, but they still know they have both a mother and a father out there looking after them. While it would have been wonderful having the opportunity to be with both my parents at the same time, that wasn't in the cards for me. But to have spent the first thirty years of my life thinking my father was gone, only to find him alive and well, I consider myself very fortunate, and am perfectly satisfied with the chance to experience them sequentially. It's more than I ever dreamed was possible.

Life is messy, and complicated. The decisions my parents made affected lots of other people's lives. We listen to our hearts sometimes, instead of our own best judgment, and the results can be devastating. I like to believe that we're not driven by the desire to hurt one another; that more often we're driven by love. But whether love makes us stay, or makes us go, in the end we have to live with the consequences.

About the Author

Valerie Joan Connors is the author of three novels, and the current president of the Atlanta Writers Club. Her first traditionally published novel, *In Her Keeping*, was released in August of 2013 by Bell Bridge Books. Valerie's first book, *Give Me Liberty*, is a historical novel set in New York just after World War II, and was self-published in 2010.

During business hours, she's the CFO of an architecture, engineering, and interior design firm. Valerie lives in Atlanta with her husband and two dogs.

CPSIA information can be obtained at www.ICGtesting.com
Printed in the USA
LVOW08s2052170614

390478LV00002B/11/P